THE SUN AND THE MOON
and other fictions

Inscribed for
Agnes & Henry
with love Pat

P.K. PAGE

PKPage
Dec 1973

Anansi   Toronto

"Kleptomaniac" from FIDDLER'S FAREWELL, by Leonora Speyer. Copyright 1926 by Alfred A. Knopf, Inc. and renewed 1954 by Leonora Speyer. Reprinted by permission of the publisher.

Some of the short stories orignally appeared in *Preview, Here and Now, Reading* and *Northern Review.*

Published with the assistance of the Canada Council.

Copyright © P.K. Page 1973.

Design by: Barry Rubin
Typesetting by: Foundation Press
Printed in Canada by: The Hunter Rose Company

ISBN: Paper 0-88784-327-1 / Cloth 0-88784-429-4

House of Anansi Press Ltd.,
35 Britain Street,
Toronto, Canada.

1 2 3 4 5 6   78 77 76 75 74 73

Introduction

With many other readers, I've long been an admirer of P.K. Page's poems: of their artistry, their bravura effects, their verbal precision and their evocation of the usually concealed layers of emotional and psychic experience. When I heard she had written a novel and had published it in 1944, under the pseudonym of Judith Cape, I was more than slightly intrigued. Apart from the visions of cloak-and-dagger and Holofernes' severed head raised by the last and first fake names respectively, I wanted to see what kind of prose the P.K. Page of that time would have produced. The only other example of it I'd seen was "The Green Bird," a short, delicate, faintly threatening piece, but not much to go on.

THE SUN AND THE MOON proved to be a much rarer specimen than I'd imagined: a Canadian romance. That is, as an example of a *genre* it suggests Hawthorne's BLITHEDALE ROMANCE, Bulwer Lytton's ZANONI and Rider Haggard's SHE rather than PRIDE AND PREJUDICE or MIDDLEMARCH. In Canadian Literature, it's more like O'Hagan's TAY JOHN with its living dead, Gwendolyn MacEwen's prose with its magic heroes, or Marie Claire Blais' MAD SHADOWS with its iconic characters and strange events than it is like AS FOR ME AND MY HOUSE or THE STONE ANGEL or THE APPRENTICESHIP OF DUDDY KRAVITZ. As a "realistic" novel it would be hard to accept; as a romance, it dictates some unusual terms, which we must either swallow whole or reject outright. Towards the beginning of the book, we are presented with the proposition that the heroine, having been born during an eclipse of the moon, has the ability to take on the identity not only of inanimate objects (a stone, a chair) but of other people as well, thus robbing them of their souls. We know then that we are not in the world of what Virginia Woolf calls "the common sitting room'', no matter in what detail that sitting room may be described.

In fact, the juxtaposition of Kristin's lethal talent and the social milieu she inhabits is at first slightly jarring. It's no lonely house on the moors, but an upper-middle class household, complete with a brittle socialite mother, her patronizing friends, frothy cocktail parties, and a stuffy, animal-shooting father. But beneath the pink boudoir setting and sometimes breathless language a more relentless allegory is being played out. The crux of the story is, quite literally, a power-struggle between Kristin and the man she loves, Carl Bridges, who is a painter of some skill and fame. It's a struggle for the possession of Bridges' soul: against her will, Kristin finds herself taking over his identity and thus depriving him of his ability to paint. Without wanting to, she shows she will ultimately win: her "gift" is greater than his. She must either destroy him, drowning her own identity in the process, or divert her attention to another object. The resolution of her dilemma is both ruthless and fascinating. Like many romances, THE SUN AND THE MOON is incredible on the level of social realism, but on the psychological/allegorical one it makes great sense.

The short stories that appear with THE SUN AND THE MOON are from the same period. A number were published in PREVIEW, NORTHERN REVIEW, and other magazines of that era; "The Green Bird" is widely known through Robert Weaver's CANADIAN SHORT STORIES. Their language is, in general, more condensed, and their footwork more adroit, than in THE SUN AND THE MOON; but they share with it both the bizarre perspective and the disconcerting insights characteristic of Page's work at its best. Several display a mordant humour ("The Neighbours," "George") and others achieve their effect by a piling-up of details about a way of life we may have forgotten or never lived (were boarding houses really like that?) but which we remember, through the medium of Page's prose, with something between nostalgia and horror.

Together, these early stories and this early novel add a dimension to our knowledge of an imaginative and important Canadian poet.

—Margaret Atwood, 1973

Contents

The Sun and the Moon   1

The Neighbour   138

The Green Bird   142

The Woman   147

The Lord's Plan   152

Miracles   158

As One Remembers a Dream   164

George   176

The Glass Box   195

Dedication

Some years ago I met a young woman who was expecting a baby. "If it's a girl," she said, "I shall call her Kristin after the girl in *The Sun and the Moon.*"

In due time I received a letter: "Kristin arrived February 20, 1971, during a lunar eclipse." The 'lunar eclipse' rang a distant bell. It was many years since I had read the book so I looked it up.

There, in my youthful prose, the book began with the birth of Kristin. During a lunar eclipse.

To this real Kristin, born in 1971, I lovingly dedicate this new edition of an old novel.

THE SUN AND THE MOON

PART 1

KRISTIN

The world throbbed to the excitement of a lunar eclipse. Astronomers and their bastard brothers, the astrologers, worked busily charting the heavens, linked at this moment by a mutual concern for the moon.

In a hospital, a pale pile of yellow brick on the top of a hill, which strove to touch the sky with its longest finger of stone, doctors, nurses and a young mother worked to bring a girl-child into the world.

The sweet smell of ether hovered in the air when the mother opened her eyes.

"It is a girl," the nurse said, "I'll bring her to you."

"A girl," said the mother, "she shall be called Kristin," and shut her eyes again. The electric light hurt them; it was a small pain compared with that of the last hours, but there was no need to tolerate it. It could be borne if necessary, but necessity was no longer a part of suffering. The baby was alive; she longed for the feel of the small creature against her body.

There was no time in this building of births and deaths, where the record of human suffering mounts on its own time chart, oblivious of the convenient man-made clock. It might have been hours or minutes when the light snapped on again, opening the room away from the young mother on the bed; pulling back the walls and reconstructing space, where space had been crowded out. It might have been hours or minutes since that first encounter with light until this one; since the moment she

1

knew it was a girl until this moment when the white nurse held something in her arms that made the mother eager to hold it too. Until this moment when the nurse said, "Isn't she sweet? Here she is," and bending down had put her in the bed.

Astronomers forgot in the period of eclipse that human life was being propagated still. Theirs was the world of mathematics; mathematics so vast and inconceivable that even their minds were made dizzy with contemplation. But the astrologers had been busy for weeks turning out articles for the pulps on the subject of birth and the eclipse: "Was Your Baby an Eclipse Baby?" headed paragraphs leading to founts of evasive prediction.

The young mother didn't care. All of importance lay beside her embodied in the small shape which was her daughter. The resentment she had felt previously, because her husband was away, was a thing of the past. What he had given her compensated for his absence. And as she thought she realized that his present to her was also her present to him and she marvelled at the miracle and smiled to the child at her side.

Kristin was so small. Surely never, never had a child been smaller, her mother thought. And she grew strangely, not with a slow continuous growth, but with sudden spurts and little unfoldings. And she was good. No baby had ever been better. She just lay with her hands curled like shells and her funny long eyes gazing beyond.

When Ralph first came to see her she had felt her love flood through her and she had wanted to say, "Here she is, our precious, whom I give you." But she had been afraid then, and it was too late to say it now. For a year was almost gone and the miracle was over though the joy remained. Oh, just to be with Kristin, to know her for her own, that was enough.

Ralph had laughed at the name. "Kristin!" he had said. "A little stagey, darling." But he had let it pass, adding as his contribution, Jane, as a middle name. And secretly she had

2

laughed in return. Ralph knew no escape from what he called the accepted-common-or-garden. Therein lay his security. But she was different; three-quarters of the way she plodded, but she skipped so frantically for the last quarter that the plodding was forgotten.

She would temper the plain Jane in Kristin with her own imagery.

It was exquisite to stand by and watch Kristin grow. The shell hands changed to two stars. Kristin walking, holding out her arms for balance and her hands two little dimpled stars. "Oh, thank you, Kristin, I had forgotten the grace of children, and their beautiful shy aloofness. I never knew that it is the very young who possess the key to fairyland. I didn't know so much."

But Grace, the mother, knew a shrinking of delight as Kristin grew older, and a small fear nagged her heart. She and Ralph had produced a queer child, someone who could not have grown from themselves. Grace now began to take refuge in Ralph's conventionality. But Kristin felt nothing of the restraint of her surroundings. Like a dream child, fair and ethereal she walked about the house, talking to people constantly who were not there. People with names and evidently shapes and weights.

At meal times her whole body struggled with the effort of lifting these friends onto chairs so that they too could eat. And she insisted they have their portion of food. The fact that it remained untouched worried Kristin not at all.

Kristin had peopled the house. And Grace grew afraid, not of meeting these people but of perpetually not meeting them. Ralph laughed at her for this. "All children imagine themselves surrounded by friends," he said. "There is nothing extraordinary in it."

"But," said Grace, clutching a book in her hands and sitting on the extreme edge of her chair, "she doesn't *imagine* them, she *sees* them, actually sees them and feels them. She asked me the other day who the funny little old lady was and what she was knitting. I nearly jumped out of my skin.''

Ralph knocked the ashes from his pipe. ''Don't worry,'' he said, ''she'll outgrow it.'' But as he saw her face he knew Grace needed more practical and immediate comfort than that. It was not enough to predict vaguely for the future, so he added: ''Tomorrow I'll play truant and we'll have a day at the sea—Little Cove—just the three of us. Like to?''

''Oh, Ralphey, yes!'' Her face lit up. Already she had forgotten Kristin.

She is very young, he thought. I must be with her more and look after her. He crossed to her chair and kissed her but as he drew away she clung to him saying, ''Kiss me again. Oh, Ralph, don't leave me yet, I want you near so badly.'' She ran her fingers against the grain of his hair cut and pressed her face to his. Here was a depth in which she could sink and submerge herself.

And so they sat together, both suddenly aware of a new relationship, aware of a new peace; neither knowing the need of speech in this strange calm that lapped over them. Then a tremor ran through Grace and he sensed her fear. She sat upright with a jump and clutched the lapels of his coat.

''Ralph, if it were to rain tomorrow I couldn't bear it.'' Her voice was tight with panic and her eyes were wide. ''I could stand everything but that—everything.''

It didn't rain. The morning dawned with no sign of a cloud in the sky. Little Cove was sparkling and clear in the sun—a dream beach that had just emerged from the sea, unspoiled. And Grace lay on the sand, completely content, happiness curled like a cat on her chest.

Kristin, with the sureness of five-year-old fingers, dug through the soft dry upper sand, smoothed it carefully and dug again. She liked the feel of it forcing her nails away from her fingers. She liked the wetness you reached if you dug far enough—the crispness that lay covered until you began to dig.

4

She enlarged the hole and smoothed its edges and sat back on her heels to admire.

"Here," said her father, joining her. "If you must be a ground-hog, be a Girl Guide ground-hog and bury the picnic rubbish." He put the parcel of papers and eggshells into the hole and scuffed sand over them.

"See if you can cover them up so no one could possibly know we've been here."

Kristin didn't move. He had spoiled it now. It had been so smooth, all patted and beautiful. Now it was just a garbage hole. She didn't want to look at it again.

"Come on, Kristin," he said. But she had turned. Mummy lifted her hat from her face and raised her head.

"Go along, darling. Do as Daddy tells you. There's a good girl."

But Kristin didn't hear. The hole was spoiled. It didn't exist for her any longer. She was no more a part of it. Already her interest had shifted. A mass of seaweed caught her eye—deep maroon seaweed swirled around a log at the high-tide mark. Kristin moved towards it slowly, stooped and fingered its crispness. Its touch on her fingers was brittle—a thin, almost forgotten touch. She broke a piece off and held it in her hand loosely. Where the seaweed curled it pricked her palm.

The day had settled to a still weight of heat. The half moon of white sand danced in the sun and there was a haze far out at sea so that the horizon was impossible to find. Kristin followed the mark of the high tide, excitedly finding devil's purses and fisherman's floats and seaweed with bubbles in it that popped if you pressed them hard. And thus, following the flotsam and jetsam at her feet she arrived at the great rock cliff at the far end of the beach. The rocks were pale and large and smooth, and waves lapped at their base and broke into laughing spray that splashed high into the air. She was hot and tired. Far along the beach she could see Mummy and Daddy like two little coloured dots with the sand dancing and wiggling between. She gazed up at the rocks and climbed carefully to a ledge of stone and flung herself down on her stomach. Up there, so high, the sun beat harder on her back, and below—a long way down—the waves broke themselves to powdered glass as they hit the rocks.

Lying there unmoving, Kristin felt something she had never felt before. A change came over her. Slowly she stiffened and became hard and still, knowing nothing but the sun beating on her back. The sun on her back and a sense of rest, nothing more. Nothing more for a very long time. Then suddenly there was movement somewhere and voices talking. But she knew without hearing, for her ears were stone; she knew only as a rock can know, by the vibrations of sound striking an inanimate thing. Then, as gradually as she had stiffened from flesh to stone she melted from stone to flesh and heard then as a person hears and knew as a person knows, that her mother and father were standing over her, worried. And her father bent down and picked her up in his arms and said:

"She's got a touch of the sun."

And her mother put her hand on Kristin's head and said, "Darling, darling!"

"Lie still, Kristin," said her father, "and we'll take you home to bed and you'll feel quite well again."

But Kristin didn't feel ill and didn't want to go home to bed. All she wanted was to be left alone on the rocks, forever, and to become a rock again, knowing nothing but the sun and the wind and the sea.

"She's so pale," said her mother.

"Course I'm pale," Kristin replied, "I was a rock."

"Ssh! dear," whispered her father shifting her higher in his arms; and her mother ran along beside them, the brim of her large hat flip-flopping in her worried eyes.

They bundled her into the car.

"Sleep, my darling," said her mother. And Kristin shut her eyes. But she couldn't sleep. The rocks were large in her head, like a magnet drawing and drawing.

6

The picnic things were stowed away. The car started.

"The day is left behind," she heard her mother say as the car moved off.

"There, there, Gracie," her father answered, "there are other days ahead."

"She looked so strange," her mother said, "as if—as if—she'd been dead. As if she knew something we didn't."

Kristin lay across the back seat pretending she was on the rocks. Almost she could feel herself tightening to stone again. But the noise of the car and the talk of her parents were with her. They were too close—they held her from the rocks, her rocks. Lying there she knew they were hers as nothing had ever been before.

"She is quiet," said her mother, one night later. "Ralph, she won't play with other children. She's not like anyone else. She sits and sits."

"School will knock it out of her, you'll see," he answered. "She'll be a different child when she starts school."

But as the years drew Kristin taller she wanted more and more only to be alone. Children bounced and ran and yelled and screamed. They bothered her. She hated quick movement, hated to jolt the quietness of her body. Grown-ups were different. At least they sat still, but they talked so, on and on, until their speech was as restless as movement and Kristin, listening, found it necessary to slip away from their chatter and withdraw into the peace of herself.

The rocks had faded for her now only because of more recent experiences. She had only to sit still long enough to know the static reality of inanimate things—the still, sweet ecstacy of change in kind. But this knowledge, this breath-taking communion, she kept to herself. She learned early that to speak of it drew the eyes of her parents back in a sudden fear, resulting in the vigilant supervision of her movements. And that supervision denied her the essence of her life. So she lived in a world of her own, like a pale sprite barely able to touch on a common ground with the people around her.

School was an interlude to get through somehow—an interlude of jarring faces and movement and speech. Her teachers resented her aloofness, her disinterest. But once, unconsciously, she centred attention on herself in the classroom. She had written a descriptive composition on a chair which had been read aloud to the class and later sent home to her parents with this note pencilled in the margin:

"Although the literary style is, in itself, negligible, Kristin has somehow in her immature way made the chair an entity, endowed it with a physical individuality that is quite unusual. It is almost as if the child had actually been a chair herself."

And of course, she had. She had known the pressure of the molecules in the wood, the massing together of atoms, the feeling of the cleats that hold a chair together and the upward surge within the wooden framework that keeps it a composite thing. It held no mystery for her; she knew with the understanding derived from personal experience.

When Kristin was seventeen she met Carl. He was in town, having been commissioned to paint Judge Lothrop, and the Lothrops were celebrating the occasion with a cocktail party. The picture was finished, the artist was to be there. And Carl Bridges was a name to conjure with.

Kristin, sitting before her mirror, running the comb through her long hair, was annoyed at her lack of calm. She didn't want to go. She dreaded the noise ahead of her, the endless talk which she could never take part in. But her protests had been useless. "Kristin, darling, this is the opportunity of a life-time. Just think, you'll meet Carl Bridges—*the* Carl Bridges, my pet. You'll regret it for the rest of your life if you don't go." And so here she was getting ready, combing her long hair back from her forehead, refusing to hurry.

"Kristin, Kristin! We're waiting."

8

"Coming," answered Kristin, picking up her bag and gloves and grimacing at herself in the glass.

She felt stiff in the car on the way over. Her hands in her gloves were numb and there was a vacuum around her heart. Long, slim, shiny cars were drawn up before the Lothrops'. The green of the lawn ran right down to the pavement. Bright beds of flowers lined the path up to the front door. Everything looked so right, so set to its pattern of correctness. Kristin almost laughed. And there was her mother, spike-heeled elegance, slim as a reed. And her father running to paunch, the successful business man, hair beginning to thin. They, too, were of the pattern. They need not question where to walk or what to say. Their pattern carried them where hers didn't. Hers didn't follow this direction. She had walked away from its certainty and was just a little afraid.

The front door was open. Like garlands flung on streamers talk came to them through its opening and Kristin winced at the noise and hesitated on the step.

"Come on, Noisey," said her father over his shoulder. He was in a party mood already. He called her that when he felt gay—as an apologetic gesture for his daughter. She didn't mind. Her mother waited and slipped her white glove through Kristin's sleeve, leaving a smudge where it had rested. "Silly baby," she said. "This is a party, not an execution," and then suddenly left her as she caught sight of Mrs Lothrop.

When Kristin turned, her father had gone too. She saw the grey expanse of his back being thumped enthusiastically by a friend.

Poor darlings, she thought, that they should have had me as a daughter, and she brushed the white patch on her sleeve and walked into the diningroom.

It was practically empty and unexpectedly quiet. Over by the sideboard stood a friend of her mother's.

"Come here, funny child," she called. "Come and let me

talk to you.'' Kristin crossed to her.

"They dragged you here after all? Your mother said you didn't want to come.''

"No, I didn't,'' said Kristin.

"You'll get over it,'' said the friend. "Cocktail parties get in your blood in time. It's just a matter of getting over being shy.'' Kristin smiled. She wasn't shy, but she couldn't explain that—not to this woman with her thin mouth and metal eyes—not here where there was no peace.

"I used to be just like you when I was your age,'' the woman went on, twirling her empty cocktail glass between pale fingers. "It's your parents' fault, they should have had more children. I, too, am the product of selfish parents. I wonder if that shaker's full.'' She eyed it, lifted it, beamed and poured herself a drink. "Oh, and one for you,'' she said. "You'll feel better with a drink inside you—limbers you up.''

"Thank you,'' said Kristin. It was clear and golden in the glass—almost the colour of my hair, she thought, and the woman caught it.

"You have cocktail-coloured hair,'' she screamed, delighted with her own humour.

"What's that?'' asked a man across the room.

"She has cocktail-coloured hair,'' she repeated, quite weak with laughter and he spluttered and put up his knee to slap it and turned to tell the phrase to a man at his side.

"You see, people want to laugh,'' the woman went on. "Make them laugh and they'll love you, is my motto. It's easy when you get the hang of it. It just needs courage to start.''

But Kristin wasn't listening. Through the doorway opposite, attended by a flurry of chiffon and little wisps of laughter, came Mrs Lothrop and a thin dark man. Kristin's fingers tightened on the stem of her glass as she watched him. His eyes are like sailing ships, she thought, quite free of his face. And his brown hands are beautifully still. His whole body is still.

"Well!'' said the voice at her side with a rising inflection,

10

"well, our Kristin is not so shy and young that she doesn't know an attractive man at any rate. I've been wasting my time on you, child. But remember, if you want to catch him, make him laugh." And as she went, her knife-blade body cut the air and sent it off in two folds on either side. But Kristin didn't move. She knew suddenly that she was glad she had come. If she never met him, if she never saw him again, it didn't matter for she had seen him once across a room—a sailboat in a harbour of screaming, bustling little tugs. And he had seen her and in his seeing his body seemed rested. His upward-pointing shoulder had fallen.

They were circling the room. Introductions fluttered before them. They stopped for a minute here, a minute there and came on again. Now they were in front of her. And for the first time she did feel shy, breathlessly shy.

"And this is Kristin," Mrs Lothrop said. "Kristin, I want you to meet Mr Bridges so that you can always remember you met a great artist the year you came out," and they were gone again.

He had swept over her like the sea. Her hand was shaking. She put down her glass and twisted her fingers together. She wanted to go now. Go while she held that moment in quietness within her; go before the encounter was jarred and broken. But still she didn't move. Quite close, in the next room, perhaps, was Carl. She liked the feeling of his being in the same house; she liked the sound of his name—Carl Bridges.

Kristin picked up her glass. She wasn't shy any more. If she did see Carl again, if he crossed to her and said "Hello" she would not know the silly panic of before.

"Enjoying yourself, Noisey?" Her father was very hilarious. There were drops of perspiration on his forehead and his face was creased from recent laughter.

"Yes, Daddy," said Kristin.

"What did I tell you?" he said, putting his hand on her shoulder. "Come into the other room where there are more people."

"I'd sooner not," Kristin said. She didn't want to leave this room where she had seen Carl, even for a room where she could now see him. This moment is like the rocks, she thought—new and wonderful. They dragged me away from that, but this time I won't move. Her father had gone again, pushed through the noise to greater noise and left her as she would be left, alone on her island.

And then he was in the room and coming to her, past the table, beside the sideboard and standing in front of her.

"Hello," she said. His whole body seemed free now—his eyes weren't so noticeable. He was quiet with the quietness of complete freedom. She didn't know what to say to him but it didn't matter. She told him so and he smiled and stared, content in their small silence. And then he lifted a hand to put down his glass.

"Your hands," she said, and there were tears in her eyes. "Your brown hands. They are beautiful." Now, now, she thought, it is no longer enough just to have seen him. I cannot bear that this be the complete experience.

"I am not leaving tomorrow," he said. "I had planned to, you know."

"I didn't know." How awful, she thought, if I had known.

"I want to stay. I want to paint you—if you will sit for me, that is." He smiled. "Please."

"I will," said Kristin. Was it only as a model that he was interested? Because he liked the way her hair grew, or because her legs were long and straight, and not at all because she was Kristin? She lowered her eyes, frightened to look at his face, frightened to read there the strict gaze of professional interest.

"But tomorrow," he said, "tomorrow we shall have a holiday. You are free, aren't you? You must be free."

"Yes."

"Can you walk?"

"Yes."

"May I call for you at eleven?"

12

I am going to cry, Kristin thought. This is stupid. But I've never loved anyone before—never—anyone. She stretched out her hand for his brown one, hoping, hoping that he would know it meant the "yes" she couldn't say.

"Darling!" said her mother, pleasure and surprise in her voice. "*Here* you are. So you've been talking to my funny little girl, Mr Bridges, my funny, shy little girl. I hope you realize, Kristin, what an honour this is, when everyone here is clamouring—but clamouring!—to talk to Mr Bridges. You mustn't let her be selfish, Mr Bridges, you really mustn't."

It doesn't matter, thought Kristin. If she wants to she can talk on and on. Everything is said. The bridge has been built, the bridge that carries today over to tomorrow. She cannot destroy it now. And as she thought, she walked onto it that it might feel her weight and she looked down at the swirling water below her.

"It is I who am being selfish," Carl said. His voice came out of the water.

"What a sweet thing you are, Mr Bridges. Kristin, tell him what a sweet, sweet thing he is. But I'll leave you now," and she went.

The bridge was firm under Kristin's feet and she wanted to say to Carl, "It is safe, we have fashioned it securely; come, step onto it and stand with me," when he said, "I'm cheating. I'm half-way across to tomorrow already."

"It's safe, as far out as that?"

"Yes, it's safe."

But Mrs Lothrop had borne down. Like a large spider, her fat body in grey chiffon, she had caught him again—her fly. He made no struggle, moving as if he wished to go, smiling as he turned and saying, "It is only a little way farther," he had gone.

Kristin trembled and ventured another step onto the bridge. Tomorrow, as she stepped off, he would be there. She felt the strong pull of excitement in her loins. This happiness was an agony. She must escape to suffer it by herself. She moved from the dining-room out to the hall where the air blew in from the garden, smelling of late afternoon coolness. She and the day were one, settled to stillness. She sat down and the hum of the voices closed about her. Reflections from the living-room passed in the mirror before her. Her eyes clung to its surface, watching the light and shade, the kaleidoscopic pattern that broke within its frame. There! Was that Carl now—his elbow jutting out from behind Mrs Lothrop's grey bulk? Or there, the back of his head, leaning towards young Katie Steen? She shut her eyes. She saw him everywhere, in everybody, and she felt, for the first time, part of the world. Carl linked her with humanity.

"Kristin, it is time to go now." Her mother, brilliantly soprano, sharply black and white, was calling from the dining-room doorway. "Go and say good-bye to the Lothrops." And her father, his face appearing red and round above her mother's, laughed loudly and added, "And apologize for making such a racket." But his face wrinkled and looked puzzled and strange when she smiled at him and said, "I'll leave the apologies to you; I'll just say the good-byes."

He nudged his wife as Kristin went. "That's the first time she's ever seemed like a normal person. Grace, Grace, did you notice? Something has happened to Kristin, she has changed."

"Perhaps she's growing up at last," Grace answered.

Alone in the back seat on the way home Kristin was silent. Her parents were gay. Occasionally they tossed words back to her for their amusement rather than hers, as people toss peanuts to monkeys in the zoo. They have had too much to drink again, Kristin thought. They'll both be bad-tempered by dinner-time. But that was incidental. It didn't matter. She could shut herself off from them, stand on the bridge and wait.

I never knew, she thought, that it was possible to lose oneself in a person. I never knew before. And feeling the fire run through her she dug her nails into the palms of her hands and shut her eyes and saw Carl.

14

"You might have told me, Kristin," her mother said in a hurt voice, pausing as she arranged the flowers and standing with one large white peony in her hand. "The least you could have done was to tell me. You know how interested I am in you. Mr Bridges of all people!" her mother went on, cutting the thick green stem of the flower as she spoke and holding the scissors uplifted so that they caught the light. "When did he ask you?"

"At the cocktail party," Kristin said, wanting to say, "His eyes are like sailboats and his hands are brown and very beautiful"—wanting to say it aloud but not to anyone.

"You've known all that time and you've only just mentioned it?" Her mother's eyes were incredulous, holding little shafts of surprise in their corners.

Kristin turned to the glass and knotted a handkerchief over her hair. May I please him, she thought, looking hard at herself. Oh, God! may I please him! And she felt young, so young; a stranger to herself.

"There he is," said her mother. There were steps on the verandah, steps in Kristin's heart. In one minute, one second even, she would leave the bridge behind her.

Her mother slipped out of her smock and smoothed her hair. The door had opened. "Could I see Miss Kristin, please."

"Just step inside," said Mary, the maid, her mouth sounding tight with astonishment. "This way, please."

Carl was in the doorway. Kristin could not move. His neck is brown like his hands, she thought. There, where his shirt is open, it is brown.

"Mr Bridges!" Her mother was beside him, holding out her hand, drawing him into the room. He was quiet. His voice came softly.

"Good morning," he said.

"You know we never *actually* met yesterday although I did speak to you. I'm so glad it's such a lovely day for your walk. Kristin's looking forward to it so."

15

"Are you?" said Carl. She felt stupid, suddenly.

"Of course," she answered.

"I've rather changed the plans," Carl said. "I've brought the car. I thought we might drive into the country and then walk. There's a place I like particularly. Unless you have other ideas I thought we might go there."

"Where?" asked Kristin.

"Little Cove," he said, "do you know it?"

"Oh, lovely, I'll get my bathing-suit."

"Kristin, you will be careful. You know I've never liked that place. Kristin got sunstroke there when she was a child, Mr Bridges, and since then I've never really enjoyed going there. Kristin," she called, "get a hat at the same time as your bathing-suit. You'll need it."

But Kristin danced up the stairs. Carl and Little Cove—together. They were part of each other—the rocks and Carl.

"What about food?" asked her mother. "You can't get it there, you know. Shall I have a basket put up?"

"I had them do it at the hotel," Carl said. "Thank you just the same. If I remember, rightly, there's no restaurant for miles."

"And such a pity! Someone could make a fortune down there if they'd start something like that."

"Oh, but it would spoil it," said Carl, "completely."

"I suppose, from the artist's point of view, yes," she handed him a cigarette. "But I must say I've reached a point where I enjoy a meal in comfort. Sand in the sandwiches is no longer a pleasure to me. You have to be young to smile on inconvenience."

"I'm ready," said Kristin from the door. She held her bathing-suit and hat in her hands. She crossed to the cigarette box near Carl. Please, said her eyes, please. He got up.

"I'll take good care of her," he said. "Don't worry."

Her mother smiled. "Do be careful, Kristin," she said. "I shall never forget how ill you were when you were young. Never!

It frightened me to death.''

"Good-bye!" Carl called.

I'm stepping off the bridge, Kristin thought. It has held, strong and straight it has led me to now, to this moment.

Carl opened the car door.

"We are here," he said as he got in, "Kristin, we have reached today safely. I thought we never should." He stared at her before he turned on the ignition.

Her mother waved from the veranda as the car started. They waved back.

"It was a long way," said Kristin settling herself comfortably, "a very long way."

The drive down was easy. Words were ready waiting to be spoken. Kristin was happy, completely at peace in the wonder of loving.

"I love to look at you," Carl said, "you are like a child."

"But I am a child. You'll laugh at me—I still read fairy stories. Truly."

"So do I, sometimes."

"Oh, Carl!"

" 'The Three Feathers' and 'Hansel and Gretel'. That frightens me still. I often feel just like Hansel—poking chicken-bones instead of fingers through at Life."

"And Oscar Wilde. Do you know his fairy stories? They are the best of all."

"I did illustrations for them when I was an art student. How I worked on them! I'll show them to you some time. The one for 'The Nightingale and the Rose' I was very proud of. That seems a long time ago... " he trailed the sentence off.

To talk like this, thought Kristin, is heaven. To be close to him saying these things. He is so tranquil, so wonderfully still underneath. And the thought of it overwhelmed her so that she had to say:

"Carl, you are like the prairies—still and even for miles

17

and miles—or like a sailboat. When I saw you yesterday I thought, he is a sailboat in a harbour of little tugs."

He didn't laugh at her. "Did you?" he said. "Do you know what I thought when I saw you? Here is the only person I've seen at this party who is not distorted. You were standing quite quietly, each line right. What were you doing there, anyway?"

"I was taken."

"Oh, taken," said Carl knowingly.

Kristin lapsed into silence. There was so much to be said. So much to be heard. But she wanted to spread it out. Wanted to leave something for the succession of tomorrows that stretched out before her. For surely, there must be a succession. If it were to end . . . fingers closed around her neck. If it were to finish today—or after the portrait even . . .

"Carl," her voice came in a cry. "Carl, you won't leave, will you?"

"Leave? When, Kristin?"

"Ever. I just thought—perhaps tomorrow or after you'd done my portrait, that you might leave."

"Don't worry, Kristin, if I leave I'll take you too. You can be my professional model. I'll paint you sitting and standing and clothed and nude and awake and asleep and——"

"You are teasing now," Kristin's voice was tired.

"Only a very little," said Carl.

If he were to leave without me, Kristin thought, if he were to say, suddenly one day, "I am going," I think I should die. To live on without him . . . . She covered her eyes and turned her face away, fearful that he would see her with the pain drawing her cheeks.

"We are nearly there. Look, to the left. Surely that beach is the one below Little Cove."

"Yes, yes!" And Kristin forgot Carl for the moment and remembered only the rocks. "Soon we'll see the rocks," she said. "My rocks. The only things that really belong to me."

"Why your rocks, Kristin? Why yours more than most things are yours?"

"One day I'll tell you." She couldn't now. Although she was sure of Carl, not yet was she sure enough that he was steady in his knowledge of her. To tell of the rocks was to give herself to him, complete. And I don't know if he wants me yet, she thought, feeling all in that moment, older and strangely guileful.

"One day—you promise?" He had slowed down and was watching her.

"One day, if you still want to know."

But he was not content. "Promise?"

"I promise." It was an oath, an oath that bound her to him. She could not escape him now. Oh, this sweet terror that held her, this terrible joy! She clutched her knees and rocked a little on the seat, feeling the thrill eating her flesh, dissolving her brain.

He slowed again and turned. "We are here," he said. "Look, Kristin, the island."

She didn't dare speak. The road was bumpy. It lifted her up and flung her against him and tore her away again. She felt the roughness of his jacket graze her cheek and she held her fingers against her face and laughed.

"I am jolted to death," she gasped through her laughter. And he laughed too.

He drew the car to a stop at the edge of the bank and she was out, out, before he had pulled on the emergency brake, out and down the bank to the sand.

Oh, the wind in her hair and the sound of it rushing past her ears! The mad glory of it as it flattened against her sides!

"Kristin!" He called to her from the bank, but she didn't turn. If she looked back now, if she called in reply, if she joined with him for one minute even, before she had time to recreate herself as an entity, it would be too late.

Escape! Escape! Down across the sands to the sea.

At the edge she stopped and took off her shoes and socks. She would not turn yet. The feel of the salt water was sharp on her ankles and feet. She swung around to wave.

"Oh, Carl," she called as she saw him, tall and thin, with the wind whipping the rug he had slung over his shoulder and his hands full with a thermos and picnic basket. Oh Carl, oh Carl, I should have stayed to help you.

She hurried back. He was on the beach now. The thick white sand was almost hiding his shoes and the wind had blown his dark hair over his face. How could she have left, how run away for a moment?

"I'm sorry," she said. "I left you. I should have helped." Will he believe me? Will he know that I mean it? She wished there was some way, other than words, to prove her words. "Carl," she gripped his elbows. "Carl, I had to go. Believe me, I had to leave you."

"I know, Kristin." He set down the picnic basket.

"You didn't mind?" She knelt beside the basket, looking up into his face.

"No, of course not. But," he paused, "it's just that I have the feeling that it will always be so."

He knows so soon, she thought. How could he know it? She sifted the sand through her fingers.

"Am I right?" he asked.

"Carl," she started. But because she could not frame her lips to words of her own, she repeated, "Yes, it will always be so." She wanted to cry out, to deny the truth, but she couldn't. If she refused to accept her own truth she faced destruction. If not . . . She could not follow it through.

Carl smoothed the rug. "There," he said, "now we have staked our plot. Not that we need to, the beach is practically deserted."

Kristin rolled on her back. "If you lie flat," she said, "you can't feel the wind and the sun is strong." She covered her eyes with the back of her wrist.

20

Carl felt in his pocket for his dark glasses, lifted her hand and put them across the bridge of her nose and behind her ears. She smiled, a little half moon of a smile.

"You look like an owl," he laughed, "a smiling owl."

"And upside down, you look like—I don't know what you look like. Look at me upside down. Isn't it silly!" She pulled a face, reached for her bathing-suit—and began to change, slipping her dress over her head and sitting for a moment in her slip, with the sun beating on her bare shoulders.

"Oh, I love the sea," she said fiercely, "love it, love it!" But feeling his eyes upon her she was suddenly self-conscious. What did she mean by changing in front of him? She blushed and covered herself with her dress. She was aware, for the first time, consciously and terribly aware of the shape of her own body; the lift of her breasts, not fully covered by her slip, and the smooth line of her leg above her knee. Carl picked up his trunks and walked back into the bushes.

What happened, she thought, that made it seem wrong and wicked? What have I done to myself, to myself and Carl? And she changed quickly and moved slowly to meet him, shy all over again as she had been at the cocktail party, but body shy, wanting to hide herself, trying to hide herself behind her skimpy towel.

"Race you," said Carl, starting off across the beach. "I'll race you into the water," and she watched him as he went, saying aloud to herself, "Thank you, Carl," before she too, ran down to the water's edge and followed him into the sea.

"You're like a porpoise," he said, diving for her ankles. But she kicked out in time and was beyond his reach and she lay on her back and laughed at him as he came up dripping, the water emphasizing his dark skin.

Oh, it is good to be here, she thought. It is good, good, good, but the water is cold—and she splashed through the shallows to the shore.

"Oh, Carl, my shoes!" There they were, a little way off,

with the water lapping around them. "They're soaked!" She picked them up and poured the water from them. "And my socks, like little drowned mice!" She wrung them out. "How silly. I forgot them when I ran back to you." And the memory made her thoughtful. "If they'd gone out to sea," she said, pushing the thoughts away from her, "I'd never have remembered where I had left them."

"Scatter-brain!" He took her arms and raced her along the sands. "Let's go to the rocks, your rocks," he said.

Her rocks. She would not let it happen again today. Not today. She would stretch out on them and feel their warmth but this time she didn't want more of them than that. She would not let them steal her away from Carl.

He gave her his hand. It was cool from the sea as he pulled her up.

"Listen!" she stopped and held up her hand, "you can hear the river. Over the sound of the sea you can hear the river." They clambered on, the heat of the rocks burning the soles of their feet.

"Here!" Kristin flung herself down on her stomach, her head jutting over the rock cliff that fell down to the water. Carl joined her. They lay like that, in silence, watching the swirling, pounding water flung high in foam.

I am here again, thought Kristin. Their warmth is my warmth, their muteness is my muteness. I have returned to my own. She began to feel the slow penetration of them, the gradual infusion of their substance into her flesh and she fought against it. Not now, not now, she thought, but her will had gone. Already her body refused to obey her mind.

"I'm getting dizzy," said Carl. "That water is almost hypnotizing me."

It was a queer floating voice in Kristin's ears.

"Kristin, I have a surprise for you."

She couldn't answer. He rolled her over and lifted her to a sitting position. "Kristin, are you all right?"

She was back now. It hadn't happened. Just in time he had come to her—another minute and it would have been too late. His face looking down was worried.

"Yes, I'm all right." She spread out her socks to dry and propped up her shoes so the sun could reach their wet insides.

"What's the surprise?" she asked, the echo of his words coming to her from far back.

"A cigarette. Like one?"

"Yes, please." She held out her hand for it.

"I've at last discovered a waterproof pouch that *is* waterproof. Look." He undid it and produced the cigarettes. " 'A miracle of dryness'," he said, "unquote. So runs the ad. Why does a cigarette always taste better after a swim?"

"Is it a riddle?"

"No, just a question."

"It sounded like a riddle. I hate riddles. They do though, don't they—taste better, I mean." If she stretched her fingers out to full length she could touch his leg, just below his knee. But she kept them curled, terrified of spoiling the moment by some too-quick movement, of breaking from her life the first moment of reality, the first swift wonder of loving. She watched him instead, his hands brown and firm and supple, economical in their movements; and his dark eyes that looked golden when he smiled. She watched the smoke lift from his cigarette and half hide his face from her, then drift away to leave it showing clear in the sunlight. And she wondered at her complete ease, her feeling of having been used to this always, she who had never felt comfortable before except when alone.

"Do you mind if I stare at you, at your queer half-enchanted face? If it worries you, pretend it's professional interest, the artist viewing his subject."

"I'd sooner not pretend." She felt the blood rise in her cheeks as she spoke, felt his personality rush over her, desired only to know the shape of his lips on hers and to hold the smooth stretch of his shoulder blades under her hands. But he came

23

no nearer and she feared that her flesh would rush out to him as steel to a magnet.

She stubbed her cigarette, needful of a definite gesture and ran her fingers through her hair. I am no longer a child, she thought. I have grown up. I am now part of the adult world.

"You are so right," he said, "every gesture, every line. Naturally, as a child would, you show yourself off as a woman." He held out his hand again as he had to help her onto the rocks. "Let's have lunch."

He pulled her to her feet and she noticed his hand was warm now from the sun. Her own looked white beside his.

"Do you never tan?" he asked.

"Never," she answered. "I don't even burn. It's very odd. We make a sort of study in black and white, don't we?"

"As the old ladies would say," he led her across the rocks, "I think we look rather nice together." He chuckled as if there were a subterranean joke he did not wish to bring to the surface.

"Oh, my shoes!" said Kristin. "I've forgotten them again," and she ran back before he had time to turn.

Lunch on the sand was lovely. Stretched out, heads supported by their left hands, their feet still bare, it seemed to Kristin to have all the romance of a Roman feast.

"Only nicer," said Carl, "for if it were truly a Roman feast, you, being mere woman, would be unable to break bread with me. And too, this simple food hardly does justice to the high-living of ancient Rome. A bottle of beer and tongue sandwiches and a banana would hardly be fitting food for those extravagant times." He rolled up the banana peels in the sandwich paper as he spoke.

He is tidy, thought Kristin. His hands are precise and neat. I should love to see him working, watch the way he holds his brush and the sureness with which he must mix his colours.

"Draw something for me," she said.

"Come then," He stowed the rubbish back in the picnic

basket and got up. Her eyes rose with his figure. "Before the tide comes in I'll draw for you on the sands."

They started across the beach. He picked up a stick, drew swiftly with it as she had imagined, barely erasing a line as he worked—quiet, concentrated; turning to her occasionally to explain or laugh or see if she was interested and then returning to his work, using his hands, building up, scooping away, smoothing, patting and bringing forth from the sands figures in bas-relief running together.

"They are like birds," she said. "They have the sweet, swift motion of swallows in flight."

"You try," Carl said. And she began, timidly at first, continuing with more courage, delighting in the ease with which figures grew under her fingers, astonished at her own ability. He leaned over and watched her. "But you are good," he said, "really good! You should study."

She shook her head. Already she had decided that this beginning should also be the end. I am using his talent, she thought, I can feel the current of his talent running through my veins. And her forehead wrinkled. Would that this had never happened. Oh, God! that I should begin to absorb Carl as I absorb inanimate things. And a weight fell through her body, growing and filling her with dread. She stopped working.

"Go on," he urged. But she wouldn't.

"No, no. The sea will only take them all away." If only the sea *could* take them all away, could erase forever her knowledge that she had stolen from Carl; stolen against her will the essence of the man she loved.

She held her head, heavy with anguish. That my love should destroy when it should create, like the parasite that destroys the plant it lives upon. I must warn him, she thought, somehow I must warn him, of the danger. But her mind recoiled at the thought. Oh no, not yet. Not yet can I tell the whole truth. I must prepare him first. I must have time before I tell him

25

the whole truth. And then she remembered a poem she had liked without knowing why and learned because something made her. Quietly she began to recite, her face still covered, her lips moving slowly as though it hurt to speak:

"She stole his eyes because they shone,
Stole the good things they looked upon;
They were no brighter than her own.

"She stole his mouth—her own was fair—
She stole his words, his songs, his prayer;
His kisses too, since they were there.

"She stole the journeys of his heart—
Her own, their very counterpart—
His seas, and sails, his course and chart.

"She stole his strength so fierce and true,
Perhaps for something brave to do;
Wept at his weakness, stole that too.

"But she was caught one early morn!
She stood red-handed and forlorn,
And stole his anger and his scorn.

"Upon his knee she laid her head,
Refusing to be comforted;
'Unkind—unkind—' was all she said.

"Denied she stole; confessed she did;
Glad of such plunder to be rid—
Clutching the place where it was hid.

"As he forgave she snatched his soul;
She did not want it, but she stole."

As the poem ended, as her lips came together again, in silence, she felt better. The weight had gone a little—she had told half. Whether he knew it or not she was playing straight with him. Already he possessed the open-sesame to the secret she was still unable to tell.

26

"Kristin, what a queer poem. What made you recite it?"

She couldn't answer. She was crying now. She wanted to say: I love you more than my life. Oh, Carl, believe me. Run away from me now while you are still free, before I have stolen your identity. But she could only sit with the tears streaming down her cheeks.

"Kristin, you're crying." He moved towards her and put his arms around her. "Darling, don't cry. There is nothing to cry about. What has happened?"

As he held her she felt better. The comfort of his nearness crept over her and washed away her fear. Already she had grown into the consciousness of his flesh and hers, warm and touching, and the fierce joy of it was like a fire sweeping through her, purifying as it went. She looked up at him. "I've been a silly little girl," she said. "I'm sorry. I shouldn't have spoiled the day."

What could she say now to rebuild the day's perfection, what do, to delete the last few minutes of pain? She shut her eyes. She wouldn't think any more. Lying in Carl's arms she couldn't think. The desire, the ability to reason left her as Carl bent her backwards and lowered his face to hers and closed his lips over her mouth. She knew nothing but the throb of blood in her veins almost tearing her body and the terrible passion with which she clung to him and the gradual ebbing of strength as she relaxed under his kisses so that she would have fallen back if he hadn't held her.

"I love you," he said, "you know that, don't you? I love you so much that it is an agony to be with you and not touching you. And until you cried I felt I had no right. Oh, my darling, if you hadn't cried I might have gone to bed tonight still not knowing how sweet you are."

I shall die from very happiness, thought Kristin. Such bliss is almost more than I can bear. "I love you, too," she said, tracing his eyebrow with her finger. "From the first moment I saw you I loved you. Carl, I feel so young and so old all at once. And so—so secure.'' She smiled, a slow smile.

"Little Mona Lisa,'' he said and kissed the hollow in her neck and brushed the hair back from her face with his brown hands.

"Your hands,'' she said. "They made me cry when I saw them yesterday. I'm an awful cry-baby, Carl. Oh look,'' she leaned on her elbow, "the fog's coming in—and the tide. The fog's rolling up like smoke. Damn!'' She got up. "It's coming quickly. We'd better get dressed.''

They walked hand in hand up the beach. "I am drunk with it all,'' she said, reeling and laughing, "drunk as a tar. I want to climb to the topmost peak of the world and call 'I love him, I love him. He is like fire in my throat, like white flame lapping me round'.'' She turned. "Look, the fog has come in. Already the sea is hidden. And it's nibbling your outline, too. We're figures in a mist, fading and forming.''

"Come, you'll get cold.''

Is it real? she thought. In the mist, like this, it seems like a dream. But it must be real, it has to be. She reached out for Carl, touched his shoulder, afraid to find his flesh unresistant, but it was firm.

"It is really true,'' she said.

"Yes, Kristin, it is really true, unbelievably true.'' He held her to him and kissed her again. This happiness is a pain, she thought, that will devour me. And I want, above all else, to be devoured by it. She laughed under his lips.

"What are you laughing at?''

"Love,'' she said. "That love could be like this. I never knew what it was like before.''

"Nor did I.''

"You?'' She drew away and looked at him. "But, Carl, you must have known.''

"Not that it was like this,'' he said, "I promise you.''

"Thank goodness for Mrs Lothrop,'' said Kristin. "Wouldn't she die if she could see us now? Fat, silly old Mrs

Lothrop—but I thank her for her party—I like her better than I ever have.'' She hugged herself and shivered. "We must get dressed.'' She ran to her clothes and began pulling them on, shivering as she did so, not knowing whether the fog or the excitement rippled her body and made her teeth chatter. She wrapped the rug around her after she dressed, tense in the knowledge that Carl had touched it, smoothed it out; feeling a sweet satisfaction in the fact that it was his rug.

A dark speck appeared in the fog, grew longer and wobbled as it moved—like a nine-pin teetering before it falls.

"Carl, you look like a nine-pin, so silly. Watch me." She walked off into the fog and came back. She heard his laughter as though it were her own, deep within her.

"There is tea in the thermos,'' he said. "Like a cup?''

Tea, with Carl. "Oh, yes, let's have it in the car.''

So in the car it was. She held the cups and he poured the steaming tea into them. Ah, lovely, there together, their hands curled around the warm china. The two of them alone in a car that floated in a white world. They were silent. Kristin tucked her feet under her and leaned back. She could feel, without looking at Carl, that he was watching her and she could keep her eyes away no longer. She smiled at him over the rim of her cup.

"Happy?'' he asked.

Happy? Could this be happiness? Could happiness be so large a thing as this joy that possessed her?

"I could stay here for ever and ever without a complaint,'' she said.

He had finished his tea. They sat together, her head against the tweed of his coat. Curiosity gnawed her. Who was this man she was with? She knew nothing. Less than nothing. Sitting there she longed to ask him and yet recoiled from asking him about himself. To know more all at once would destroy the keen delight of piecing together little by little the fabric of his being. So she asked nothing, more anxious to learn as he told her.

29

The waves pounding on the shore were the only sound.

"It is high tide," she said, "it sounds like wind in the trees."

"The sea has claimed the figures we modelled," he said.

Yes, yes. The sea had them. They had gone. She was glad. She wouldn't think about them again, would forget that she had stolen from Carl. There was nothing to worry about. It was enough to be here with him, her head rising and falling with his breathing; the silence being broken occasionally with words bright and swift as a school of minnows, flashing upon the moment and going again. This is what I have been looking for always, thought Kristin, without knowing it. And now I have tumbled upon it by chance and am still breathless from the discovery.

The drive back was slow. At first the fog was so thick that it was impossible to hurry. But as they drove inland it disappeared. With each mile of the road, thought Kristin, a part of me, a part of my happiness is being left behind. She did not want to return, to go back to the eyes of her parents searching out her face; to their questions. She could hear her mother carefully choosing her words, "Did you enjoy yourself, dear?" And then, "And Mr Bridges? He is an attractive man—quite the most attractive man we've had here for some time." And her eyes would wait for the remark Kristin must make, the remark that would tell all or nothing of the afternoon. But she felt equal to it now; she had grown older since the morning. She could speak with the surface of her mind, saying words that told little more than a silence.

"Tomorrow," said Carl. Kristin waited. "Tomorrow," she formed the word in her mind.

"What would you like to do tomorrow?" She couldn't think. To be with him was enough.

"How about driving up the river? I'd like to see more of the country."

The bridge is built again, thought Kristin. "We can drive to the Rapids and swim and have lunch. It's lovely there."

30

"And I'll call for you about the same time." He stopped the car. "We're nearly into town," he said. "We'll stretch out the return a little longer." He put a cigarette between her lips, took it out again and kissed her. "You're very sweet," he said, "so unafraid to be generous."

She didn't understand. Generous? How could she be anything else? But he didn't explain. Instead, he held out his lighter for her. She watched him, watched the stoop of his head as he leaned forward, the tightening of his lips as he drew the first puff of smoke into his mouth, the lift of his thumb as he released the lever to snuff the flame and the bend of his elbow when he returned the lighter to his pocket. She was greedy for knowledge of him, greedy to know where he lived, where he studied, who his friends were. She wanted to be able to think of him as a student—in Paris perhaps, or Italy. Wanted to see him in his home, tall Carl, having lunch with his family, sitting with them in the evenings. But where and what were they like?

"I want to know your province, Kristin," he said. "Want to see the places you have grown up in, the background of your life. It's strange," he said, "I somehow never expected to come down here. But it's a beautiful province and now I shall see it with you; you showing me, not like a guide, but as though you were showing me yourself. We shall have a week together and then I'll paint you."

A week! Seven days stretched out one after another with Carl. And then the painting and . . . then? But she didn't ask.

"Don't make promises," she said, "don't make plans. Something may happen. You may grow tired of me. Anything might interfere. And if there are no plans it will be easier."

He took her hand, laughing at her, and stroked it. "All right, we won't plan, then, but it will happen just the same; you wait and see, nothing will go wrong."

She could hardly hear him. Her hand had turned to satin under his touch. Her whole body was satin with little breezes playing over it. He held her again, his arms around her, his lips taking hers. Nowhere was there an ecstasy as sweet as this.

"Oh, Kristin, Kristin," his voice was muffled, "we must go back." He drew away. Kristin smoothed her hair.

"Yes, we must go back." She wanted to be alone, to give herself up to thinking of Carl, almost more than she wanted to be with him.

He started the engine. Once again they were on their way back.

"Till tomorrow then." That was what he had said last, standing on the door-sill, his hair still untidy from the wind. Kristin drew the curtains in her room hardly knowing what she did. Till tomorrow.

Her mother had greeted her as she came in, "Kristin, surely you asked Mr Bridges in to dinner?"

"I never thought," she said.

"Rush out and see if you can stop him."

Kristin moved to the hall window. "He's gone," she answered, watching his car move out of the driveway.

"But if you hurry..." She hadn't wanted to hurry. She hadn't wanted Carl across the dinner-table. She knew so well how jovial her father would be as he stood weighing the carving-knife in his hand and how her mother's staccato voice would have risen above the dishes. "Don't you like him?" her mother had continued, "I'd have thought you would have enjoyed having him to dinner."

Questions, questions, leading questions and all she wanted was to be alone. She turned down the covers of her bed and undressed. As she stood in her nightgown before the glass she felt a fierce joy in her own figure. It was slim and supple and straight, hardly hers. She felt as though she was looking at someone else—this white skin, not hers at all, the skin Carl loved. She moved closer. And this face. She examined it closely, tracing the outline of the lips, the lips Carl had taken for his. Her fingers moved over them in a dream, as though half expecting to find the ghost of his kiss still there. Oh Carl! She was a living wire with awareness of him. Somewhere, in a hotel room, perhaps, he moved and she could not see him; moved in surroundings she did not know. Her body tightened with the desire that possessed her, the desire for him to be with her, folding his lips over hers, whispering, "Kristin, it is true. I love you." How could she bear this loneliness, sweet as it was with thoughts, how bear a life not linked to Carl's forever?

The wonder of it all. Oh, the wonder! Her mind went back to the beach, to the moment when she had feared his closeness, wanted him closer and yet dreaded the actuality. And the eventual blind surrender of her lips followed by a surprise that it was possible to be touched as she had been touched; possible to be harbouring, unknown to herself, this new creature within her which could sweep aside the other, the known self, in the ecstasy of Carl's kisses.

Oh, Carl, Carl. She turned over. Sleep was farther from her than the tomorrow she struggled towards; the moment when once again the sea of his caresses would break on her body.

But the thought of the bas-relief figures on the beach drained her to a hollow stem holding a thin fear. It must not be, she thought, shutting her eyes in an agony, it must not, must not be. She could feel the tears under her eyelids and she fought them back. I love him too much, she thought, surely I cannot hurt him, loving him so. But she was not convinced and the night stretched out before her—a tunnel of torment that she could not quench; interminable darkness leading to the reality of Carl.

Part 2

CARL

Carl was waiting. His board was ready. Any minute now Kristin would come. He would hear her steps first on the stairs and then she would stand, framed in the doorway. He walked up and down, lit a cigarette, gazed at the glowing end and leaned on the window-ledge. He was happy and he wasn't happy. The past week, now that it was over, was bright with unreality. The pale child who had grown to become so important to him was like quicksilver—always just when he thought he had her she was gone. And it was that that kept him so alert in his love. When he thought of the women he had known he wondered at himself. Many were more beautiful, certainly most were more intelligent, but none was so fascinating, none had captured him like Kristin. There—her steps sounded on the stairs. He moved forward. She stood in the doorway as he had imagined. Cool, in white, like a lily. She smiled.

"My darling!" He went to her, took her hands. She held up her mouth for him, unselfconscious, simply.

"The stage is set," he said, "shall we begin?" He was eager to start.

"Here," he held the chair. He didn't want to pose her, wanted instead to catch the lines of her own natural position. He waited for her to settle, watched her sit half sideways, cross her long legs and lift her head to look at him.

"How do you want me to sit?"

"Like you are," he said. "Just like that." He drew a chalk mark around the legs of the chair and shifted his easel. It was over a week since he had worked. He picked up a stick of char-

34

coal. It was easy to draw her, he knew her features so well—her small, intense mouth, the wide sweep of her hair-line, the distance between her eyes. His hand moved easily. At this rate, he thought, I'll have finished the sketch at one sitting. Tomorrow, if the varnish is dry, I'll be able to start on the tempera. He worked on, carried away, forgetful of Kristin as more than a model. It was good to be working again, lost in the moment of creation. The sketch was complete. He stood back, critically, and was pleased; he had caught her exactly. For a background, rocks, her rocks and the line of the sea. Kristin, white and pale against the rocks.

He looked at his watch and frowned. "You must be tired," he said. "I forgot the time. You've been sitting an hour." He watched her get up, saw from her movements, the stiffness of her body, watched her stretch. "Weary?" he asked.

"Only stiff," she said.

"It was selfish of me." He put his arm around her.

"Oh, no." She leaned against him, "I love to watch you work, see you become absorbed in something."

There is a deathly quietness about her, he thought. It is only in moments of passion that she is wakened to vitality and then it's as if the vitality will destroy her. How can she give herself so completely to love, so unfearfully? She trusts and she follows and she creates all at once.

He could feel her shoulder against his ribs. He turned her towards him, lifted her face to his and stared into her eyes. Her eyes are wide, clean, green, like buds unfolding, he thought, and her body still and clean as if the sea has swept over it. He couldn't help wondering what she would say, how she would react, if he suggested she become his mistress—she so young, so unused to the ways of love, who accepted them without alarm. But she was safe from that. He would never ask her. He was only curious. He didn't want her as a mistress, he wanted to marry her. He stopped in his thoughts, surprised at the line they had taken.

35

"Carl, what are you thinking of?"

He led her to the sofa and she curled up against him, her hair fanning out behind her head, falling in one piece—sculptured hair, forming a fan, a shell, for her head to rest on.

"What a funny face you have, Kristin. It's not a Canadian type at all. It's Scandinavian, with its high cheek bones and wide forehead. Have you Scandinavian blood in you?"

"Not a drop," she said. "My name—that was simply because Mother liked it."

"It must have affected your appearance. You hear of things like that happening."

"But what were you thinking of?" She had returned to her question. Like a child again, he thought.

"I was thinking about marriage."

"Oh." She said, "Oh," and said no more. It was an "Oh" that gave him nothing. She had a sharp sweet note in her voice as though she held a bird in her throat. Her "Oh" was the bird's note.

"Marriage," she said, ignoring the bird, stretching the word out.

"Yes, marriage," said Carl, the word beginning to sound silly. "What do you think of it?"

She spread out her arms, one lay over his chest. "I hadn't thought very much," she said. "What can I think, knowing so little?"

He smiled. No theories, so devoid of theories, this Kristin, with her eyes like green buds and her white, still flesh.

"Let's go and have lunch," said Carl, "somewhere quiet."

"There is nowhere quiet," she answered. But she was animated now. She got up—a swift, silken movement, like a bolt of taffeta moving. Her eyes were unfolding, her mouth drawn up small—silken too—a patch of red satin in her white face, below eyes unfolding to leaves.

"Carl, Carl!" the bird was back. "Your paintings, I want to see your paintings."

36

"I have so few with me."

"But those you have. How can I know you, not knowing your work; not knowing that which is more you than anything else?" There was a light behind her face, her skin was translucent.

"And I, how can I know you, not knowing the secret of the rocks?"

Her face clouded. "Not now. Not now." She brushed it away. He persisted. "A moment will come," she said. "I will know the moment. It will come and I will speak because I cannot help speaking, not because you have asked me but because it will be inevitable."

He bent over his canvases. He would not persuade her. Perhaps, when she knew him better. He would try. There was a rod between them; he would remove the rod—her way. He leaned his canvases against the wall. There were so few of them. Despite his many moves there was dust powdering their edges. He ran his finger along them and looked at the black smudge on it.

She stood in the middle of the room... quite still... but her mouth was tight again, a little pattern of red satin; and her eyes were bursting to leaves and her hands clenched, clenched. And then, "That is good," she said, "but good." She pointed, her long pale arm held forward, the white sleeve of her dress hanging straight.

"You know plates and fruit and weight on a table top. You know those things as though you had felt their shapes against your heart. Oh Carl! you know too much to be happy. It is hard for you to escape unhappiness, for even your happiness drains you. It falls like lead through your whole being. And that is why you can paint."

Kristin! Kristin saying this. Kristin speaking as his being spoke. "And to be happy, to escape to happiness?"

"To escape to happiness is to run from happiness. There can never be happiness for you, Carl."

37

He felt to touch her would be to touch a live wire. What did she know, how did she know, know, that which he was only just beginning to discover as a certainty?

"And there," she pointed to the portrait of an old man, "you have been old too. Oh Carl, had you been spared the humiliation!"

"It is over now," he said.

She smiled a little, sad smile. "Not really," she said. "It cannot be really over. It is there still in your bones, in your heart. You can never be truly young again." And she came to him, humble, bowing her head. But he couldn't kiss her, nor did she hold her mouth to be kissed.

"Thank you," she said. "You have been very generous, you have given me so much."

It is all suddenly mad, thought Carl. Suddenly it is "Thank you, you have been very generous." Party talk.

She linked her arm in his and threw back her head. "To lunch then," she said. "As we cannot go where it is quiet let us go where it is most noisy, so the noise will carry us."

It was hard to keep up, hard to keep step with her sudden moods. She seemed secure now, different, he thought; all week she has been groping, oh, silently, unobtrusively, but groping. Now she has found; now she knows of me what she wants to know. But I? He felt less sure of her. The more he knew the more she evaded him; it was like trying to catch a cloud in a butterfly net. How could the child know this, or the woman act so?

Over lunch in that crowded room they sat at a table for two and their eyes flew across the table top like moths to meet each other. Carl Bridges, artist, thinking like a poet, he mused, and laughed. Her fork was half-way to her mouth but her eyes were on him.

"You're laughing," she said. "Why?"

"I was thinking of Dick."

38

"Dick?" She lifted her fork higher and he saw her small white teeth.

"He is a friend of mine," he said, "and he watches me like a hawk and makes bald statements, bald personal statements: you are in love; your work has been hurt by a woman—that is Dick."

"And so you were thinking of Dick." Her fork was on her plate now and her hands were folded under her chin. "And laughing."

"And laughing—because now, if he could see us now he would say to me, 'You are in love'." He expected her to follow the conversation up but she said instead, looking very serious, her eyes closing back to buds:

"People—you talk of people, friends. Carl, I don't know people and I have no friends."

She said it without a trace of self-pity as though she were saying: "Charles Morgan—I don't know Charles Morgan and I have no books." He looked at her. There could be no doubt but that she meant what she said. But why, he wanted to know.

"Why?" he asked.

"I've felt no need of people, ever, until now. My life has been like your still-life—plates and fruit and table tops."

"And rocks," he said.

"Yes, and rocks."

"But if," he was still not clear, "if you don't know people, Kristin, how did you know about that portrait? How did you know I'd been old?"

"My grandmother," she answered. "When I was very young Mother was worried about me. She sent me to stay with my grandmother and I used to sit and watch her, watch her hands, twisted with rheumatism, slowly sewing; watch as she read, her magnifying glass tracing the lines of print. Day after day, day after day, watch her doing little things in slow motion with that dignity that age brings. And I grew old. For a whole month

I was as old as my grandmother.''

He was fascinated. The thought of a child Kristin, pale as winter sunshine, sitting as old as her grandmother with gnarled hands.

"Then you do know people, Kristin."

"No," she smiled and unfolded her hands and they flew off away from her chin, like two doves and fell into her lap. "I don't know how they talk or what they talk about; I don't know their anger or their happiness or the reasons for them."

"But family life," he kept at it, anxious to know more. "To live with people as you have, is to know them."

The doves flew again, to her plate this time, and one flew back to her mouth carrying a piece of lettuce leaf.

"And Dick?" She had returned to Dick. "Tell me of Dick."

"He is fair and he can't resist making puns and he..." But Carl stopped. Damn! he didn't want to talk of Dick. He was stupid to have mentioned him. He wanted to go, get away from the crowd, go somewhere where he could touch Kristin and so prove her reality.

"Ready?"

Kristin nodded and he rose and pulled out her chair, glad to be going from the noise, glad to be going off alone, with Kristin. She let her hand rest on his arm as she got to her feet and he grabbed her harshly almost and pulled her along past the counter.

"Carl," she stopped him with her voice, "the bill."

He felt silly now. The girl at the counter smiled at him as he groped through his pockets and then went back to the table where the bill lay on the plate as it had been when it had been put there. No change, he thought miserably, and rather than go back to the counter again, he left a dollar for a tip and returned, knowing already the half scorn of the waitress who would grab it with eager hands.

She was waiting, a stalk of loveliness, standing still as a shaft of sunlight, wearing friendliness on her face. When they were outside he felt better and when they had reached the corner the anger had died. He turned to her, seeing her anew as a landscape after a storm.

"Tonight, then," she said stopping, "we shall see you at seven."

"You're not going?"

"I must."

"Kristin . . ."

"Yes, Carl?"

He must keep her a moment longer. "I had hoped we might be alone a little while this afternoon." But it was no good, she was going. As she went he thought he heard her say, very quietly, over one white shoulder, "I love you." He was after her.

"Then stay!" he said, catching her up.

"No, darling. Not now. See you at dinner." And she went, a slim white figure through the heat and the crowds, alone.

Carl walked back to the hotel, lost. He was a fool to be angry. She loved him, she had told him and he knew. But he wanted to be with her and as the heat of the pavement stung the soles of his feet he grew angrier. In the hotel room he sat on his bed, hurt. It was stiflingly hot. He flung the window up to the top and took off his coat, sitting in his shirt sleeves, angry. And then he poured himself a drink—a large strong drink of whiskey—and drank it in a rage. Not thinking, deliberately not thinking, just sitting with the drink in his hand, the second drink, while the last of the first one still smouldered in his throat.

There was not enough wind even to lift the silly hotel curtains and beneath, in the square, in the green light, people walked listlessly and the flower beds shone as though planted with jewels, packed tight against each other—rubies and sapphires and diamonds and opals and emeralds, emeralds, emeralds. Hating them, he moved to the window to see them more closely and he leaned on the sill and sipped his drink and the green light of the trees rose up and filled his eyes.

Kristin was—where? If he could only imagine where. Other women, yes, he could see them, any of them, under dryers, at bridges, having fittings. But Kristin? Always she escaped. He turned away from the square, the drink unfinished in his hand, bewildered now, angry no longer. Sitting at the desk, the hotel paper before him, he began a letter to Dick.

"It is almost a month since I first arrived in this city. It is a quaint place with a waterfront which should be an artist's delight. Too, the surrounding country, sea one way and dignified rivers the other. But there is no use trying to persuade you that such is the reason for my prolonged visit."

He stopped, ran his pen through it all, lit a cigarette and began again.

"It is hot here today. I wish you were here with me to expound your damn silly theories of colour and fling your arguments at my head. No doubt, in the middle of all your talk you would look at me and say, 'You're in love'."

Carl crumpled the paper in his hand and threw it on the floor. It was no good. What could he say to Dick that didn't sound childish and absurd. Love on paper was an infantile thing, to be laughed at by the adult mind. Yet, in reality, he thought, a man's loves are no laughing matter, however puerile; they shaped him to the ultimate man. What would he, for instance, be now, if he had not met Denise, so vulgarly called Student's Delight? Denise, who had, for some unaccountable reason, given him, an angular shy lad, one-quarter of her so valuable time. Denise, the wanton with the kitten's eyes, who drove him to a youthful frenzy in those mad Paris days, so that even now he could not think of Paris without seeing her. Denise, absurdly small, with her little rounded behind stretching her tight dress even tighter; Denise, speaking always so quietly that it was as if her eyes spoke; who could make a shy boy forget his shyness even while she laughed at him for it.

And Marmo—shrill, acquiline—with such an exaggerated sense of the ridiculous, who could not observe the conventions

42

for two minutes together. An *enfant terrible,* striding about hatless with her short, dark curly hair waving like tendrils about her face. To be out with Marmo was to be a brave man, for she delighted in breaking the surface dignity of people. Action, she cried for action and always got it by her unprecedented behaviour. How high her heels were! She was tall but wanted to be taller, wanted to be the tallest woman in any gathering, "For it is absurd for a woman to be tall," she would say, "but it is exceeding absurd for a woman to be six-foot two, which is what I am with my shoes on."

Carl lay on his bed thinking. But forever his mind returned to Kristin, Kristin so unlike anyone he had ever met. It would seem, he thought, that the only similarity between the women I have known lies in the fact that they have all had strange names. Never has a Jane or a Peggy or a Mary or a Betty left a mark on my life. Denise and Marmo and Egbert, "The Egg", those were the three. "The Egg" had carried her bad shape courageously and filled the quiver of her mind with stolen arrows, sharply brilliant. He hadn't known that at first.

He had met her in Carnegie Hall . . . in the intermission. She was standing beside the picture of Wagner, he remembered very clearly, and they had just heard Ravel's "Ma Mère l'Oye". "The Egg" was standing there beside the picture, her left hand in the pocket of a heavy sweater that dragged down her low breasts. "There is Egbert," Dick had said, pulling him through the people, "leaning against the wall by herself."

"Egbert!" Dick had called and coming nearer, "Egbert, this is Carl Bridges, a friend of mine."

"Why Egbert?" Carl remembered asking.

She had taken the cigarette out of her mouth with her right hand and looked at him from beneath her half-moon lids. She spoke through smoke.

"It was the christening," she said.

He felt stupid.

"My father drank," she went on, "and arrived at my christ-

ening very much under the weather just at the time that the
clergyman was asking for my name. Mother caught sight of
father at that exact minute and called out in a loud voice,
"Egbert!" She was a very unrepressed woman, my mother, and
my father's name was Egbert.''

He had felt even more stupid. It served him right for asking
personal questions. And then she had smiled, a smile born in
the cave of her mouth that forced her lips apart and leaped out.

"You don't believe it either," she said. "No one believes
that story but myself and even I am sometimes doubtful." She
put the smile and the cigarette back into her mouth. "Ravel
is a very funny Frenchman," she added, "and you a very funny
American."

He had wanted to tell her then that he wasn't American but
the crowd came between them and they were forced apart. The
thought of Egbert had remained with him throughout the rest
of the symphony and when it was over he had searched through
the people to find her again.

Egbert! They had had good times together before that last
night when he had felt the blood rise in him to form another
man, a harsh, cruel, irritable man and he had called out in a
voice that astonished him, "God, God, God! Can you never
say anything that you haven't pilfered from other brains? Can
you never say anything of your own? When I want La
Rochefoucauld or Heine or Lawrence I can read them for myself.
A man cannot live on your second-hand conversations presented
as your own."

The half-moon lids had lowered. The harsh, cruel, irritable
man within him had died as he watched her face. And he had
almost moved to her side when she said:

"Ah, Carl, you have hurt me. But it is all right, all right.
'I've always known what it was to accept an enormous emptiness
round me, echoing and echoing, and I sitting there in the middle,
like a paper doll reflected in hundreds of mirrors.' ''

Poor child, he thought, starting impulsively towards her. And then he had remembered. That too, he had read. The words suddenly took form on a page and he saw it all. It was blue-covered, the book. He couldn't quite remember but he knew those words. She had thought he wouldn't but he did. The harsh, angry man had risen again and he had walked from the room. As he reached the door he had swung round, ready to speak, seeing the book in his head. "Wolf Solent," he had heard his own words and seen her cover her mouth and sag in her chair. He had opened the door and gone.

Carl glanced at his watch. It was time he changed, time he changed to see Kristin. The thought of her, coming fresh from "The Egg" was clean and sweet. He turned on the bath water and laid out his clothes for the evening. The thought of seeing Kristin was like a whistle in his mouth.

Standing on the veranda, waiting for the door to be answered, Carl felt caught up in the green evening light thrown out from the leaves of the trees. And he felt for one moment as if he were standing at the bottom of the sea, with marine vegetation growing thick and strong about him. If he moved it would be with the slow movement of flesh against water.

The door was open now; the inside light shattered the sea illusion. He stepped over the sill.

"If you would leave your things in the den, sir," the maid said.

He held out his hands and shrugged. There was nothing to leave. "Oh!" gasped the maid, "I'm sorry, sir." And he laughed.

"Ah, Mr Bridges!" Mrs Fender came to meet him. Her dress of black was tailored and severe as a man's dinner jacket and the white front of organdie was crisp and fresh about her slim neck.

"Come in," she said. "Ralph's mixing the cocktails and Kristin should be down in a minute."

He liked the room, cool, green, low, with two vases of white stocks.

"I'm glad you're not superstitious about white flowers," he said, "I love them."

"So do I." She was pleased, he could tell, but her eyes guarded her pleasure. She reached for a cigarette and put it in her mouth. He paused before he lit it for her.

Standing there, slim and straight, with her black plastic hair, the black and white of her dress and her pale face, she made an astonishing figure.

"You look very lovely," he said, and held his lighter for her. She fluttered just a little and looked up from the flame.

"Oh, Mr Bridges, you flatter an old woman." She said it with an air of having said it often, the "old woman" emphasized. But she touched his hand as she bent again to the lighter. And at that moment, he felt, with some extra-sensory power, that he held the key to her in his hands. He knew now more than she could ever tell him of her life. Grace Fender had travelled a long road to this surface serenity. And now that she had attained it her husband ceased to love her. The two things had happened simultaneously, he felt certain. His consciousness leapt to a point of interest—laboriously Mrs Fender had built her own shell. As he thought this, Kristin entered. She was in white again, casual, the top of her dress like a shirt, open at the neck, the skirt plain. But as he noticed, as he took her in, as he said "Hello!" and she came forward to him, so was he aware of Mrs Fender's shell stiffening. The mother had fortified herself for the daughter's approach.

Kristin sat and hung her long hand over the arm of the chair. "What did you do this afternoon, Carl?"

"Yes, tell us," said Mrs Fender. "What does an artist do in the afternoon?" She said it lightly, scoffing at her own words.

"Nothing, Mrs Fender, I assure you. I started two letters and then abandoned them. It was too hot to follow them through."

"It *was* hot!" said Mrs Fender. "I'm told it was the hottest afternoon of the year, though how people know these things

I can't imagine. I wish Ralph would hurry with the cocktails. He must be making—oh, here you are, Ralph.''

Carl got up. Mr Fender carried a long tray gay with old-fashioneds. "Good evening, sir," Carl said.

"Evening, evening, Bridges. Sorry I've been so long." Beaded perspiration marked his hair line. "The kitchen is hot," he said, passing the tray.

"It is cool in here, Ralphey; sit down and enjoy your drink." She prodded at hers with the muddler.

"Always," said Kristin, "I think the cube of pineapple is a sugar lump and wonder why it won't dissolve. Always."

"I should think, by now, you might have learned." Her father laughed at her. They all laughed. There was something just a little bit strained, as if iron girders held the family together but also held them apart. Carl felt that he alone was free. He could go near or escape entirely.

"I'm very taken with this part of the world," he said. "It's beautiful country."

Mr Fender put down his drink and slapped his knee. "Don't know where you'll find anything to equal it," he said. "Why, take the rivers alone, if we had nothing else here but the rivers it'd be a prize province. And the fishing here! I tell you, boy—why, Lowell Thomas wrote a book about it. Ever read it? I haven't myself, I must admit, but we've got it here somewhere if you want to have a look at it. And the hunting—if you're here for the hunting season I'll take you out. I've a couple of good dogs in the kennels. A little pointer bitch, she's a wonder. If there's a bird in miles Nettie'll find it. And the springer—he's young yet—but a good dog. That dog can carry an egg in his mouth for miles."

He paused. And this is Kristin's father, Carl thought.

"Get on with your drink, Ralph," Mrs Fender said. "We're all ahead of you. Finish it up and mix us another round. The dinner's cold, it can wait."

"Good idea," said Mr Fender, draining his glass. He got

to his feet quickly for a fat man.

Kristin has hardly spoken, Carl mused. She is sitting, holding silence to her. Mr Fender collected the glasses.

"Not for me, Daddy," Kristin said, keeping her glass and still exploring it with her muddler.

"One day," said her mother, "you'll bite the end off the muddler mistaking it for the cherry." Her voice had risen a little. Kristin smiled—a smile that crumpled the satin of her mouth to the petal of a shirley poppy.

"How did the sitting go?" asked Mrs Fender so suddenly that Carl felt the words had come at him from a catapult and hit upon his skin rather than his ears.

"Very well," he said. "Your daughter is an excellent model."

"I must come down and see it some time, that is, if you'll let me. And if it's for sale we'd very much like to buy it."

"Oh no," said Carl, feeling thin with discomfort. "Oh no, there is no obligation. I mean you are under no obligation at all. It was as a favour to me that I asked Kristin to sit, I assure you."

"But," said Mrs Fender, "you don't seem to understand. We should like to have it."

Carl rolled his cigarette between his fingers. He could feel the warmth of the old-fashioned coursing through him. He looked at Kristin.

"If," he said to Mrs Fender, "if it is good, if you like it, let me give it to you."

He noticed the mother's eyes jump to Kristin's face before she said: "Mr Bridges, it is sweet of you, but really . . ."

"Let's leave it like that," he said, wanting to escape the subject, knowing that in saying what he had he had given the first real clue to Mrs Fender of what existed between Kristin and himself. He tried to find some indication on Kristin's face as to how she felt at this moment, now that he had given them away to her mother. But Mr Fender entered with the tray. His face was red.

"Here we are then," he beamed. But the mood had changed since he had left. He looked bewildered.

Carl took his drink unhappily.

"And now," said Mr Fender settling himself, "tell me, how is this painting job coming? I don't know much about art," he said, "but I'm always ready to learn, always ready to learn."

Carl winced. "I'll be able to tell you more about it later, sir," he said, anxious to hold the conversation away from Mrs Fender. "It's a slow business, like anything else. You have to have the patience of a fisherman and the eye of a hunter to do a good job of work."

"Jove! patience," exclaimed Mr Fender slapping his knee again, scampering off with his own subject. "D'you know, last year, I sat four hours on a rock above a little pool in my favourite stream, waiting. Four hours," he said. "I knew there were trout there, I could see them, great big sleepy fellows. Every so often I'd change my fly and try another sort. And d'you know what fly eventually did the trick?"

"No, sir," said Carl, looking at Kristin and noticing a flicker of laughter in her face. He heard her father's voice but the words were smudged like the words of someone talking in his sleep. He had done it now, they were safe for the moment. He took a long drink of his old-fashioned and relaxed. Mrs Fender was sitting, her feet under her, disinterested.

"And that was the little beggar," said Mr Fender loudly, "that, if you can believe it, was the little beggar that made those trout rise."

"Was it really, sir?" Carl tried hard to be serious but he wanted to laugh. For no reason that he could possibley name he wanted to give himself up to laughter.

"That was the one," Kristin's father continued, "and the funny part is I can hardly get a soul to believe it." He chuckled.

"No more fisherman's tales tonight, Ralph," said his wife from the sofa. "Not until you two are having your coffee, at any rate. Kristin and I are lost. Tell me, Mr Bridges, where were you before you came here?"

"Wandering," said Carl. "Just before I came here I was in Montreal, but before that I was up North and before that again, in the West Indies."

"Ah," Mrs Fender's face softened, as though remembering something lovely and sad. "Were you in Nassau?"

"No," he said. "Trinidad and Barbados chiefly—and Martinique."

"But not Nassau?"

"No."

"It is lovely there," she said. "But I suppose the islands are all more or less alike." She seemed to shake herself with a sudden resolution. "And now," she said, "if you've finished your drinks perhaps we ought to go in to dinner."

During dinner Carl was enchanted. The two old-fashioneds had done their work. Kristin across the table was like the water-lily that floated in the bowl between them. Mr Fender was very jovial; he brandished the carving-knife like a familiar butcher, thumped the table with his ham-like fist and grew redder and redder so that his fair-grey hairs stood out almost singly against his scarlet scalp. Mrs Fender had tightened up imperceptibly. Carl didn't mind. He was caught up in the stream of his own good humour and opposite him, drifting in a pool of stillness, was Kristin smiling through her eyes.

Mrs Fender wanted to know about places. Throughout the meal she asked him questions about the countries he had visited. It is as if she has a lover wandering through the world and she wants a background for him, he thought. He was glad to tell her, for in so doing, he supplied for Kristin the bare stage-setting of his life. Still Kristin scarcely spoke. There is something unreal in all this, Carl thought—the candlelight polishing the silver, the shiny surface of the table, the two women, as different

50

as the two poles and over all the weight of Mr Fender, the mad butcher, expanding, growing louder as the minutes passed. He could feel Mrs Fender's eyes on him when he turned away from her; so close was her scrutiny that he felt he dare not look at Kristin, for to look was to have the love he felt for her break on the surface of his face and proclaim itself.

"Do you ever lecture, Mr Bridges?"

He laughed, remembering his one and only lecture. "No-o," he said. "I did once, that was all." But why, he thought, has she asked me that? Surely she is not hoping to book me up to speak at some women's club. Women's faces in rows, as though planted out by the supreme Gardener and then left, without nourishment or sunshine. He had seen them before.

"It's your voice," said Mrs Fender. "I like your voice and your hands. I can see you standing on a platform with a pointer in your hands."

"It would be painful," he said. "I can't think how people do it."

Mr Fender put down his fork with a clatter. "Nothing to it," he said. "Why, it's as simple as just talking here—simpler really, because you know the thread of what you are going to say and you follow it, while in conversation you never know what is going to be said or expected of you two sentences ahead." He paused, considered his words. "Why, that's quite a point," he said, pleased, "quite a point! I'd never thought of it just that way before. But the important thing about speaking," he said, "is to talk slowly, give yourself time to choose your next word." He wagged his thick forefinger in Carl's face.

"I hope, sir," Carl said, "I sincerely hope I shall never have the opportunity to take advantage of your tip. That's the trouble with making any kind of a name for yourself, people immediately expect you to be able to do anything."

Why is Kristin so silent? he thought. Is she unhappy, is she cross with me for running after her this afternoon? But as he thought she spoke.

51

"That is true, I think," she said, "about people expecting you to be able to do anything if you can do one thing really well. And the opposite is true too. If you have never proved yourself skilful in one thing, people think there is nothing you can do at all."

"Perhaps." Carl considered it.

The fact that this had been the first attempt at conversation Kristin had made all evening gave greater importance to her words—as if, he thought, she is saying more than the surface of her thought implies. Is she speaking to me? he wondered, wanting to atone for her lack of talents, wanting to let me know that there is something she can do?—she, the perfect woman, unaware of her perfection, trying to build herself up. Or is she—his mind rested a minute in satisfaction, feeling that this second thought was the right one—is she talking to her parents, warning them of what is to come? He smiled at her across the water-lily. She is mine now, surely, he thought. And the desire to go to her swept over him so strongly that he forced himself to return to the frozen dessert he was eating. He scrutinized it carefully.

"Don't eat it if you don't like it, Mr Bridges," Mrs Fender said.

"But I do, really." He began eating hastily to prove his words, too hastily. I am making them ill at ease, he thought, and he looked at Kristin quickly for a clue. She looks golden in the candlelight now that the room is darker. I wonder, he thought, how they would feel if I sold stocks and bonds, whether it would have made a different atmosphere for them, whether they would now be laughing, throwing out small, smart phrases at each other and resting on them?

Mrs Fender lit a cigarette in the flame of a candle and leaned her pointed elbows on the table; Kristin wiped her mouth carefully and gazed long at the smudge of lipstick on the napkin; the only sound came from Mr Fender, who, with a schoolboy's zest, was finishing up his frozen dessert. Each one, he thought, absorbed, complete, and he looked away from them to the candle flames, feeling that in looking at them now he was looking at them exposed and naked as though he were peeping at them alone in their bedrooms. No two out of the three, he thought, share a common ground and he was glad of the knowledge, glad of the further understanding of Kristin that lay embedded in it.

"A cigar?" asked Mr Fender, passing Carl his case. And Carl took it, unwilling to hurt the boy butcher by refusing.

When he looked again at the three of them they had each risen from their moment of isolation. He could look now without feeling ashamed. But the air still rippled like water from the movements of arising.

"Come, Kristin," said Mrs Fender, "we'll leave the men together. You and I will have our coffee in the other room."

As Carl watched them leave he wondered what the two of them would talk about when they were together. Sitting in that low, green, peaceful room, Mrs Fender with her feet tucked under her on the chesterfield, Kristin draped like a length of taffeta on one of the chairs.

But Mr Fender had begun. "To get back to fishing," he said, winking, "now that the wife can't object." The maid entered with the coffee and liqueurs and Mr Fender stopped.

"We have no choice of liqueurs," he said apologetically, "it's Grande Marnier or Grande Marnier," and his face crinkled with amusement.

"Then Grande Marnier it shall be, sir," said Carl.

"An excellent choice," continued Mr Fender, delighted with their make-believe.

With the first sip of the liqueur Carl had the strange sensation that his brain had warmed, swelled and divided. One part was with Kristin, the other part was here with her father, laughing at his obvious and rather crude jokes. Mr Fender had already started his second liqueur and passed the bottle to Carl.

"Kristin," said Mr Fender, changing the subject abruptly, "is a very queer child."

"She is a very beautiful child," Carl amended.

"Beautiful—" he stopped. "Hm, I hadn't thought about that. She's put together well... But beautiful, well, I dunno. Confidentially," he said, leaning forward, "Grace and I are almost frightened of her. We wouldn't have her know that, of course, but she's different. Grace sometimes thinks she was a changeling. These hospitals, you know," he said, "how they can ever keep the babies identified. God, they all look alike!"

Carl laughed. Mr Fender poured another drink. He is feeling them, Carl thought, they evidently make him fanciful. I wonder if later he'll be sorry for what he is saying now?

"This is very much between the two of us," Mr Fender continued, curling his fingers around the cigar, "but Kristin is sometimes queer," he dropped his head and rolled up his eyes. "Sometimes," he said, "she goes comatose—or so it seems. She won't move or speak."

"She's just naturally quiet," Carl said hurriedly.

"You may call it that," Mr Fender went on. "You may call it that if you will. But it's queer. Grace and I don't understand her at all."

Carl could see her with her mother now and he wanted to go to her, the pale child who held his thoughts.

"Well, we may as well join them," Mr Fender said: "But don't let on I've spoken to you in this way, I wouldn't have them know I've told you."

He looks old now, Carl thought. He is worried.

"Ah, here you are," said Mrs Fender. "You've been a long time over your coffee. I hope," she said, "you've talked yourself out on the fishing subject, Ralphey."

Kristin stretched out her legs and looked at the tips of her evening shoes, speaking slowly as if to them. "There's an eclipse tonight," she said to the left foot, "an eclipse of the moon.

I should love to drive up to the park to see it.'' She inclined her head towards the right toe. "Let's all drive up to the park.''

Carl noticed a look of concern pass between the parents.

"I'm simply too lazy to move,'' Mrs Fender said. "Why don't you two young things go? Ralph and I will stay here.''

"Oh, come with us,'' said Carl, "it's a beautiful night.''

"Not for me,'' Mr Fender said, settling himself and lighting another cigar. "I'm too old for such things. You and Kristin go, as Grace suggested. Have you your car?''

"No, it was such a nice night I walked.''

"Well, you can have mine. I'll go and get it.''

"Let me,'' said Carl.

"He never lets anyone back that car out of the garage but himself,'' Mrs Fender said. "You run along, Kristin, and get a coat.''

"You two don't want us butting in,'' said Mrs Fender when they were alone. "I'm only glad Ralph had the sense to realize it. When Ralph gets an idea there's no changing him... and he does get funny ideas,'' she laughed lightly, lightly moving about the room as she spoke. "Kristin hates a crowd anyway,'' She went on. "You noticed her at dinner. She's a strange child; most people don't understand her. But I have the feeling you do. She comes home happy when she's been with you.''

The father, thought Carl, is trying to frighten me away; the mother, meanwhile, is anxious to encourage me.

Mrs Fender stopped in front of him and put her hands on his shoulders. "Carl,'' her eyes were worried as he looked into them, "Carl, don't hurt her. I couldn't bear my Kristin hurt. She hasn't the normal defence mechanism. She doesn't know how to ward off blows.''

"Do any of us?'' he asked.

"Yes, yes! I do. I've had to. I could walk through hell fire now.''

Is she acting? Carl thought. Why is she talking like this? She walked away; she was just a little bit dramatic.

"I shouldn't speak like this unless it was necessary." She smiled suddenly, touched the petals of a stock. "She was born on the night of an eclipse," she said. "I was happy that night. But I've learned since that happiness is unimportant."

"No," said Carl, "not unimportant; but not the only importance as so many people think."

"That," she said, "is over my head. And now good-bye." She held out her hand. "I hear Kristin coming and the car is in the front, I can see the lights." She looked young, brave. He wanted to assure her somehow that Kristin was safe with him. He squeezed her hand.

"It's awfully good of you, sir, to let us have the car. I'll try not to bash it up too much." They were on the steps. Mr Fender was telling him it had the new gear shift and that the emergency brake was under the dash-board.

Kristin snuggled against him in the car. "Darling," she said, "was it a hideous evening? I'm no help at a party. I find it so difficult to talk."

"It was a very enjoyable evening," Carl said. "I know you so much better for it."

"Do you? You know about them?"

"Your parents? Yes."

"It's strange," said Kristin, "they've been awfully patient. You've no idea how hard it's been for us all. It may sound silly, this talk of not being understood, it's been so overdone. But it's not a case of not being understood or of misunderstanding—there's not enough touching of hands for that. It's more like the stars—from a distance we look part of a pattern as the stars do, but actually we are miles part—there is no contact."

"Do you feel the same way with me—miles away?"

"No, no." Her voice was suddenly intense. "Oh, perhaps I do," she added, "but differently. It's more as if you're the sun and I the moon; you the strong, vital element and I but a pale thin light—and yet in spite of the difference in quality you are able to eclipse me and . . ." she stopped.

56

"And you able to eclipse me?" He waited a long time for her answer.

"Yes," she said at length, "yes."

"Well, darling, this is evidently my night." They had reached the park. He turned the car off the road and stopped it. "But I wouldn't mind being eclipsed by you one little bit."

"Don't say that!" She clutched his knee firmly. "Carl," she said, "don't say that, or even think it, ever again, will you?"

"Darling, why?"

"I can't tell you. Just *don't*. Please!" She sounded so desperate that under the night he had to smile as he gave his promise—a strange, solemn oath to satisfy her childish whim.

Clouds had rolled up out of the west and covered the sky. "Damn," he said, "we shan't see that eclipsed moon after all." He expected her to be disappointed.

"It doesn't matter," she said. "It doesn't matter a bit. It is there just the same, the feeling's there."

"Could you tell by the feel?"

"Of course," she said. "I was born during an eclipse." She seemed to think that was explanation enough. "Let's walk down by the lake."

"Won't it ruin your shoes?"

She laughed at him. "You are cautious, darling."

He caught her hand. "Only for you," he said. Why, because she had laughed at him, did he love her more; why because of that laugh, ever so faintly mocking, did he want to hold her, bend her to him, lose himself in the length of her kiss?

A small wind blew her hair across his face like a tent. She drew away, stood stork-like on one leg and began taking off her shoes and stockings.

"See," she said holding up her long skirt, "my shoes will be saved from ru-in." She threw them into the car.

She moved white against the darkness, like a silver birch swaying. I am in love with a moon-child, he thought. She will never be mine, never. And as he started after her he was filled with the same fascination, the same melancholy he felt when swimming at night, following the path of the moon.

The second sitting was not successful. Carl, though eager to begin that second morning, had, as he worked, felt incompetent. With his eyes on Kristin he was sure of what he wanted, but brush in hand, eyes on the canvas, a lethargy crept through him.

"I'm in poor form, this morning," he said repeatedly. "Perhaps I'd better leave it. I'll only ruin what I've got."

But he kept on. I can't give in, he said to himself. If I give in now I only make it too easy to give in the next time, and using every bit of creative energy he could gather he fought against the feeling that someone else had taken over his hands. Perhaps I have tried too hard, he thought. Tomorrow it will be different. Even Kristin is remote this morning; I can't reach her.

At the end of the sitting as she pulled a comb through her hair he said, "Stay for a minute and talk." But she only shook her head. And he was half glad. The morning had depressed him. He didn't want to excuse himself to her.

Waiting next morning for her to come he worried at his canvas. God! he thought, I worked with a heavy hand yesterday! But he was confident. He felt enthusiastic. Until she came he would take out, paint over, undo the heaviness of his own work. And when she came he was pleased.

"Darling," he went to her, holding her with his wrists so that he shouldn't smudge her with the paint on his fingers. "Look, I've undone it. Yesterday's botches are hidden."

He began again, working easily, finding a thrill of power in the mastery over paint and canvas. But gradually, imperceptibly at first, the lethargy returned, the stiffness. It is almost, he thought, as if someone is using my faculties, or I using someone else's. And he grew frightened. What was happening? Have I suddenly lost my ability, he thought, am I no longer Carl

Bridges, the artist? What strange force is sucking my body's strength?

"Kristin," he began, but it was no good. Kristin was more remote than ever; if he spoke to her she seemed barely conscious of his words. It is all like a bad dream, he thought. But soon even his thoughts trailed away from him and he worked with a mechanical lack of talent and pitiful lack of power. On and on, on and on, on and on, on and on.

At last Kristin moved. He saw her shift on her chair and get up. The dream-like quality remained, she was the other side of a veil and he could not move to her or touch her. Then suddenly the veil vanished, the dream was over. He was alive, fresh, energetic. He felt like a dog coming out of the water; he wanted to shake himself. It was all behind him now. Those strange muddled movements, that sick fatigue, the woodenness of his body—finished, ended.

Kristin seemed barely able to move; she said nothing, as if to open her lips was the ultimate in exercise. Walking with the quietness of death upon her, she reached the couch and fell on it.

"Kristin," he went to her, contrite. Again he had made her sit too long. "Kristin!" He bent over. Already she was asleep. Her breast rose and fell with deep, regular breathing. Poor darling, he thought as he spread his coat over her, poor little thing.

He tiptoed over to his easel. What had he done, he wondered, in that interval when consciousness slept? He looked at his watch. Two hours he had painted—what had come of those two hours? But as he reached the easel he felt sick. His own eyes mocked him out of the thick mess of paint. He covered his face, shuddering, trying to remember. It was Kristin he was painting. And there, for proof, on the couch, Kristin lay sleeping. Hold to that, hold to that, he thought. It is Kristin you painted but uncovering his eyes again, staring at the canvas he felt the sick twist in his stomach, the ice creep along his jaw.

Kristin or not—the canvas mirrored him.

Two-inch headlines formed: You are mad, mad.

He had painted Kristin, but instead, crude and terrifying was his own face to contradict him. His own lips shaped, "Do you not know me? Will you not acknowledge me? You and I—we are one."

He felt his mind break into hundreds of black pin men, each screaming, "We are one, we are one, we are one!" If Kristin were awake, he thought, crushing the pin men, she would tell me, she would explain. He would call her. It was all quite simple. He would call her and she would waken and the bird in her throat would say, "Darling, you're dreaming. Look—the portrait is me, not you. Look, Carl. It is Kristin." Yes, yes, Kristin would tell him.

But as he opened his mouth to speak all thought of Kristin vanished in the sudden desperate realization that he was going to be sick.

PART 3

CARL AND KRISTIN

"Darling, darling, darling! Wake up. It's a beautiful morning and there's a telegram for you."

"I am awake," Kristin said, sitting up. And then stretching out her hand, "A telegram, for me?" Shivers ran down her legs.

"Do you think it could be Carl Bridges?" Her mother was excited. "Do open it, Kristin."

Kristin looked at her mother. Certainly she would not leave until the envelope was open, until she knew the message that lay, secretly, behind that opaque envelope. And so I may as well get it over with, Kristin thought. But she wanted to wait. Wanted to hold the envelope in her hand and then very slowly open the flap and all alone read those typed words that perhaps would, surely must, end in the word "Carl".

"Hurry, darling." Her mother was sitting on the bed, her eyes flashing little sparks, her long white hands held together, fingers interlocked.

Carl had been gone a month now—over a month. After that terrible morning when she had awakened on his sofa to the sound of his nausea she hadn't seen him again. And she had only had one short letter: "Forgive me, I had to leave. The cold impact of fear was more than I could face. Another experience like that would send me mad. But my painting's all right now, I've been doing a lot. My work, as you must know, is not only my livelihood but my life. That is why I was so frightened. I love you, Kristin. Try to hold that as truth." She remembered every word of that letter.

"Kristin, are you trying to pique me? If you don't open it I will myself." Her mother moved impatiently on the bed as Kristin held the envelope to the light and tore the end off it. "Arriving at one o'clock Tuesday meet me if you can. Carl." Kristin tried to hold herself steady.

"It's Carl," she said. "He's arriving today."

"Today! How exciting! Kristin, I believe I'm more excited than you are. What a funny child you are. Aren't you glad?"

Glad! What a word, thought Kristin, stretching her legs straight and thinking her heart would surely break the barrel of her ribs. Glad!

"Yes, mother, I'm glad." Oh, go now, she thought, please go. Leave me alone with this moment.

But her mother crossed to the cupboard and sorted through the dresses. "You're going to meet him, of course. What will you wear?"

Wear, thought Kristin, wear? What does it matter what I

wear, she thought, what does it matter if I go as I am? What does anything matter beside the reality of Carl returning?

"Why don't you wear this pretty green dress, Kristin? You've hardly had it on more than once and you look sweet in it. I can't imagine why you don't like it."

"All right," said Kristin.

The mother looked inquiringly at her daughter. "You are a funny child," she said. "I should think you'd be excited."

Can't you see, thought Kristin, that I'm so excited I daren't use words? Can't you see that life has begun again for me; that this long, dead interval is finished? Don't you realize that it is true that he loves me? The core of life that dissolved with his going has formed again.

Waiting at the station, pushing through the heavy swing doors, walking onto the board walk of the platform, Kristin could hardly bear it. It is to breathe again, she thought, lungs that were cramped are free again. The tether that staked me to death has snapped.

"Miss Fender," a crisp voice came over her shoulder. She turned. Miss Gillespie was there with her notebook. "Are you expecting someone on this train?"

"Yes," said Kristin, "Carl Bridges."

The reporter's eyebrows lifted. "Is he to be here long?" She was making little marks in her book.

"I don't know," Kristin replied.

Miss Gillespie stopped writing. "Perhaps I'd better wait and interview him," she said. "After all, he is news. Ah, here she comes now." Miss Gillespie looked at her watch. "On time to the minute. I only hope there are a lot of people getting off. The society column's been poor the last few days, no one's entertaining."

No one's entertaining, no one's entertaining, thought Kristin to herself as the train roared in. She tried to catch a glimpse of Carl in the windows, but saw only a blur of faces. The train stopped. Carl, Carl, Carl! She scanned the people getting off.

He hasn't come, she thought, he must have missed it. And the ache in her emptied her, left her drained. Of all the people who are getting off, of all the people who have been waiting, I am the only one left, the only one not feeling happiness surge in me.

"Oh," she took a breath. "Oh!" There he was. She began to run. "Carl!" she called, for he hadn't seen her. "Carl!" He was in a jumble of luggage and porters and people.

And then he saw her and broke free from the jumble. He pushed the people away. He took her hands. He looked the same—exactly the same—still brown and tall and thin. She wanted to cry again. He was like music, sunlight.

"Darling, you came."

"Yes, I came."

"If you knew what I've suffered, wondering, wondering—will she come? What if she's busy? What if she doesn't want to see me? The thousand 'ifs' that tormented me, dragged me apart." He held her hands still.

"Mr Bridges," said Miss Gillespie, arriving, "I represent the press. May I say that you are in town?"

Carl hardly turned from Kristin. "Yes," he said, "yes."

"And are you going to be here long?" Miss Gillespie continued.

"I've made no plans yet," said Carl.

"Perhaps I could see you later," said Miss Gillespie, "when you have decided."

"Certainly," said Carl. "I'll be at the hotel."

"Thank you." Miss Gillespie moved off.

"Let's go," he said. He turned for a porter. "Those are mine," he said to the red-cap.

"Will you want a taxi, sir?"

"I have the car," said Kristin.

They followed the porter. "It's good to see you, darling."

"Oh, and it's good to see *you*."

"Missed me?"

63

"I've hardly lived since you left."

"Why didn't you write?"

"I couldn't. I felt dead."

"Oh, my darling, I was a beast!"

"No, no. I understood."

They had reached the car. The porter stowed away the bags.

"Just let me look at you," Carl said, "for a minute, just let me stare and stare." They sat together in the car. Kristin wondered if she would ever be able to drive, she was trembling so.

"I had to leave," Carl said, "and I had to come back. I had to leave to make sure of my work. I had to come back to make sure of you. Now I'm sure of both. Kristin, I've never been as happy in my life."

"We must go," she said. "Mother's expecting us for lunch." She stepped on the starter. "Do you want to book a room at the hotel first?"

"I can phone from your place," he said.

Mrs Fender met them on the step. "Carl," she said, "how nice to see you again. How more than nice." She gave him her hand, drew him in. "You must be hungry," she said. "One always has breakfast so agonizingly early on a train. And it's after one now. We won't stop for a drink. You can have one with your meal . . . oh, and you know where the bathroom is. You'll probably want a wash up."

"Thank you," said Carl. "I think I will, if you don't mind."

"Kristin, why didn't you wear a hat? I did ask you to."

"Forgot," said Kristin. "simply forgot."

"I'm sure Mrs Lothrop would like to see Carl," said Mrs Fender. "Perhaps I could get her to tea."

"Oh, Mummy, don't. Wait and ask Carl. He's probably tired."

Kristin couldn't eat, nor could Carl very much and Mrs Fender looked at the food and at them in despair. But even her glances didn't lower their exuberance. They caught each other's eyes across the table and laughed. Carl kept lighting cigarettes throughout the meal.

He said, "I've never worked as hard in my life as in this last month. I've brought some of my things with me. If you'd like to see them I'll——"

"But we'd love to, Carl." Mrs Fender was delighted. "Love to. Let us see all we can while we can." She smiled at him. "For we never know when you are suddenly going to disappear again."

"That time I couldn't help it; I wasn't well."

"You look well."

"I am now." It is hard, he thought, to remember Mrs Fender when I am conscious only of Kristin.

And Kristin thought, if only mother would realize the ecstasy of this moment and not keep pinning us both down with trivialities. We are like two moths, impaled on the feelers of her curiosity breaking free only to be caught again.

In the hall as Carl untied the canvases Kristin thought, this is as it should have been, as it should always be. This moment is rounded with communion; the ends of the circle are joined; it is complete.

"That," said Carl propping a canvas against the hall table and speaking for Kristin's ears chiefly, "was the first thing I did after I left." A red-headed boy against a background of brick buildings, crude and powerful. Poor Carl, thought Kristin, what an effort to escape from me. But she could say nothing.

"It's very queer," said Mrs Fender, "not exactly my meat, though I'm certain it's very good."

Oh, can't you feel, thought Kristin, Carl's terror, Carl's daring? Can't you feel the reassertion of his masculinity?

Does she understand? Carl thought. I hope she knows. I want her to know, want her to see that I am all right now and this is my only means of telling her.

As the other canvases were unwrapped, propped up, Carl felt better. He had told her everything now—his fears and his ultimate triumph. And as he watched her, he saw her eyes return again and again to the red-headed boy.

"I like it," she said. "I like it so. It is not as good but it's more courageous than the others—like the beginning of a journey."

She knows, she knows, he thought.

"How strangely you talk, Kristin," said Mrs Fender. "I don't even know what you mean—like the beginning of a journey." They laughed then. "Do you understand her, Carl?"

"I think so, Mrs Fender." Of course I do, he said with his eyes to Kristin, of course.

The maid appeared in the doorway. "The telephone, Mrs Fender."

"I wonder who it is?" said Mrs Fender as she left.

"Darling, you know." Carl went to her, tipped up her face.

"Carl, how you've suffered!" And I can never tell him, she thought, how I've suffered. Can never tell him I stole his identity. "Kiss me," she said, "quickly, Carl. Mother will be back."

"Oh, my sweet, it's been so long. Kristin, I want you to have the painting—that first one. I feel somehow that you must have it. Would you like it?"

"More than anything you've ever done; more than anything in the world." Having that I am safe, she thought, it is the part of Carl I cannot touch, the upspringing kernel that I cannot destroy.

And Carl thought, how did I ever live away from her? How can I ever bear to be separated from her again? He led her out of the open door onto the veranda.

"If everything were to stop now," she said, "if the bells tolled out the end of the world and darkness fell upon us and washed us into oblivion I should not care. I am happier now than I have ever been."

"It is exactly two twenty-five," said Carl, "to the minute. Remember that time, Kristin, for on such a minute do I ask you to marry me.'' He looked out across the lawn. She must say ''Yes'' he thought. Surely, she will say ''Yes''.

At two twenty-five exactly, he wants me to be his wife—his wife, she thought. Oh, Carl, is it true? It all feels unreal. She turned to him, looked at him. ''What is the time now, Carl?''

''Two twenty-seven,'' he said.

''At two twenty-seven,'' she said, ''exactly, I answer that I will.''

''Oh, my darling!'' He kissed her. ''Now all that's left is to ask your father for your hand, in the time-honoured custom.''

''Really?'' She laughed. ''It seems so silly—as if it's any affair of daddy's anyway.''

''I'll ask him tonight. We'll look at rings this afternoon.''

''Oh, Carl.'' She looked at her hand. ''I never dreamed that I'd be engaged. Isn't it funny?'' He kissed her fingers.

''I suppose everyone can see us. Does it matter very much?''

''Children, children!'' Mrs Fender's voice called, ''That was Sarah Lothrop, she wants us all to go to tea this afternoon.''

Carl and Kristin looked at each other and laughed. ''What does it matter,'' said Carl, ''what does anything matter now?''

''Did you accept?'' asked Kristin as they returned to the hall.

''Why, of course, darling. You know it was through the Lothrop's that we met Carl. It would be very ungracious to try to monopolize him now, wouldn't it?''

''Well, Mummy, Carl wants to get a room at the hotel and take his stuff down. Would it be all right if we went and saw to that now and then collected you in time for tea?''

Mrs Fender eyed them both. Does she know? thought Kristin. And Carl bent down and began to strap his canvases together, not daring to trust his eyes under her probing.

''That'll give you a little over an hour,'' she said. ''Sarah likes tea promptly at four o'clock.''

Kristin couldn't help laughing—what did Sarah and her stupid ''on the dot of four'' matter? How absurd to regulate life by hours when life was a flower unfolding, unfolding in the face of time.

"You haven't packed 'The Boy' ", Mrs Fender said.

"He's given him to me, Mummy."

"How good of him." Mrs Fender's voice showed she was glad he had not given it to her.

Good, thought Carl, good! When I would have given her wings, given her the world if only I could. It is a poor substitute, he thought.

"Don't forget a hat this time, Kristin."

They packed the car again. It is as if, Kristin thought, we were off, as if we were leaving for good. And Carl thought as he stared at Mrs Fender on the veranda, she is sad, her happiness has ebbed from her. I hope she will find a new happiness in our delight. I should like to feel that somehow she will know happiness again through us. But as the car turned out of the driveway he forgot her, forgot everything in the miracle of knowing Kristin for his own.

"Darling, there's so much to talk about."

"I know," she said. "I know." How queer, she thought, that I know nothing about him, where he lives, his early life; but it hardly seems to matter.

And he thought, the rocks—surely she will tell me about the rocks now.

"The world goes on just the same," she said, braking the car. "The policeman at the corner holds up his hand to me and the square is full of people. But the gods are smiling on us a little," she added, drawing into the curb. "Look, we have parked right in front of the hotel." His hand closed over hers as she pushed the gear into neutral.

"Don't," she said. "Don't touch me or tell me you love me until we are in your room."

The bell boy took the bags. Carl carried his own canvases. He's tall and straight and slim as a weir pole, thought Kristin, in the dim light of the hotel.

"Ah, Mr Bridges, nice to see you," said Mr Seely at the desk. And then, "Good afternoon, Miss Fender."

"Are we going to have you with us again?" Mr Seely asked.

"If you can give me a room that overlooks the Square," said Carl.

"I think we can, I think we can—yes, there we are." Mr Seely slid the key onto the counter. "I hope you'll be comfortable," he said, beckoning the bell boy with a backward shake of his head. "Room 810," he said. "Take Mr Bridges' things up."

They walked behind the boy, their steps making no sound on the carpet. It is like a dream, thought Kristin, everything feels new. It might be a hotel in a strange city; familiarity is gone. She could say nothing.

But Carl chatted to the bell boy. "Were you here earlier in the summer?" he asked.

"No, sir. I'm new."

"I didn't remember your face," said Carl.

Kristin hardly heard. Carl, Carl, Carl, she thought. Carl's wife. Mrs Bridges. Kristin Bridges.

And Carl thought between the chatter, her green eyes, the satin of her mouth, the bird in her throat; and his hand tightened on the canvases.

Along the corridor, dark and heavily carpeted; the clatter of the key in the lock, loud in the quietness; the sudden burst of white light as the door swung open.

The bell boy put the suitcases on the stands, looked about him to make sure everything was in order. "Will that be all, sir?"

"Yes, I think so, thank you." Kristin watched Carl's brown hand move against the pale city flesh of the boy's as he tipped him. She watched the boy turn and go to the door and she moved toward Carl, unable to stay away a minute longer, as though she had been separated for years.

Oh, sweet, sweet, this moment as he held her, this poignant

flight, this upsurging miracle of loving.

"I hate this," said Carl, "kissing you in a hotel bedroom. There's something sordid about it."

"Oh, no!" Kristin exclaimed. "There's nothing sordid in loving. Already the room is beautiful." She closed her eyes, swaying a little before him.

"You have made it so," he said, looking only at her, at the pale star of Bethlehem on its slim green stem. And he drew her to him again, feeling the pulse in her white throat under his lips, tracing the long ivory column of her neck.

She sighed. "I am complete only when I am with you. Only in these minutes alone with you do I know myself to be three dimensional. Carl," she said, "to be loved is to know rebirth."

"If that's the case you'll be born again and again. I'll never stop loving you, Kristin."

She pulled away then, her fingers on his collar, her eyes serious. "Don't say that, Carl. Don't make promises. Love me now as I love you, don't think of the future."

"But if it's true, wise one?"

"Truth is a changing thing. We only know the truth of the moment. Love me at this moment completely." She moved away. "Your bed," she said, sitting on it. "Oh, my darling, if this moment could be forever."

"What a funny wife I've chosen," he said. "And now, what sort of a ring do you want?"

She looked at him suddenly then, in surprise. "I hadn't thought," she said.

"Try to think now. They probably won't have what you want. We'll have to order it."

"I think a moonstone," she said. "Something pale and cool."

He had started to unpack. His brushes and comb were on the dressing-table and his dressing-gown on the chair.

"Not diamonds?" he said.

"No, not diamonds. They flash. I hate things that flash. I

70

like to look and look at things and feel no splinters in my eyes."
She ran her hand over the counterpane as she spoke.

He leaned over her then, laughing. The square line of his
shoulder jutted against the light. She smiled up at him, slipped
her hands under his coat to know the strong line of his back
beneath his shirt.

"Carl," she began, but he covered her words and she sank
back under the eagerness of his lips, hungry as he from the
long time they had been parted. But in the back of her brain
a bell tolled out:

> "She stole his mouth—her own was fair—
> She stole his words, his songs, his prayer;
> His kisses too, since they were there."

And a small voice answered the tolling, "How can I steal what
I am returning? It isn't true."

"We must go," she said, "or we'll be late for mother."
She got up and stood before the mirror, running Carl's comb
through her hair. And he stood behind her watching her movements in the glass, watching her fill in the small patch of mouth
with vivid lipstick and smooth her hair to the texture of gold
satin.

"Sweet," he kissed the top of her head and she leaned against
him, their eyes meeting in the mirror. "When can we be married?" he asked.

"Oh, soon," she said. "It must be soon."

"Come then and we'll look for that ring."

She picked up her hat and walked out into the dark, silent
corridor and he, shutting the door on the strange room already
grown familiar, said, "And they celebrated their engagement
with a tea party at Mrs Lothrop's! Kristin, how we'll laugh about
it later—'Well, Mr Bridges, how nice to see you again and
you've brought little Kristin with you.' "

" 'Yes, Mrs Lothrop, little Kristin *would* come along.' "

" 'Well, how sweet; how pleased we are you returned to us.' "

Their laughter echoed in the corridor, making the hotel sound inhabited, gay, in spite of the darkness. But in the jeweller's their gaiety was subterranean. Kristin held her laughter in check as she heard Carl telling the shop girl confidentially that he was wanting to buy a ring for his sister as a birthday present; and she listened with grave eyes when the assistant suggested that perhaps her birthstone would make a nice gift.

"No," said Carl, turning to Kristin. "Hasn't Mary *always* said she wanted a moonstone?"

And Kristin heard herself replying, "That's what she always told me. I remember her saying the last time I saw her—moonstones, moonstones—over and over."

"We've not a very large choice in that particular stone," the girl continued, "but I'll show you what we have." She bent and scooped out a tray from the case, staying out of sight just long enough for them to turn to each other with ghost laughter on their faces.

"There," said Carl, picking one ring from the tray—a large moonstone set with small diamonds in a thin white-gold band. "Do you think Mary would like that one?"

"I don't see how she could help it," Kristin said, knowing that of all rings, she could like no other better.

"I do so want to get her something she'll really like."

"If she doesn't," Kristin said, "she's not the Mary I thought she was."

"That decides it," said Carl to the shop girl.

"You don't know her ring size?" the girl asked practically.

Carl showed mock annoyance. "I am a fool," he said. "Now what can I do?"

"She could always have it made to fit, of course," said the girl, but Kristin rushed into the breach just in time.

"I think her hands are about the same size as mine. We could wear each other's gloves anyway, if that's anything to

72

go by." And she stretched out her right hand and slipped the ring onto her fourth finger. "I'm certain it'll fit," she said, "quite certain."

"So that is that," said Carl as they left, "easy as can be. Do you really like it, darling?"

"Carl, I love it! But love it!"

In the car he opened the box. "Oh," sighed Kristin, seeing it again, "let me hold it, Carl." It was like a soap bubble in her hand. "It is beautiful, beautiful!"

"Try it on," he said, pushing it onto her engagement finger.

She sat staring at it, turning her hand right and left. "I wish I didn't have to take it off," she said. He bent, kissed the palm of her hand. "After tonight, after the formalities are over you need never take it off again."

After tonight! She put it back in the box and started the car. "Are we late?" she asked.

"We'll just make it."

Mrs Fender was waiting for them on the steps. And Carl thought, as he opened the car door, always she is on the steps; my mind holds a myriad images of Mrs Fender standing just here, welcoming us, waving us off.

"How punctual you are," she said, "and I'm ready. Kristin, your hat?"

"It's here," said Kristin.

"Well, put it on, darling."

Carl held the door for Mrs Fender. "No, no," she said. "I'll sit in the back. You two sit in the front." She got in; there was no time for persuasion, already she was settled.

The drive over amused Kristin. She couldn't help thinking how, two months ago, she had driven this route exactly, but driven it with a heart filled with fear and discomfort. And now, two months later, she was driving it again, this time with a heart almost too heavy with happiness. Where before there had been insecurity, now there was security.

Carl talked over the seat to Mrs Fender and Kristin heard

him only partly, heard his voice which she loved but failed to hear the words he was speaking. And as he talked, Carl thought, I can see Kristin in the mother. Kristin is what the mother might have been and has sacrificed for propriety and conventionality—sacrificed it to such an extent that she refuses to recognize herself in Kristin—refuses to acknowledge her old basic self.

The lawns are less green this time, Kristin thought as she brought the car to a stop, and the flowers in the border have changed. The air of festival has gone. It is nicer this way. The sweet tang of surprise will not be here today, but sweeter than surprise will be the awareness of a familiar Carl, the Carl I know, the Carl I'm engaged to.

As they walked up the path Mrs Fender lingered over the dahlias that flanked it. "Ours are so poor this year," she said. "And these—look at them. Beauties!" But Kristin was barely conscious of anything but Carl. Even tea with Mrs Lothrop was important, with Carl there.

"Sarah, dear!" said Mrs Fender as Mrs Lothrop came forward to greet them, the spider again in her parlour. But Sarah wasted no time on Mrs Fender, rushing instead into a profusion of greetings for Carl, her fly.

"Ah, Mr Bridges, how charming to see you again. I quite thought you had gone out of my life for good. Ah! Ah!" She sidled around him, fluttered and exclaimed. Kristin was laughing, remembering Carl's conversation in the hotel. "And Kristin," said Mrs Lothrop, hardly glancing at her; realizing Kristin's amusement as she turned away and turning back to say, "Is there a joke, Kristin?" But she didn't wait for a reply. Instead she went on, "I have invited a few of your old friends, Mr Bridges; just a few. They're so anxious to see you. Of course at this time of day it's almost impossible to get men, but I knew you wouldn't mind. You don't, do you? Now let me see—that's right, Grace, help yourself to a cigarette and get Kristin to pass them to Mr Bridges for me."

"Let me," said Carl, anxious to get away from the tirade

74

of words and thinking he had spoken the truth in the hotel when he had said, "We'll laugh about it afterwards." It would obviously be much funnier in retrospect.

He lit a cigarette for Kristin. Her hand trembled and his did too, a little, both of them aware so fully of each other's nearness, a nearness unbridgeable. She knew he was amused because his eyes were golden. To touch his fingers was to touch dry ice.

The doorbell rang. Mrs Lothrop was up, fluttering to the hall. "Ah, ah," she said, "I expect that's dear Katie Steen." And over her shoulder, "She admires you *so* much, Mr Bridges. I know you'll be nice to her, she's such a *sweet* girl." And Carl, sitting in a sudden silence, thought, today I can be nice to anyone.

Mrs Fender seemed far away. She watched the smoke of her cigarette float upwards in the still air of the room. Carl and Kristin were unspeaking, as if by mutual consent, hating to interrupt the stream of her thought. But the room shifted to a swift attention, an alertness that provoked a quality of geometrical precision as Katie Steen's excited, confidential voice came like a snake into the room.

"D'you know, you'll never guess, but Tiny phoned just before I came out and said that she was buying a wedding present this afternoon and who should she run into but Mr Bridges and Kristin—Kristin of all people!—and they were at the ring counter."

"Sh!" said Mrs Lothrop; whispering followed.

Mrs Fender turned her head with a jerk; Kristin, feeling the blood rising to her face, reached for an ashtray behind her. Carl crossed his legs very carefully and thought, damn gossiping women. Damn them! They'd have known tomorrow, surely they need not have interfered with our secret of today.

"Carl," Mrs Fender's voice was small. He looked at her, trying to read the expression on her face. "Carl?" her voice rose, a young bird trying to fly. She said no more. It was a question and he didn't know how to answer it. Mrs Lothrop ushered Katie Steen into the room. The question was suspended.

"You remember Katie Steen, Mr Bridges?"

"Of course," said Carl. "How do you do?" She held out her hand to him.

"How very nice to see you again," she said. "I do so hope you'll stay longer this time than you did last. Are you down on business?"

"A painter is always on business," Carl said. "That's both one of the joys and one of the drawbacks of my profession."

"Ah, Mr Bridges," Katie Steen answered, "how elusive your replies are."

"Simply because, in a sense, my job is elusive too." He smiled.

Kristin listened to him and was glad Katie wasn't questioning her. At this moment, she thought, I am defenceless; my joy is as exposed as a wound. But Carl would manage. He would be polite and charming and evasive and Katie would soon fall under the spell of his charm and forget.

More people arrived. The room grew thick with them. They built a wall between herself and her mother, herself and Mrs Lothrop, herself and the curious eyes. If she sat still no one would bother her. Carl, poor Carl, would take the brunt of the questioning faces. He was passed round the room, from one pair of hands to another, from one woman to another; the only shuttlecock among hundreds of bats. She saw him again as she had at the cocktail party—his shoulder up-pointing, the tenseness of his whole body concentrated in that shoulder—the sailboat in the harbour of tugs, holding stillness in his eyes.

And Carl, talking, moving his lips to repartee, remembered the cocktail party, remembered as he caught a glimpse of Kristin how she was the only person free from distortion, the only person complete within the confines of her own form. He could bear it all—the words, the flattery, the brittleness of women's voices and conversation, when he looked at Kristin. Kristin, whom soon he would take away from this world to his own world; the world of Birchlands, of Dick, of solid people following a pattern built securely upon the rock of their own integrity.

When people grouped together beyond the hearing of Carl and Kristin they talked quietly, excitedly, and their eyes darted towards Kristin or Carl. She could feel the current of excitement that ran through the room—a forked, electric current unlike the steady stream of her own happiness. Soon, she thought, soon, we shall be able to leave. Her mother came towards her. She looked tired, older than usual.

"Have you asked Carl back to dinner?" she looked at Kristin, but there was a curtain across her eyes.

"No," said Kristin, "I haven't."

"I think you'd better," she said.

Kristin put down her cup and took a cigarette. She stared long at the end of it. What does mother know, she thought, and what does she think? There is no happiness in this secret. I don't like it. I should like to stand up now and tell all these whispering women that I am going to marry Carl. All my life I've kept secrets but these women have made this one seem wrong. She wanted to go to Carl and feel his arm strong about her and together with him walk out of the house and down the path to the car. If he would only come to her now! But she couldn't even see him, he was hidden by women, women's voices covered his deep voice. She got up then and crossed to her mother. I must tell her, she thought, out of fairness I must tell her. All these people are certain of the truth of our engagement. Mother, alone, is not sure.

Forcing her way through the people she realized that she felt a sudden affection for her mother, a feeling she never remembered before. She went to her, took her arm instinctively but awkwardly; gradually she turned her away from the conversation she was involved in.

"Mother," she said, speaking close into her ear, "it's true. I can't have you not knowing when all these people have discovered it. We were going to tell you tonight."

Mrs Fender gave no indication that she had heard; her face kept the same expression but the curtain was drawn back. She pressed her daughter's hand. "Thank you, darling," she said, "I'll say nothing."

Kristin felt better. The party seemed almost normal now. Nothing that these old friends of Carl's could say mattered.

"Perhaps we can escape," said Mrs Fender. "You collect Carl."

Walking through the room, dodging elbows and cups, she felt indifferent to the atmosphere. She was walking to Carl; surely, happily, she was walking through chaos to peace. He was in the thick of a small circle; Katie Steen was flapping her long eyelashes and looking up at him. "Oh, Mr Bridges, you're so modest. Now if I were an artist I'm certain I'd make the most fantastic demands on everyone." She ended her words with a streamer of laughter.

"I shouldn't," said a woman Kristin didn't know, who was obviously taking advantage of this opportunity to appear spiritual. "I should shut myself up all alone and let my divine talent pour through me uninterrupted by the demands of society and responsibility."

"And for stimulation?" Carl queried.

"Ah, stimulation!" the woman breathed. "Stimulation would come from within. Stimulation would issue from the fount of my talent."

It was then Carl saw Kristin. He raised his eyebrows.

"Mother's thinking of leaving," she said.

He turned to the women about him. "I'm afraid I must go," he said.

A protest went up:

"Oh, Mr Bridges!"

"Why don't you stay and I'll drive you home?"

"Such a pity to cut short this delightful conversation."

"Surely you could stay a little longer."

Carl smiled at them all. "It's awfully good of you, but I'm afraid I must go."

The spiritual woman came forward. "We must meet again," she said. "Perhaps dinner some night. You know I've always felt that I have a talent and it only needs drawing out. Colour means so much to me. I'm fascinated by colour, aren't you?"

Poor Carl, thought Kristin, what a lot of talk. How silly women are! He smiled away from them, tossing them phrases as he went, little empty phrases especially designed for the occasion.

"Need we ever do this again?" he asked Kristin as they fought their way through to Mrs Lothrop.

"Never!" said Kristin, so violently that he was surprised.

"I am jealous," Mrs Lothrop announced when, at last, they reached her. "You've hardly spoken to me all afternoon. I had so hoped that we could have a nice talk."

He was suddenly deflated; he could think of no answer. He had used up his supply of pretty speeches. "I'm sorry," he said, "but it's been a lovely party and you were far too kind to go to all this trouble."

She held his hand. "Mr Bridges, Mr Bridges; why didn't you reserve just a few minutes for your hostess?"

He knew no way out. Kristin, watching, felt, I must help him, somehow I must set him free. She moved forward, stretching out her hand. "I'm sorry, Mrs Lothrop, but we really must go. Mother's waiting for us." She almost forced her hand between the two locked ones. "Good-bye," she said, "and thank you so much."

"I knew no escape," he said, "every exit seemed blocked."

They were free now. Mrs Fender had joined them and they were in the hall. It was quiet by contrast and cool.

"Really, Sarah might have warned us," Mrs Fender remarked as she went down the steps. "I wasn't prepared for such a mob." But Carl and Kristin had no words to speak; they were bursting with the spate of other people's words which must form in them, sink and fall away before they could find their own vocabularies again.

"Did Kristin remember to ask you to dinner, Carl? because we want you to come." Mrs Fender spoke from the back seat; her voice sounded smoother than it had in the house; ironed out like a long sheet of ribbon.

"Thank you," said Carl. "I'd love to."

"You can come right back with us now," she said, "there's no need to change."

And then Kristin remembered the ring. How could she have forgotten for so long the small, square box in Carl's pocket? The symbol of their love. She wanted to see it again, feel it firm between her fingers; she wanted to know that it had not evaporated as it looked as though it so easily might. That so small and frail a thing could be subjected to that noise and heat and still remain whole astonished her. But if symbol it is, she thought, it is intact still. Heat and noise can never destroy the texture of our love . . . it will be silence and the ice of fear. Her fingers tightened on the wheel as she thought—silence and the ice of fear. Surely, surely—she fought against the thought, tried to build a door in her mind to shut against her self-knowledge. But like ivy, like morning glory tendrils the knowledge twined up and over the door, forced their way through the slits of its faulty structure until the door was shut behind the thought; the thought locked into her consciousness.

"Kristin, dear," her mother called, "you must be more careful. You drove right through a stop light."

The sinuous green growth was cut down. The moonstone, pale and beautiful, filled the cavern of her skull, shone in her head. Carl watching her, thought, she has gone through a pain and come through to beauty. Peace of mind shines like a jewel in her forehead.

Traffic was thick. They crawled slowly through the old streets with their close-packed houses but as they climbed the hill across the bridge and drove round past the convent it was possible to accelerate, possible to breathe. Turning at last into their own drive a restraint seemed to fall on them all, so that, even when the car had stopped, they sat as they were for a few minutes before they opened the doors and faced the new scene. Mrs Fender moved first. "I must go in and speak to Mary about dinner." Carl opened the door for her. And then Kristin moved with a sudden concentration of movement, frightened of the thick foliage of her fear growing up again.

She stretched out on a veranda chair and held out her hand for Carl's, gazing at him long and steadily as he took it, feeling love leap through her like a white panther and curl up, live but momentarily stilled, at her side.

"Carl, I told Mother. I had to. All those people at the tea whispering and pointing. Mother looked dazed and uncertain. It was awful for her."

He didn't answer. She knew and yet she had said nothing. Uncertainty touched him, like a finger on his heart. Parental disapproval; he had not allowed for that.

"Are you annoyed?"

"No, darling. It's just—I was wondering what she thought."

"Do you mind?"

"In the final instance, no. But for the moment, yes."

"I think she was pleased, Carl. How could she be anything else?"

"And then there's your father. You know I've never approached a father before about such a matter." He passed her a cigarette. She looked at him through the smoke, opening her eyes very wide. And then he told her about Denise and Marmo and "The Egg" sketched them into his life with wide strong strokes.

She listened like a small girl, seeing Paris, London, New York for the first time; seeing Denise, Marmo, "The Egg", less vividly, unable to picture women so different from those she had known; seeing them only as the smile on Carl's face, the curl of his lips, the movement of his hands. Seeing them as part of him.

His story only ended when Mrs. Fender joined them, stood uncertainly beside them and said, "As Ralph's not home yet, I wonder if you'd mix us a drink, Carl? I'll show you where the things are." He got up then and Kristin sat still, living over Paris, London, New York; feeling that a strong net of knowledge had formed about her, about her and Carl, holding them together. Soon, soon, she thought, we will know each other so well that our love, a wiry little plant, will grow tall. For, she thought, love thrives on knowledge—my knowledge of Carl, his knowledge of me. As long as we are still discovering each other the growth is slow.

She moved. The white panther at her side rose from his sleep and followed her into the house and upstairs, waiting beside her as she tidied herself for dinner. "The Boy" was in her room, Carl's boy. She had forgotten him in the excitement, the multiplicity of the day. Her mother must have brought him up for her. He looked strong and virile and masculine against the pale femininity of her bedroom. Here we have it, she said to herself, the sun and the moon together, and she looked from the painting and felt secure. Carl will predominate, she thought, as he does here; but as she thought the apple-green curtain billowed out with a sudden gust of wind, billowed out and over the picture and left the room untouched, free of Carl. Ah, she said, forcing the curtain back and seeing the painting dark as old brick against plaster, ah Carl, I love you so. The white panther stirred at her feet. She dipped her fingers into the cold cream, made up her face and then stood, hands crossed over her breasts, leaning a little to one side, saying, "Ah, ah," over and over.

"Kristin!" It was Carl's voice in the upstairs hall. "Kristin, the cocktails are ready." Oh! she went to the door. He was standing there. The white panther leaped. "Sweet, sweet,

82

sweet!'' he said. He kissed her lightly and held her to him. ''I must wash up,'' he said, ''I'll see you in a minute.''

She walked down the stairs and into the livingroom. ''Daddy not home yet?'' she asked.

Her mother ignored the question. ''Kristin,'' she said, ''are you happy?''

''Terribly!''

Her mother was holding her elbows and looking at her with no smile in her eyes. ''You love him?''

''Oh, yes!'' Her mother's grip relaxed.

''You are very lucky, Kristin. Your Carl is a darling.''

''Oh, Mother, you're glad, then?''

''More glad than you'll ever know. I've not been so happy in years.''

''Don't tell Daddy, will you,'' Kristin pleaded, ''Not until Carl has spoken to him.''

Her mother went back to the sofa. ''No, darling,'' she said. ''This is the very first secret you've ever trusted me with and I won't let you down.'' She laughed then. Carl came into the room. ''To happiness,'' she said, lifting her glass, and then, ''Carl's made Planters' Punches, darling, see if you like them.''

It is nice sitting here, thought Carl, jutting into the smooth circumference of family life again, feeling a part of the old formal pattern of the family. For Mrs Fender has accepted me, he thought, and Kristin, sipping her drink, with a faint line of nutmeg on her top lip, watches me over the rim of her glass as I watch her.

''Mother,'' said Kristin, ''Carl knows you know.'' She lifted her glass again to hide as much of herself as she could.

Mrs Fender's face lit to a city of lights. She patted the seat beside her, looking at Carl, and he went to her. ''I feel young,'' she said. ''A grown-up daughter makes me feel like a child instead of an old woman. But Carl, I'm terribly happy—truly.'' She took his hand. ''I could never have wished anything more for Kristin, or for myself,'' she added. ''Of course,'' she said, "it's rather sudden. You've not known each other very long."

I've known him all my life, thought Kristin. Carl is bound up in the knowledge of the rocks, in the knowledge of stillness.

"Long enough to be sure," Carl said.

The room was out of focus with restrained excitement. They felt strange to each other, these three. Carl faced his wife and mother-in-law; Kristin her husband and mother; Mrs Fender her daughter and son-in-law. It was a new arrangement—an arrangement the heart had accepted but one which still knocked on the surface of the mind; and the mind, prompted by the heart said, "Come in, open the door and walk in," but the door was barred. To speak with the heart, thought Carl, and disregard the shyness of the mind is something we have not been trained to do, something which we have always been led to believe verges on the maudlin; something we have been brought up to consider "not done", slightly indecent. And yet, and yet, he thought, what can we speak of at such a time? What can we say with the white-livered mind, the anaemic brain, that the full-blooded heart will tolerate?

"You think Daddy will approve?" asked Kristin breaking the long disordered silence.

"I know he will. He'll be as thrilled as I am."

But it wasn't as easy as that, thought Carl later. After dinner, closeted with Mr Fender, Kristin and her mother in the living-room, Carl sat in the utmost discomfort, waiting a chance to broach the subject. Mr Fender, unaware of what was to come, talked on and on. And Carl, at last, in desperation, interrupted him—driving through the seaweed of his words and saying loudly, briefly, "I want to marry Kristin, sir."

Mr Fender continued with his story and then suddenly pulled himself up. "What's that?" he said astonished, hearing the words after they were spoken. Carl repeated it, this time more graciously. Whatever reaction I had expected it was certainly not this, Carl thought, as Mr Fender jolted forward in his chair, mouth open, eyes startled. Carl felt ill at ease, but Mr Fender collected himself, stopped long enough to light a cigarette slowly and take one or two puffs before he spoke. When words came Mr Fender was transformed. He was the business man. Carl could see him sitting behind his desk, highly efficient, quick as a trap.

"You want to marry Kristin," he said.

"Yes," Carl answered.

"Why do you want to marry her?"

"I am in love with her, sir."

Mr Fender took another puff, blew the smoke out in a thin swift stream. "No doubt you've been in love before?"

"Yes," said Carl, "I have."

"Then what makes you think that this time you want to get married?"

"Because," said Carl, watching Mr Fender's demanding eyes, "this time I'm in love with the sort of girl I'd like to have for a wife and because I'm in the position to give her the sort of life she's been used to. And," he added, thinking of the years Kristin had lived remote from human contacts, "I think I could make her happy."

"How much have you a year?"

Mr Fender was not making it easy but Carl began an account of his finances. "To begin with, sir, I make with my painting alone enough to keep us comfortably. I am lucky in that; my work is popular. And quite apart from my own earning capacities I have a private income. My parents are dead. They left me . . ." He continued, explaining in detail his financial situation. Mr Fender's face relaxed a little, Carl thought, but he spoke brusquely still.

"There is Kristin," Mr Fender said. And Carl saw her—pale, slim, generous—saw her when he had proposed; saw her at the station, her face alight, her eyes unfolding, her bright satin mouth; and he said, "I have spoken to her, sir. She wants to marry me."

"That is as it may be," said her father. "She may think

she does, but had you ever stopped to consider that Kristin is barely eighteen? She has never in her life before had a man take any interest in her whatsoever. No doubt she is flattered by your attentions, she is attracted by your glamour. How is she to know, with no experience to help her, if she is in love?"

Carl felt exasperated. "How is anyone to know, for certain, sir, however much experience they have had before?"

"Then you are not certain?" Mr Fender shot the words out.

"I am certain enough to know that living apart from her is not worth the food I eat." He wanted to say, can't you remember being young, can't you remember that to be in love is like exposing your cuts to salt water? Can't you try to make this easier for us all? And then he thought: he doesn't approve of me; in his eyes I'm not suitable. And the words "Kristin is barely eighteen" made him feel helpless. If Mr Fender chose he could refuse to allow Kristin to marry. Carl lit a cigarette himself. He was silent during the first puffs too; he used Mr Fender's tactics.

He said, "I am thirty-seven. I am old enough to know my own mind. Kristin needs an older man, she is wise beyond her years. As to my family—my father was a well-known Montreal lawyer—you may have heard of him—R.C. Bridges." He thought he detected a flicker of recognition in Mr Fender's face but he kept on. "He was raised to the Bench and he died four years ago, leaving me a house in the Laurentians. You needn't fear, sir, that I'll take her to a life of bohemianism. I'm hard-working. I paint, I don't talk about painting. But most important of all, I love Kristin and she loves me." He stopped. Mr Fender's face was inscrutable. There is nothing more I can say, Carl thought, I have no trumps left.

Mr Fender crossed his legs carefully, pushed his coffee cup away from him and said, "That is all very well, all very well, but you forget Kristin."

Forget Kristin! thought Carl, forget her, when she is my only thought; when I would go through this for no one in the world but Kristin. He wanted to cry out, wanted to sweep the dishes from the table in a large desperate gesture. But he sat silent and concentrated movement to the precise flicking of his ash in the saucer of his coffee cup. He heard Mr Fender's voice continue, building obstacles, forming hazards.

"You forget that Kristin has never been trained to do anything. She has no more idea how to run a house than to fly. She can't cook or mend or manage money. And on top of all that, she's queer. In no way is she a normal child. I believe I've mentioned this to you before—she has comatose periods."

"I know what you mean, sir, but it makes no difference. I still want to marry Kristin." Whatever you say will be of no use. His mind set to a letterpress: I still want to marry Kristin.

Mr Fender looked at him through half-shut eyes. "Nothing I say will change you?"

"Nothing, sir."

"And Kristin? You say she wants to marry you?"

"Yes, sir."

"You've not known each other very long."

Does he not know, thought Carl, that you recognize the qualities you love in a person immediately and that the length of time you know them only verifies those qualities, shows them up as true?

"I know, sir," he shaped his lips to understatement, "but we've seen a great deal of each other and I promise you we know each other well for we've seen each other alone and so know one another better than we should had we been meeting at parties for months."

Carl felt that he was losing ground with ever word. Somehow, he thought, I must win him over. But how, and how long will it take? How can you convince a man of the insistence of love when he has long since forgotten the sound of its clamouring voice in the night? What a topsy-turvy social system that demands that the young man must approach the middle-aged on a matter they no longer know of themselves. He looked up from his thoughts to find Mr Fender smiling. He had the smile on his face that proclaims a successful business deal, well handled, well carried off, to his advantage.

"Well, Carl," he said, passing him his cigarette case, "the opponents always shake hands after a battle, don't they? And the loser takes his defeat with good grace." His smile was broad and Carl, watching him, listening to his words, felt the sickness of failure gnaw at him.

"And the winner, sir," he couldn't help saying, for fury rose in him like a long, high tide, "takes success with modesty."

"That," said Mr Fender, "is for the winner to decide."

Carl wanted to punch him, wanted to stand up and show him who was the better man, which of them was most fit to look after Kristin.

"I think," Mr Fender went on, "if I were the winner it would be hard for me to take this success modestly. If I had had to go through this to marry Grace I doubt if we should ever have been married."

"I thought," Carl began, but Mr Fender waved him quiet. "However," he said, "this is a strange battle, for there is no loser, is there? It's the old story—I don't lost a daughter, I gain a son." He laughed immoderately at that and thumped Carl on the back. Carl laughed too, laughed because his heart was light, laughed with surprise, laughed with delight, laughed, laughed until his throat ached.

Kristin, hearing the laughter, sighed. "Mother," she said, "I think it must be all right. Listen." And then, "Oh, mother, I was so frightened, they've been so long." She dropped onto the sofa then. "How awful this part of marriage is," she said, "and how much you have to love a person to bear going through it." She found it easier to talk to her mother than she ever had and she remembered how the first time she met Carl she had felt that he linked her with humanity. Now he had managed to link her with her own family. Carl, Carl, she thought, how much you have given me. Oh, my darling, oh, my very dear!

"I'll take your father out," her mother said. "You and Carl will want to be alone."

"Thank you, Mummy."

"Kristin, I'm so happy, darling." She slipped her arms around her and held her close. "My funny little daughter," she said, "to be Carl's wife."

"You do like him, don't you?" She knew but she wanted to hear it again. It was important beyond importance to hear her mother say, "I think he is perfectly sweet." And it was comforting to sit there with her mother, knowing that for this minute at least, they had met on a common ground; that she had not been alone in the long agony since dinner and was not alone now, in this delirious happiness.

They opened the door then, Carl and her father, laughter still ringing in their voices.

"We must celebrate," said her father, "Celebrate the happy occasion." He carried a decanter and glasses. The talk flew about her head; her father kissed her; everyone kissed everyone else—she and Carl didn't kiss; the room seemed to hold many more people than it actually did. Glasses were raised: "To Carl and Kristin. Carl and Kristin." She smiled, she laughed, she talked, she lifted her glass to her lips. Noise was loud about her, but Carl, like the thin, clear note of a wood-wind, sounded close to her; it was all she heard.

"When do you plan to be married?"

"Soon, soon."

"But the arrangements, the invitations, the trousseau?"

"Soon, soon."

"And your linen and china and silver?"

"And fittings and parties and showers?"

"Soon, soon, soon."

The clatter of glasses; voices falling to a diminuendo, rising again, falling; smoke in the room and a space in Kristin's head where the wood-wind played and she added her own accompaniment—soon, soon, soon, soon. And then silence—silence stretching out like a sea about her, her glass empty and Carl saying, "Darling, they have gone, we are alone." Alone and close to Carl and engaged. "Was it very awful?" she said. "Was Daddy difficult?"

"Very cautious," he said. "I didn't enjoy it very much."

"Poor darling, You were in there so long. I didn't think I could bear it. I was so sure he was finding a hundred and one objections."

"He was. I wish you could have seen us. But it's over now and, oh my darling, it won't be long before you're my wife." He felt in his pocket for the ring and Kristin waited for the sight of it again, waited to have him put it on her finger, waited solemnly upon the ritual, the white panther rampant at her side.

Kristin wakened. He is here, she thought, for a week now he has been here, under this roof. She held up her hand and looked at the moonstone on her finger. For a week he has been here and we have been like mad things, going to parties and coming back. We have seen each other only in little intervals, intervals short and sweet as cointreau. But this morning, she thought, we have claimed for ourselves. And the thought was like waking again. She got out of bed, she got dressed; she could lie there no longer when Carl, perhaps now, was up at breakfast, listening for her coming. "The day is lovely," she said aloud, pausing a moment at the window, "So we must get away early and have every possible moment together."

The morning is sweet as hay, she thought, as she went downstairs, sweet as hay. She hummed a little, a tune that came out of the air and settled on her lips. By the time she had reached the bottom step the words joined the tune—"Upon the shore I fou-ound a shell, I he-eld it to-oo my ear." And then the words went off into the air again and she was at the dining-room door and Carl was there alone.

"Was that you singing?"

"Yes."

"I've never heard you sing before."

"I don't very often but sometimes songs just—come."

"You look sweet, darling."

She pushed him back into his chair. "I'm excited—a whole morning with you and no one to say, 'Ah, Mr Bridges,' and tear you away from me." She poured herself coffee. "Where is the family?"

"Your father has gone to work and your mother went with him—had an early appointment with the hairdresser."

"Oh." The sunlight fell in a shaft across the table, lighting one side of Carl's face. She buttered a piece of toast.

"Where shall we go?" he said.

Ah, what were places, what did it matter? "Anywhere, anywhere," she said. Like foam, she felt, like cow parsley blowing in a field; Carl the wave behind the foam, the wind in the meadows. He passed his cup for more coffee, his brown hands moving like wings. For a moment their minds united; they saw the foam and the wave, the cow parsley and the wind, the sun and the shade, brown wings flying against the sky, the breakfast table and then their own breakfast table; they saw the trees change, the leaves fall like gold wafers thick about them, the snow gather in the grey sky and drive to earth, bright as fireflies; they saw, with one mind, their lives revolve like a merry-go-round, the dark horse, the white horse, following on each other to the sound of a thin tune—a wood-wind and a humming voice. They saw—but Carl thought, I have seen a vision—and saw nothing more. And Kristin thought—I have seen a lie—and the shutter fell. They looked at each other then and Carl smiled and noticed the concentration of Kristin's mouth; the patch of red satin was a ruby.

"Let's finish our coffee on the veranda." They took their cups into the sun and sat together, the smoke from their cigarettes forming similar patterns on the air, joining and disappearing.

"I wish," said Kristin, "we could be married without all this fuss. I wish," she said, "there need be no parties, no bridesmaids, no invitations, no wedding—just marriage.''

''I wish it too.'' I hate, he thought, this long period crammed with unimportance that holds us from each other. But, he thought, it's worse for Kristin than for me and after all, and after all . . . but the thought faded, went up with the smoke as he looked at Kristin.

''Let us go,'' she said. ''Carl, let's escape from telephone and doorbell. Let us waste no more minutes here, lovely though it is.'' She got up; when he turned she was gone.

They drove to the country. He had hired a car again as he had earlier in the summer. As soon as he had checked out of the hotel he had made arrangements for it. For, he had thought, if we are dependent on the Fender's we shall never be alone.

Kristin was gay, the child Kristin today, exclaiming, delighting in everything; holding the world in her hands for her joy.

Stopping at last by the river where the water fell deep away from the bank and the trees hung over the river and stared at their own reflections she gave a long anguished sigh. ''Carl, Carl,'' she said, ''we shall never be happier than this, never.'' She clung to him then with a desperate finality, so that happiness ebbed within him and he knew only the awful melancholy of love.

''But darling,'' he tried to soothe her, ''we shall always be as happy.''

She covered her face. ''It is awful,'' she said through her fingers, ''to have reached the peak, to be able only to stare at the stars from this perilous position or slip down; slowly, perhaps imperceptibly lose ground, fall away.''

''It's only that you're tired,'' he said. ''This last week has worn you out.''

''No, no,'' she said, ''it's not that—it can't touch me. There is a centre within me the rush of people cannot approach.'' I am frightened, she thought. Even holding Carl close is not enough—even feeling the strength of him under my hands and knowing his love is not enough. She shuddered. For a long time he felt her against him, shivering and then she became still. He was relieved, but Kristin feeling the peace steal over her knew with a dreadful certainty the danger of this moment.

It's happening again, she thought. Carl, save yourself from this, run away from me, leave me. She felt the change come over her gradually—the change of texture—and she couldn't speak. Carl, Carl, she screamed out, but no sound came; she struggled but her body didn't move. Before it reaches my mind I must set him free; now that it is only my flesh, while I still have a chance, I must, must, must. But each moment it became more difficult, each moment the sensual pleasure of absorption coursed through her more strongly. I love him too much, she thought, too much, too much. He moved, he shifted her. It was like a shock striking her nerve ends, it was like sunlight after darkness striking her eyes. Now, she thought, now. She shaped her lips to speech, it took all her concentration.

"Carl," she said, "take me swimming."

They were safe now; it was over. She drew a long breath and moved as in her sleep; the crisis was past. She looked at the water and shook her head.

"Kristin," Carl's voice behind her made her turn. "Kristin, did you feel anything queer happen then?" She didn't answer. What could she say to him, how explain? "It was funny," he said, "almost as if I didn't exist."

"What a silly husband I'm going to have!" She held up her face to him. Oh, if only she could tell him, if only she could share this old ecstasy that had turned to misery since she had met him. Instead she went for her bathing-suit. "Look at the water," she said.

But Carl, as he began to change, felt that somehow he had come through a queer experience. It was as if, he thought, as if I were a—he felt for the word in his head—a Zombi. Just body. As if my mind, my soul—he rejected the word as it formed—were sucked from me, the essence gone, the container alone, remaining; useless, empty. But, he thought, why should

93

such a thing have happened? I've probably imagined it. And he dived into the smooth surface of the river and forgot.

Splashing together, laughing, Kristin's memory was washed clean like a slate in the rain. They raced; Carl with his strong overarm fighting to keep up with her minnow side-stroke. And when they arrived breathless on the small beach and flung themselves down, dripping, in the sun, they looked at each other with water-clear eyes, free from the shadow of doubt or dread. Kristin took off her cap and ran her fingers through her long hair. "Like corn tassels," said Carl, touching it, "corn tassels damp in the early morning."

Ah, to lie here beside Carl, to hear his voice, to hear him saying, "We'll go to Birchlands for our honeymoon, unless there's anywhere you'd sooner go."

"No, no," said Kristin. "To Birchlands where it is quiet and we can be together—like this, always."

"You'll love it," he said. "The lake, the woods—it's a gorgeous place."

They lay in the sun a long time. Carl talked. He told her of his early life, of his mother and father and sister. And Kristin, listening, pieced together the jigsaw of his life.

"My father was quiet and infinitely patient," Carl said. "He never told me to do anything or not to do anything but when I behaved badly he would call me into his den and we'd discuss it, just like a law suit. He would line up all the aspects of the offence and then he would say, pointing with a long forefinger at an old ink-stand, 'There is the prisoner. I shall defend him, you will prove to me he is guilty.' And so we would haggle—he putting forth marvellously lucid arguments why I was not wrong—I pitting all my intelligence to prove I was. No punishment ever followed. But I always left his den feeling wise and grown up and very responsible. He did the same with my sister too until he learned that these "cases" as he called them, upset her far too much. She would leave the room so cowed with the thought of her own wickedness that she turned with a sort

94

of fanatical desperation to religion and sang hymns constantly and read nothing but the Bible. He was frightened that the small print would ruin her eyes and he didn't believe in burdening her with such an overwhelming sense of sin so he had to stop. But for me he applied the same tactics until I was more or less grown up. I think he always had a secret hope that I would follow in his footsteps; but at seventeen, when I left school, I knew I wanted to do nothing but paint. He took me into his den—we had moved by then and the den was a veritable study, large and booklined. The old ink-stand was still there.'' Carl paused to light a cigarette.

Kristin opened her eyes and watched the trees blowing a little in their top branches. They seemed woven together, Carl's story and the movement of the leaves.

''My father sat for a minute and then pushed the ink-stand into the centre of his desk. 'There,' he said, pointing, 'is the boy who wants to be an artist. The case is open.' He began. He stated the joys of a life given over to art, the joys of creation. He was very generous. When it came my turn to speak I could hardly think of anything to say. I remember the light hitting the glass of the ink-stand and flying like splinters into my eyes. I said, 'An artist may work for years and get nowhere.' I said, 'Popularity fluctuates. Even when an artist is accepted he may suddenly fall from favour.' I said, 'He must suffer more than a man should and then perhaps have to prostitute his art—turn commercial to keep alive.' I don't remember if I said anything after that. It was like pricking my own toy balloon. I do remember wanting to cry and being disgusted with myself. And then my father said, 'It means a lot to you, boy, doesn't it? Where do you want to study?' I knew then from the tone of his voice that he had agreed. Fortunately he lived long enough to see his faith in me part way justified.''

''And your mother?'' Kristin wanted to know, wanted to know all about the family.

''Mother? I don't know how to describe her. She was some-

95

one who never seemed quite real to me and now that she's dead I find it hard to believe she ever lived. Not," he said, "because she was insignificant. She was more alive than any person I have ever known. She flashed. She moved like lightning. She laughed unexpectedly and the world seemed like a chandelier; she cried and all of life was misery. She was the vital core of the family and yet father was the skin, the binding whole that kept the family together. She died when I was in Paris. I didn't hear until a month afterwards, but during that month I felt incomplete. It was a wretched feeling—and quite apart from my actual life and work, for during that time I had my first picture accepted for exhibition. I should have been happy. Father sent my sister over to join me then. She was terribly upset. I was glad to have her near me; glad to have someone to talk to about Mother. And it was fun showing her Paris. But she was there so short a time. She met a chap—Henri Bateau—and married him. He was home from the States on holidays. As soon as it could be arranged—for she had to become a Roman Catholic—they were married. She lives in Boston now. If only she weren't having a child she'd come up for the wedding." Carl stretched. "What a lot of talk," he said. "Am I boring you?"

How could he ever bore her? No matter how small, how ordinary, the details of his life, she wanted to know. But they weren't small, they weren't ordinary. It was like having someone read aloud to her. Another family—a family as unlike hers as any could be and he spoke of boredom! What can I give him, she thought, to compare with what he's had? How can I make life a gay and a sad thing for him as his mother did, or a steady and just thing, as his father did? All I can do is love him as I've never loved before; not even, necessarily, she thought, as he's never been loved before. And she wanted to cry out at the bar of her own horizon and knock down the city limits, the signs that marked her boundaries. "Do you think," she said, for she wanted to know badly, badly, "do you think they would have liked me?"

He caught her then, pulled her to him. "Silly darling," he said laughing, "they'd have loved you even as I do. Through me they love you now."

Ah, she thought, this is security, this is happiness, this is fulfilment, and she lay for a moment, complete in her love. He raised himself on his elbow and looked down at her. The pattern of the leaves dappled her face. "Oh, darling," he said, "my own darling!" I hate, he thought, to leave her even for a week, as I have to, to get ready for the wedding. "Look," he cried, jumping up suddenly, "I'm going to do a painting—of the river—this part of it where it's deep and the trees bend down to meet themselves. The light's perfect."

He went to the car and collected his things. She watched him as he tacked paper onto a board, unscrewed the top of his paint jar and laid out his paints.

"I haven't done a water-colour for ages," he said. "I'm quite excited."

Once again she was fascinated by the way his fingers moved cleanly, economically; brown and certain from paint to paper. This, she thought, will never weary me—to watch Carl at work. As long as I live I will find delight in watching his hands and the magic that lies under his touch. She saw him sketch in the bank and the huge bole of the tree, rising like a monument from the river's edge and then she saw colour grow on the paper, the trunk brown, but not brown, solid, twisted, holding up its green crown. And though he painted loosely, each leaf was there and the wind too. His brush moved to the palette; her mind moved with his hands—back and forth, back and forth, caught in the rhythm, carried by the rhythm, until thought dissolved in motion and swam like a fish in the current of a stream.

Carl mixed the colours for the water with an insensitive eye. For the second time this morning, he thought, I feel queer. I feel—invaded, he thought at last. Invaded. There is no other word. It is as if I have surrendered my being to an alien force and it has made me less. He looked at his painting and groaned. "Something is wrong," he said aloud, "the invader has ruined it. It's a case of too many cooks, too many cooks. They are spoiling the broth." He laughed then, a hysterical laugh. The broth, he said, that's good. It's the river they're spoiling—the broth. And then the sensation left him. He painted quickly, unconsciously. The invader marched in, stormed his defences, hoisted the invading flag, took possession smoothly and entirely. The city that was Carl knew foreign leadership; foreign colours waved from the ramparts; foreign primitive workmanship ousted the easy-running talent. Night fell on the city that had been Carl, dark and still—a silent abyss—but the fingers moved on relentlessly, unwittingly.

Kristin stretched. He turned to her and her eyes were ugly with terror.

"Kristin! What is it?" Her face was whittled with fear—sharp and white. "Are you ill?" She rolled over, burying her face in her hands, unspeaking. He saw her body heave, but she made no sound. "Kristin, my dearest," he bent down to her, his arm across her shaking shoulders.

She forced her voice to come, struggled to keep it steady. "Carl, do something for me."

"Anything, darling."

"Get the lunch things and go up the river about two hundred yards and light a fire. I brought sausages. They'll need cooking. I'll join you later." Don't question me, she thought. Oh God, don't ask me why! "Please Carl. I wouldn't ask you if I didn't love you."

Kristin, he thought, what has happened? What has come between us twice today and kept us from each other? But he went, went without questioning, feeling that in some way, his obedience to her wish might close the gap.

Oh, oh, wailed Kristin when he left. Why must this happen, this power for happiness turn to destruction, turn inward upon my love and destroy Carl's identity? Why, why?

She walked to the river and dangled her legs over the bank; the water on her feet made her feel better, brought her back to reality, smudged the horror of her metamorphosis. If only, she thought, I turned into trees or stones or earth when I'm with him it couldn't hurt him. But this way, this way I am like a leech, a vampire, sucking his strength from him—the moon eclipsing the sun. Oh God! And the more I love him, the more perilous the danger. I cannot be with him without stealing into him and erasing his own identity. Why should it be, she asked, why, why, why? But the leaves above whispered in the wind of their high branches and the river flowed past and the world was still. My love is like a blight, she said, lowering herself into the water to wash away the pain from her face. Insidious, evil, she thought as she trod water, like an octopus, like a cobra; like a leech, like a vampire, she repeated. Oh Carl, what can I do, my darling? She swam with the current, letting it carry her. If I were brave, she thought, I would let it carry me out to sea. But the thought of it made her struggle towards land and as she felt the shore under her feet she knew safety again. It will be like this always, she thought—the surrender to the water and dry land emerging just in time. It will be so; it must be. The texture of our love cannot be destroyed.

She walked back to the car and rubbed her face and hair with a towel. There will be interludes, she thought, but they will pass and perhaps, eventually, they will cease altogether. We shall come through them. How little my love is worth if we give in now—if I give in, she amended.

The vision of "The Boy" in her bedroom reminded her of the male mind of Carl that would not tolerate submersion; that would rise up again strong as a weed and as swiftly, no matter what she did to him.

Still rubbing the water from her hair she ran along the path by the river calling, "Carl, Carl! Oh, my darling, I'm coming, coming."

She saw him tending the fire, squatting before the teepee of wood that rose in a spiral of blue smoke. He is invincible, she thought, I cannot hurt him, and she slowed her pace, waiting for him to meet her, waiting for the agony to be finally over as they linked hands, and standing together she searched his eyes for the reassurance that she knew lay hidden there.

PART 4

KRISTIN

Kristin held her arms above her head and slipped into the dress. It is lovely, she thought seeing herself full length in the mirror.

Her mother, looking her up and down with critical eyes, said to the fitter, "It doesn't hang quite right here." She pushed Kristin in the small of the back with her fingers. The fitter grunted. Her mouth was full of pins. She used her hands to speak with, her hands and movements sharp as the pins in her mouth.

"It is so simple," her mother said. "Long and slim and plain. You will look as if you are taking a vow of chastity." The fitter snorted and the pins shot out—bright projectiles from her tight lips.

Kristin was tired of it now. Tired of being pulled and pushed. The dress was a dream. If she had to have a white wedding, well, she was pleased with the dress. But the fittings exhausted her. She wanted to go home, back to her own room and write to Carl. For he has gone, she told herself. Gone, gone. The form of the word in her mind was a hollow echo. It is the loneliest word I know, she thought.

The fitting finished, there was still no escape. As they opened the door of the house piles of presents and letters greeted them. Her mother was excited.

"Oh, Kristin!" she said, "look. Come and open them. See who they're from."

And Kristin obeyed. She sat surrounded by tissue paper and excelsior.

"Don't get the cards mixed, whatever you do," her mother warned. "What a pity Carl isn't here to see these lovely things."

The letters came next.

"Dear Kristin,

"I'm so happy for you. Although I've never met your Carl Bridges I know he must be perfectly sweet. And what a lovely bride you'll make. I wish it were possible for me to get to the wedding to see you both. They say he is very attractive . . ."

"Dearest little Kristin,

"I've not seen you since you were a strange, tiny girl and it seems impossible to imagine you a bride. What an interesting life you will have, married to an artist! I am sending you a little gift—getting it off tomorrow—and it carries all my wishes for your future happiness . . ."

They were all alike—on and on—it was hard to tell where one stopped and another began. Kristin put them in a pile.

"You'd better write more thank-you notes," her mother said. "Once you get behind, you're done for."

"How I loathe it all," Kristin complained.

Her mother looked hurt. "Oh, darling, don't say that. When we're doing everything we can to give you a lovely wedding."

Kristin couldn't answer. What can I say? she thought. I can't tell her the truth—that if they had asked me I should never have considered even for one moment this sort of a wedding. "I'll go upstairs and begin," she said. She marked a description of the presents on the cards. "I'll try to get all these done this morning." And her mother smiled.

"Write to them nicely, dear. People have been so kind."

Upstairs at her desk, Kristin stared at the pile of cards and shuddered. Thank you so much for the cake plate, it was just exactly what I wanted. The sugar tongs are the prettiest I've ever seen. I don't know how to thank you for the . . . She pulled the paper towards her and sat for a long time, pen in hand. Then,

"Darling," she wrote,

"How I wish you were here. I realize now that it is only when you are with me that I can bear all the fuss of marriage. How much sooner would I go with you into the woods and stand beneath a tree and be married by a solemn squirrel than go through this endless business that is before us. Don't for one minute, imagine that I don't think it worth it. I'd go through death first if I knew I could live with you for a week even. But the letters! Oh, Carl, the letters people write! For all *they* know of you I might be marrying an idiot.

"This is a silly letter, darling. I didn't mean to write like this but it all came over me with a rush. What I meant to say was I love you and miss you.

"This morning I had a fitting for my wedding dress.

"Come back as I remember you. Oh, Carl, Carl, I can't believe it was only yesterday that you went and that it will be eight days more before I see you. When I get terribly lonely I look at 'The Boy' and feel better. 'The Boy' is more comfort to me than your photo even. The photo is something you can give to anyone, something that anyone might have seen—'The Boy' is yours and mine.

"When I think that soon now we'll be at Birchlands together, with no interruptions, no parties, no people, I get almost dizzy.

I feel like a very young child one minute and so terribly grown up the next. Do you think I seem older than I did when I first met you? I *feel* so different. I seem to fit into the world in a way I never did before. I lie awake at night thinking of you and hoping and hoping that I can make you happy. I'd love to know what you are doing at this exact minute.

      "I love you,

        "Kristin."

She read it over and sighed. I wish I were a writer, she thought, so I could really say what I want to. But now, she twirled the pen in her fingers, I must start on the letters. Her whole being revolted at the thought, massed together, became heavy. She addressed Carl's envelope and sealed it, chose a fresh piece of paper and began: "Dear Mrs Eliot." She held her pen tightly and wrote with the deliberate care of a child who is learning to write.

The sunlight fell in a pool on her desk and she sat there, pale and fair, her mouth tight and concentrated. But it is hard to focus the mind, she thought. I feel swimming in a pool of light, no part of me touching anything—just adrift in sunlight. She tried to gather her thoughts again—loose threads swaying in the sun—tried to draw them together with her fingers and knot them, so, to form a solid cord. "Dear Mrs Eliot. Thank you so much for the beautiful ... The lampshade is love-ly ... Carl and I are so grateful ... "

The cord had formed. The pile of letters grew; the sunlight thinned to a single beam that fell, steady and strong, on the paper before her. The rest of the room disappeared and Kristin at the desk knew nothing beyond the white squares of paper marked with small, carefully shaped black hieroglyphics, that she pulled towards her, pushed away. She worked at the desk in silence and "The Boy" watched over her shoulder.

The week passed. Letters came and went. Parcels arrived, were unwrapped and placed on the tables in the living-room.

People called, exclaimed over the presents, drank tea and sherry and left again. Fittings continued: dresses were taken in, let out, smoothed over the hips; lingerie chosen, hats tried on. The clergyman called and Kristin dashed from party to party. But all the time, though too busy to stop and relax, Kristin's heart said, Carl, Carl, come back and take me away. Her mother moved through the days, smart and two-dimensional as a fashion-plate, loving the people, the clothes, the fuss; dealing with the caterers, arranging about the church, inexhaustible, smiling, cap-able. And her father, returning at night, signed cheques, com-plained that his chair was moved from the living-room and chided her self-consciously and constantly.

At night, in her room, Kristin read her letters from Carl, scribbled notes to him in bed and lay tossing and turning in the darkness, calling for him, crying out against this life in which she had no time to be quiet, no time to be still. But the week passed, passed at last, like the traffic passing from the high street in the early hours of the morning.

Today, cried Kristin, wakening, today he comes! She hugged her knees, shut her eyes and moved to music. "Today," she cried, jumping from her bed. "And in less than a week," she said, leaning on her dressing-table and gazing at herself in the mirror, "in five days time we shall be married! And then...?" she questioned, "and then...?" It rushed over her then, the fear, the fear that the busyness of the week had quelled, pushed under. But if I fall like a shadow on him, blotting his personality, destroying his work? "What can I do," she called to the mirror, "to keep him safe from me? Where can he turn to escape? And who can help us, who but ourselves? I am the enemy," she said, "with a love in my heart more dangerous than hate."

But she was torn from herself, drawn into the tempo of the house.

"Kristin!" her mother called, opening the door, "Oh, you *are* awake. We've a busy morning," and she stopped. "Do you feel all right?" she asked. "Kristin, you look ill."

"I am tired," said Kristin, "that's all." She tied the belt of her house-coat.

"I've turned on your bath," said her mother. "So hurry, darling, there's so much to do."

Yes, hurry, hurry; sink thought into the whirlpool of speed, sink like a rock away from reality, disappear in the eddying light and darkness of motion. Allow the wings of your imagination to be bruised and broken by the actuality of things to be done. Forget, forget!

She bathed, she dressed, she ate. She moved like a swirl of wind, brushing aside the partitions of her mind, counting the morning which, like a wedding cake, rose before her, tier upon tier, until she stood, high on its topmost layer, waiting for the train to come in.

"Carl!" He was off first this time, his brown neck hidden, his brown hands gloved; but like a rocket of light behind her eyes he came to her over the platform. "My darling!" The world can go hang, she thought as he kissed her, die out from the sterility of its own restraint, fall with a splash upon the still surface of conventionality.

"This," he said, "is the last time we shall ever be parted. The worst is over; the best waiting upon our readiness. You are as lovely as I remember you. Oh, my sweet!"

To look into his face, to look at the firm brown lines of his face, the stillness of his eyes. I am at peace again, she thought. What has been jarred is mended.

"What have you done? Tell me, tell me," she said as they walked through the station.

"Missed you and missed you again."

"Ah," she laughed. "But seriously."

"I was serious."

"But all these days——?"

"I went to Birchlands," he said, "to get the place ready. It's looking lovely. The trees are turning. The lake is blue."

"And then?"

"I spent the rest of the time in Montreal. And you?"

"Parties, fittings, thank-yous. Terrible!"

"But now!" he said.

"Yes, but now!" Oh, to be with him again, to know the long ache ended. I can hardly speak, she thought, such is my happiness, such my delight, when I am with him. The white panther is attendant and no fall frost can touch us.

"Let's," she said, stepping out from the station, "let's buy a sandwich and eat it in the park. I'd hate to share you with the family so soon and I couldn't bear the noise of a restaurant."

"We can buy food here, at the station counter." He supervised the loading of his suitcases and then left her. She watched him push through the swing doors . . . her Carl, tall and straight. He burns, she thought, with the steady flame of an Aladdin lamp and I am a candle beside him, to be puffed out by the first gust of wind, inconstant beside his constancy. But no! She swept the words away with a little gesture of her hand. That is not true, she said. The truth, she thought, running her finger around the steering wheel, is not so easy. We both are constant to ourselves, both faithful to the form of our own lives, but my faithfulness is like a drum, sounding at intervals and his is a whistle, steady and endless. But importance lies, she thought, not in the drum or the whistle so much as in the combination of both; the combined sound falling upon a still air through the years ahead. She leaned on the wheel. Now, she thought, watching the people passing before the car, he is saying to the girl at the counter, "Thank you very much," and perhaps he is turning with the sandwiches in his hand and coming to me. And I, she thought, am like a small animal behind the wheel, stiff with desire for him, bearing this moment only through the tenseness of my body, holding myself like a shield against the day, until he returns to me.

And here he is, she said to herself, here he comes with the sunlight falling on him and his hands full and his eyes golden. He was beside her now. She moved along the seat. "You drive,"

106

she said. "I simply don't dare trust myself at the wheel. I'd probably run over everyone in sight."

"I'm no more sure that I won't, myself." He gave her the parcels. "Sandwiches and two pints of milk and chocolates and cigarettes. All right?"

"Lovely! Oh, Carl."

"Yes?"

"Just, oh Carl. I can't get used to the idea of you really being here, can't believe that it's not just imagination. When the house was at its maddest I've sometimes told myself, 'He is here now,' and for a moment believed it and felt the weight lift, only to fall again, heavier than ever, realizing you to be in Montreal." She sat sideways in the seat so that she could watch him—the tilt of his head—the way he signalled definite clear signals to the cars behind.

"When we meet," she said, "it is like fashioning a new building with turrets rising; endless turrets rising up clean and tall and white."

"Sometimes," he said, "you almost take the words out of my mouth. It's as if you know me from the inside—an empathetic knowledge of me."

"What is empathetic?" She sat up straight.

"Well," he hesitated. "It's a psychic term really. An inner knowledge resulting from the projection of the mind of the observer into the thing observed."

"Oh!" Why are we talking like this, why already are we on the subject I dread? She raised her hand to her mouth to hold it steady. "Is there any cure for it?" she asked.

"Cure?" said Carl. "No, I don't think so, darling. It's a sort of extra sense that leads to a fuller understanding. I don't think it's a thing people try to cure."

Oh, but they do, she thought. Carl, they do, they do.

"At any rate," he said, "I was only joking—about you, I mean."

She covered her mouth again. It's no subject to joke about,

for it's true, true, terribly true. But he interrupted her thoughts.

"I've brought you a present, Kristin. See if you can guess what it is."

"Another painting?"

"No-o-o. Not altogether."

"Oh, Carl, I can't guess. I was never any good at guessing. Tell me." She was excited. "Please."

"I'll show you when we have lunch. I have it with me."

"But tell me now, please, Carl."

"Don't be so impatient." He laughed at her.

"Will I like it?"

"I hope so." They had turned into the park. "Where shall we go?"

"Left here. To the place we were the night of the eclipse. On the little hill that overlooks the lake. Oh," she said, "the trees are turning, I haven't had time to notice. How lovely it is."

He stopped the car then and she leaned against him. Before he had pulled on the brake or turned off the engine she cried, "Kiss me, kiss me, Carl."

"Oh, Kristin. Little Kristin." He held her close and they sat together, forgetful.

"Pity the poor city lovers," she said at last. "Oh, Carl, to have nowhere to be together except in the dark shadow of some house. How can they bear waiting until the darkness falls? How can they bear it—people who love each other as you and I do?" She curled her fingers around his neck. "You look so different, up close, like this. Isn't it funny!" They laughed and they kissed and grew serious again.

"Kristin, I do hope you love Birchlands. I want you to so badly."

"But I will. How could I help it? With you I could love any place."

"But I want you to love Birchlands for itself—apart from me."

She smiled at him. "Darling, when all my love is centred in you I could only love it *through* you. I couldn't love separately. You see," she said, with her head in his lap, looking up at him, "I'm so very one-track." She sat up then. "Oh, show me the present. Carl, please!"

"Shut your eyes," he commanded.

She obeyed him and waited, wondering what the present would feel like in her hands, wondering what it could be, as she heard him rustling through his suitcase.

"Here," he said.

It was in her hands now. It felt hard. She opened her eyes. *Fairy Stories,* by Oscar Wilde. "Oh Carl!" She could feel him watching her as she opened the covers and turned through the pages. "And pictures," she said. "Carl, how beautiful!" And noticing CB at the bottom of the illustration, "Darling, they're yours. But Carl . . .?" She couldn't understand. She looked up at him and saw him laughing. "How," she said, "how did you——?"

"You remember that first day I spent with you I told you I had done illustrations."

"Yes, yes." She was impatient.

"Well, I found them when I was at Birchlands. So I bought a copy of the book and had an old bookbinder I know rebind it and put my illustrations in."

"Oh, darling!" She touched the pages as if they were velvet, then reached for his hand. "Carl," she said, "how I love you. How sweet you are."

"You like it then?"

"Like it! You couldn't have given me anything I like better. Thank you, thank you." She pulled him to her and kissed him, feeling the sweetness of an ebbing summer live again. "Thank you for so much—for everything. If I live to be eighty I shall never be able to thank you properly for—yourself."

"Nor I," he said, "for you."

She clung to him. He is my strength, she thought, my strength

109

and my happiness. Let the world crumble and we, together, will know it for bliss. Oh, my love, my love that grows like a flower in my heart, unfolding the curve of its petals like the loved hand opening; unfolding to beauty throughout the years. But the thought was dammed.

"Carl," she said suddenly realizing, "you must be starved. What a selfish wretch I am." She reached for the parcels and carried them under the trees. But for the moment she couldn't eat, herself; she was content merely to sit there, beside him, watching him eat, while the lake stretched out below like a great arc of blue and the knowledge of Carl fell about her, surrounded her, held her to a composite entity, aware only of her love for him, her love for him and his nearness.

Kristin sat in the garden alone. Alone for the first time since—she couldn't remember. She felt numb. The effort of thought was too much. It meant prising through the cotton-wool wrapping that swaddled her brain—layers and layers of it. But she had to think, had to make the effort now that she had the chance. The last hours had been a nightmare—fear rising upon fear and growing too large to hold within her. It hurt to think, hurt with the physical pain of an incision in her scalp.

The sun is quite hot on my face, she thought, and the strap at the back of the deck chair is firm across my back. These things I can feel, as acutely, more acutely than usual. If I start from here, start from this consciousness of the physical, perhaps, she thought, I can work through. The sun and the strap of the deck chair and the pressure of my knuckles on each other as my hands are twisted together. These things are all quite clear. But, she thought and she sat upright, straightened to a rod with the realization, I can't marry Carl. Loving him as I do I cannot marry him. She held her hands to her head.

"I met him,"—she spoke out loud to keep her mind concentrated—"I met him at the station three days ago. I met him and my love rose like the flight of a bird. We took sandwiches to the park and had lunch there and I remember the shaft of my love on the air; his laughter and his lips; the blue of the lake and the golden trees. All that, I remember," she said, "as though it were etched on my mind. And then," she said—and the fear rose like a mad thing in her head—"it happened. I felt it happening and fought against it but the waters of his being closed over me quickly," she said. "I was drowned in him. And this morning," she went on, forcing herself to follow the course of what happened, "this morning I came to the surface, I emerged from the sea and reclaimed myself." She shut her eyes, trying to shut away the sight of Carl's face that floated before her. He looked like death, she thought. When he came to me after breakfast he was an old man. Carl! Her hands went out for him as she thought, and touched nothing but the air. Carl! She held her hands together, then pressed them palm against palm. "He is not here," she cried. "He is"—she narrowed her mind to touch the thought—"he is at the railway office buying tickets for our honeymoon."

She saw him then, tall and brown, leaning slightly on the desk in the great shiny room and she began to cry. If I could forget his hands and his up-pointing shoulder, she sobbed. She turned in her chair and pressed her fingers against her eyelids. If only I could forget. All my joy has gone, all my happiness. I am left with only my fear and my anguish. Drawing her hands from her eyes she saw her mother coming across the grass and Mary behind her carrying a tray.

"I've had Mary bring a cup of tea out here, darling." Her mother sat beside her and Kristin could feel her gaze searching out her face. She watched Mary put down the tray and arrange the cups and saucers. Watched her hands moving, turning the silver teapot, putting the blue plate with the thin bread and butter on the table, saw the little cakes.

"That will be everything, Mary, thank you."

111

It is all remote, Kristin thought. It has nothing to do with me. She tried to centre herself, to hold reason in her head and stand steady.

Her mother poured the tea and passed her a cup. "Feeling better?" she asked and Kristin stared at her tea, finding no words.

"I've phoned the people who are giving parties and told them you're simply too tired to go. Carl doesn't mind and they all understand. You'll get a chance now to rest. Two days with nothing to do and you'll be all right."

If only it were as easy as that, Kristin thought. And she wanted to scream out against her mother's phrases that treated her despair like the neurosis of an hysterical woman. Anyone seeing us, Kristin thought, sitting here having tea on a green lawn that stretches out about us to the tall trees, could never guess at the panic this moment holds.

She watched her mother light a cigarette. She took one too, puffed at it and stubbed it out. There was no consolation anywhere. Like a record in her head the words of the poem repeated themselves over and over.

> "She stole his eyes because they shone,
> Stole the good things they looked upon;
> They were no brighter than her own."

On and on, verse after verse.

> "As he forgave she snatched his soul;
> She did not want it but she stole."

That would come. Unless she could hold herself apart from him, know the end of her love, she would steal his soul too. She could see the inevitable stealthy approach; she could see him standing, an empty thing, possessor of nothing but his physical shape, while she, unhappy, laden down with him, hugged his soul to her and could not let it go.

Light stirred through the words in her head, cut them up, destroyed them. He was coming across the grass, dragging his long shadow behind him.

"There's Carl," said her mother, her words announcing her relief in his coming. "Carl," she got up, "you're just in time for a cup of tea. Come along."

He was beside the tea table. "No sugar," he said, and her hand holding the sugar-tongs paused. "Of course not, how silly of me."

"Feeling better, darling?"

She nodded. He is trying so hard to be natural, she thought. Oh Carl, my darling, if only we need never have met.

"I must run off," her mother said. "There are still a thousand and one things to be done."

Carl sat down. "I have the tickets." He took them out as he spoke. "Just think, in two days' time we'll be at Birchlands." He stretched his legs and took a piece of bread and butter. "In two days' time," he went on, "the hell of this last week will be over, forgotten."

She pushed the words that formed away from her. "It has been hell, hasn't it, darling?"

"Your tiredness has, in some way, affected me too. The last few days have been like a mad dream in which I've had no control over myself. I suppose I must have been more tired than I realized. But soon it will all be behind us." He looked at her but she couldn't meet his eyes. Numbness rose in her again. My brain is bruised she thought, beaten with worry.

"Kristin." He was reaching across to her, trying to build another bridge; but she couldn't help him. She gazed at her moonstone until it grew large and blurred. He took her hand, lifted it to his cheek. "Oh my God, Kristin, I love you!" His voice was sharp. He hurt her hand as he held it. The panther moved from the darkness to her side, her veins were studded with light, fireflies moving in her blood stream.

113

"Oh, love, love, love!" she cried in a voice so shrill it startled her. But calling out against it as she did, mocking it with her mind, the long tide reached out and drew her to Carl. Sitting in his lap, her face against his, knowing his delight and her own, the thin wail continued in her head, like a fire siren against the night: it is over, this is the end; Carl, Carl, this is an interlude only; love me and turn your head away.

Her father was in high spirits at dinner. Carl, in his happiness, was talkative and gay. Kristin watched them all. Her father grumbling good-naturedly, Carl telling stories and her mother's words, like mice, running in and out of their talk. "The wedding cake has come. Darlings, you must see it." And, "Ralph, did you know Lucy Smart sent a cheque for a hundred dollars?" And, "I wonder why my dress hasn't come yet? They promised to have it here by six." The door-bell rang and the phone rang and when Mary called Kristin to answer either her father said "No. We must have our meals in peace." And then, "Perhaps it's something important, you'd better go." Kristin was glad of the phone calls and the door-bell; glad to escape from so much happiness she could not join; glad to be alone for the few minutes in the hall, coming and going; glad even of the letters that still had to be written, which released her from Carl's eyes.

As dinner ended her mother looked at her watch and said, "Well, children, we must get ready for the rehearsal."

Kristin had forgotten. The party after the rehearsal had been cancelled and she had forgotten. They got into the car, Carl finding her hands and holding them, no one saying very much. At the church the bridesmaids were already there and Johnny, the best man—a makeshift for Dick who couldn't get away. They were talking in the porch. Some of the ushers had arrived. The church was grey and cold inside. It was too early for lights and just dark enough to be depressing and dreary. Kristin wanted to run away. But the colour of the stained glass windows seemed peremptory, demanding and held her there. The clergyman arrived, grey and sanctimonious. He said, "My dear, my dear, this is a beautiful moment in your life, the moment when God sanctions the love in your heart and makes it a sacred, holy thing." He said it several times and Kristin wanted to cry out to him, scream that her love was evil. He showed them how they walked up the aisle. The ushers were referring to lists and plans, learning the seating arrangements; the bridesmaids were excited, pretending already to be in their dresses, holding their hands as though carrying flowers. Her father was enjoying it all, walking up the long aisle with her, doing it a second time to make sure. Carl looked nervous. Kristin could see him, standing apart, the light from one of the windows just touching the end of his nose, turning it purple, like an amethyst set in the end of it.

The clergyman explained the wedding service to them. He intoned the phrases, "Love, honour and obey." "In sickness and in health." "Till death us do part." "I plight thee my troth." And Kristin heard them with a sick heart. Till death us do part. It is only, she thought, death that can part the awful unity of us, the unity that must destroy our love. She wanted to take off her hat, run her fingers through her hair, block her ears to the sound of the clergyman's voice and her eyes to the tall figure of Carl standing apart from her, yet within her. She wanted to cry out to them all: "I cannot go through with it; I cannot marry Carl, marry a man in whose eyes I only see my own when I look; marry a man to destroy him." But the harsh words within her evaporated, lifted. For he stood there, complete, strong, virile as 'The Boy', contradicting her thoughts— something apart from her, a rock—steady, self-reliant—something she could not destroy.

The rehearsal was over. The bridesmaids and ushers joined together, called to Kristin, "Come to the party after all. We're having it anyway." But it was her mother who answered, "No, really, I must be firm. She's too tired."

"Carl, then," they called. "He could come."

Kristin watched him smile at them and refuse; watched them tumble into the cars; heard their words flung across the half-light, "We'll see you at the wedding."

"Get a good rest, Kristin."

"It's a pity to miss such a good party."

She took off her hat, reached for Carl, feeling that now, at this minute, he was safe from her and she could turn to him. He pressed her fingers, whispered, "Oh, darling, how I wish that had been the wedding." They got into the car, her parents still talking to the clergyman on the steps. He kissed her then, quickly, touched her hair. They were apart, Kristin thought, quite apart from the rest of the world, sharing a strange vacuum that no one else could approach with words or gestures. For the moment she was happy—the fear gone—safe in the knowledge that Carl shared this dislocation of life with her, the wrenched moment that was apart from all normal living; this sudden right-about-face of being. He stroked her hand, holding her close to him. Now we are Hansel and Gretel, she thought, holding to each other. But as the moments passed she grew so light that she felt they were both floating, flying high above the world, knowing only the wind and the clouds, detached from the solidity, the squareness of an earth life. We are Peter Pan and Wendy, she mused. Hansel and Gretel are gone.

"Good night, good night," her mother called on the church steps. They could hear her heels as she moved on the pavement; they drew apart.

"Such a good man," said her mother getting into the car.

"He's too serious for me," her father added. 'I must say I enjoy a laugh and a joke."

As they drove home through the tree-lined streets, watching the night settle about them, the fear returned to Kristin. Nothing is secure, she thought. Everywhere there is change. The hand stretched out to give is refused; the hand stretched out to receive finds ashes in its palm.

Her father stalled the car at a crossroad and swore loudly.

Her mother said, "I wonder if my dress has come yet?" Carl whispered in the darkness, "Dearest, dearest!" and then they were home again and her mother was hustling her off to bed. All of time is cut up into pieces, Kristin thought, little lengths of this and that; the reel never unrolls to full length. The images in her mind faded as she lay down. Fear, bright as a sword blade in the sun, dimmed and grew grey; the moment of happiness in the car that shone like the cup of a buttercup grew grey; everything grew grey as the inside of the church. She was sleepy; she couldn't think any more. Falling off to sleep she saw Carl with the purple light like an amethyst set in the end of his nose. She sighed and slept.

The next day was over like a promise broken. No sooner were jobs done than others cropped up that called for attention and Kristin threw herself into the work despite her mother's pleading. Only this way, she thought, can I bear it. Only this way, too busy for Carl to touch the core of me, too busy to think, too busy to question, can I cross the endless chasm. By night-time she was exhausted.

"You look pale and tired, darling," her mother said. "No way for a bride to look. I suggest an early bed."

Yes, Kristin thought, yes. She was willing.

Her father kissed her self-consciously. "I hope it is nice tomorrow," he said. "There are storm clouds in the west."

"It's sure to be," her mother announced. "We'll all concentrate."

Upstairs, saying good night to Carl, Kristin felt the tears forming in her eyes.

"I've only seen you in little flashes," he whispered. "All day long—little glimpses. Oh, my darling!" She leaned against him, holding him tightly, still unwilling to look into his face. "Tonight," he said, "is the last night I'll kiss you outside your bedroom door." He held her chin and kissed her. The whole world was alight. If it could always be so, she thought, Carl always dominant... She left the words suspended in her head, for-

117

getful now of all but Carl, all but the blind magnificence of him.

"Ah, my love!" He let her go then, leaned her backwards, and stared at her. "Little Kristin. Dear heart!" She held him again, loathe to leave him at this moment, frightened of turning her back and going to her room.

"Whatever I may tell you after we're married," she spoke slowly, carefully, "remember that now, at this moment, I love you more than my life." She held up her lips. "Kiss me again," she said, "and then I must go to bed."

He kissed her. She turned then, not looking back, and opened the door of her room. She heard his footsteps move off and she sank on her bed and sobbed into clenched hands, "I love him, oh God, I love him and our love is nearly over; married, our happiness will be a torn and finished thing."

She looked up at "The Boy". It is no good, she thought, he is not strong enough. Even "The Boy" can't convince me now, and she turned the picture to the wall.

She undressed, stared at the boxes in her room lying open still for last-minute things to be thrown in, looked at the tags she had written—red tags with "MRS CARL BRIDGES" printed on them carefully. Her room looked empty. Empty cupboard, empty drawers—empty of everything but her wedding dress, long and pale in her cupboard and her going away suit; her drawers empty of all but her wedding lingerie and her make-up and accessories. She couldn't look at them; they were part of Carl's destruction.

She walked to the bathroom. In sickness and in health, she thought, turning on the tap. I plight thee my troth, I plight thee my troth. She leaned out of the bathroom window. The sky was dark with clouds, not a star showing. The wind sounded large and angry. Storm clouds in the west—she remembered his father's words. Little Kristin, dear heart. Oh, oh! She held her face-cloth to her eyes, seeing light and colour form beneath her lids as she pressed her eyeballs; feeling the slow white pain creep into the tissue of her eyes.

118

She could hear the wind howling as she returned to her room. The storm is a symbol, she thought, getting into bed—a pointer predicting the course of our love. Lying in the bare room, the room stripped of her personality, "The Boy" turned to the wall, she felt alive with the reality of Carl. Everywhere she looked Carl was there, like a ghost, filling her with terror. She could bear it no longer. She reached her hand up for the light switch; the room opened to darkness, large, with Carl all about her. She felt his hands, saw the lift of his half smile, heard him whisper. Terrified, she drew the covers about her neck, covered her face. No blind was permanent; each shutter she drew down was nothing more than the slide of glass in a phial which held two acids apart—a slide that was destroyed by the acids and ultimately brought them together to react.

Desperate she lay there, checking the desire to cry; knowing that before tomorrow, tomorrow that loomed like a giant, so immense that she couldn't see it as a whole, she must find a solution that would protect Carl from her. For, she thought, as we are, the steady whistle of Carl's integrity will be torn to tatters of sound by me. As we are, if I marry him, it will mean the complete merging of two personalities. But the truth rushed to her out of the night: it will mean the obliteration of two personalities. That is, she thought slowly, the words like heavy sacks that had to be carried together to form a sentence, that is, if I have a personality of my own. For I am a chameleon, she thought, absorbing the colours about me and our marriage will submerge us, wipe us out as sun obliterates the markings of water on a stone.

Fear sucked her down.

One plus one will equal nothing, she cried, clutching her pillow until her finger nails ached. Mathematicians know nothing, nothing at all. There is another field, a field beyond the realms of accepted mathematics where allowances are made for figures and they can and do add up quite differently. One and one equal two is a truth no longer—it is an instance only.

119

She felt calmer for a minute, considering her discovery and she heard the wind again, increasing now, like a gargantuan bellows blowing outside her window. The wind held the house and dropped it. Quite suddenly the world was still, suspended in a void—for a second only—and then the rain came, released like cattle into the corral of the roof—wild, flint-shod cattle tearing the structure of the house.

She listened. She could hear the wind again, pulling at the trees, whipping their branches. The night had risen for the furious stampede that held the sea and all emotion in its intensity. And she felt part of it, like a branch torn off and carried by the wind, hurtled through the air, drained of emotion—a chance body that the night had taken and robbed; empty now, left on her bed, tranquil, at peace. No worry could touch her. The problem was solved though the answer was still not in her possession. She lay immobile, a branch the night had tossed and forgotten. She slept, knowing sleep, conscious of it, aware of its quality of slow germination, of gradual growth. She remembered nothing before it, nothing more than the stirring, the easy evolution of the seed that was herself.

And then suddenly she was awake, knowing her strength to be in jeopardy; knowing she must put forth every effort to stay alive. The wind was like a mad creature tearing at her branches and the strain on her roots made her entire being ache and throb. She knew only an instinctive desire to stay standing, to battle with the wind and so remain upright and invincible, to dig her roots into the earth, clutching at the soil, bracing the trunk that was torn and twisted with the force of the wind. Muscular soreness wrenched her, surged through her, but with it a joy in living, a fierce happiness. She was pitting her strength against the wind in a battle for existence and she was winning. For a moment she cried out, remembering something undone. She cried, "Carl, I've never told you about the rocks," but the wind stopped her mouth, caught her branches, swung them out, stripped off the leaves and she was forgetful again of all but the fight; conscious of the deeper grip of her roots in the earth, the greater bracing of her trunk against the air. Exultant, she fought, knowing her supremacy; knowing the re-creation of self in the united forgetfulness of self; she pitched her strength at the night and her strength was returned to her.

Gradually the wind weakened, the rain lightened and died and the air fell like velvet about her—soft and sweet. She released her grip and submitted herself to a peace, a peace more surely permanent than any she had known. She was strong, upright and intact. The long night was behind her, the fight over.

As the morning sun dropped honey on her leaves and fell in warm patches on her trunk, so, too, did it creep through the Venetian blinds of the bedroom and stripe the waking shell on the bed that had once contained her. The sun touched them both, the past, the future, equally.

Graceful, swaying slightly, she faced the calm of the day and drank from the rich, wet earth—steady in the security of her fibre and bark; content in the sweet uprising form of her growth, holding her branches up to the sky in the simple, generous gesture of the victor who knows victory to be within.

The day settled to warmth. A breeze lifted the fallen leaves at her roots. Two sparrows perched on a branch and pecked at the clustered red berries she held out for them, turned from their eating and preened the brown and grey of their bodies with their small beaks. One soft feather floated downward to the bronze leaves below. Mary, at the back door shaking the mop, said, "My, but the leaves sure fell in the storm last night, but it's a lovely day for the weddin'." The shadows shortened and the sun grew hot.

PART 5

EPILOGUE

The sun and a small wind broke the surface of the lake to glinting sword blades. On the far side, where the trees marched unchecked, right down to the water's edge, there the lake was a shifting pattern of scarlet, vermilion and burnt orange—but bright, bright, so that it hurt the eyes and the pain crept like a thin red line of infection through the whole body.

This was beauty to a happy heart. A wild, intense kind of beauty and the red line became a current of recklessness, no mean stream of fierce pain.

Beyond the trees and the trees' reflection hills ranged higher and higher like the backs of large amethyst elephants and camels. A fantastic and gargantuan circus parade, monochromatic, motionless.

Kristin sat in the glassed-in veranda that hung out practically over the water. Beside her on the window-sill was a bottle of nail polish. As she dipped the brush in the varnish she lifted her eyes no higher than the neck of the bottle. She knew no need of the view; she knew no need of shutting the view from her. She knew nothing but a pallid desire to perfect each oval nail and leave each in turn shining, smooth and vivid as a rowan berry. As vivid as an autumn rowan berry.

The whining groan of wet wood brushed against wet wood made her lift her head. Below, at the wharf, Carl was getting out of the row-boat. She watched him a moment and returned to her nails.

Nine were finished.

She dipped the brush in the varnish again, as relentless in her continuance as the lake shifting, eddying and rippling.

Ten were finished.

She placed her hands in her lap and sat gazing passively at the coloured tips of her fingers. A small unamused smile nipped the corners of her mouth. The veranda door opened. Kristin continued to stare at her nails.

"Hello, Kristin," said Carl.

"Hello," she answered. Only her lips moved.

"It's beautiful on the other side of the lake," he went on. "I cut through the woods, blazing a trail as I went. It's a splendid walk. Takes you clean up to the top of Old John's Hill. We must clear it some time—scrap the cedar that grows as fast as the mushroom——"

"Cedar?" said Kristin.

"Yes. Lop off some of the lower boughs of the maples and spruces and we'll have a fine path."

"Maples and spruces," said Kristin.

Still she hadn't raised her head. He crossed to her and lifted her face so that she looked at him. The small blank smile still played about her mouth. His hand was under her chin. He could feel the young firm flesh of her throat and the steady pulse in her jugular vein. Her face presented only a mask for him to look at. It was like living with an idiot. His fingers tightened and he felt her pulse strengthen under the pressure. By God! he would make her feel something, force an expression into her face, if only one of loathing. He bent her to him. He would kiss her until she struggled to escape from sheer exhaustion. He would pit his manhood against her aloofness.

Emotionless, passive, she accepted his prolonged kiss. When he released her, longing for some show of feeling on her face, she turned back to examine her nails, as though merely interrupted by some trivial thing which neither annoyed nor pleased her.

He drew away. Thick with anger he moved with the jerkiness of a puppet over to the windows. The colour and brilliance of the lake cut into him until he hated the place. She hadn't even resisted him. He moved her neither to love nor hatred. She was indifferent; coolly indifferent to his attentiveness and neglect. He forced his knuckles against the frame of the window until pain gnawed at the white blunt joints, hoping that perhaps physical suffering would waken him from this honeymoon which had from the outset been like a hideous nightmare pressing close about him, stifling him, terrifying him.

He'd noticed she was different on the wedding day and dismissed it, thinking she was tired; but a week had passed since they were married and now . . . what could he do? His knuckles were numb. In his desire he had treated her always as though she were completely normal, talked to her about little things, pretending that both she and he were interested in them; while all the time he knew that this heightened casualness was but a cloak to cover her unconcern and his distress. The anger had gone now. The waters of his rage had ebbed, leaving him a smooth beach, washed clean of all signs of turmoil. He turned to her again, emotionless as she. Together they could play this game of apathetic living. This was the time when pods burst open, scattering their contents and leaving themselves empty and light. He and she could join in this mad carnival of empty things. They could and should dance frantically, wantonly, to the pipings of September winds. The comparison amused him. With a mind tuned to minuteness he followed the images intricately. Their place in the autumn festival grew to assume importance and with the swelling of this importance his apathy diminished; gradually his vulnerability returned.

Kristin was apparently immovable. She sat as before. As Carl looked at her again he sensed, rather than saw, a certain grossness smudging her almost translucent features. It was as if the flesh had murdered the spirit and risen triumphant from the scene of the crime. He shuddered. The Kristin he first knew had seemed to have been hugging to herself a personal spiritual ecstasy.

He remembered their meeting at the Lothrop's party. He hadn't wanted to go. It wasn't shyness—rather an awareness of the ridiculous—his own particular sense of the ridiculous, admittedly. It had, in the end, been a splendid, garish affair. Shrill *soigné* women had laughed with tense, immaculate men after the initial gush of enthusiasm over the painting. And he had been tossed carefully and quickly from guest to guest by a hostess adept in the arts demanded of her by society.

"And this is Kristin," Mrs Lothrop had eventually said, considering it unnecessary to mention her last name. "Kristin, I want you to meet Mr Bridges so that you can always remember that you met a very great artist in the year you came out." And she had dragged him on unmercifully, eager to show him off to her guests, careful to monopolize him herself.

"Now, Mr Bridges, another cocktail. I think we both deserve one." Mrs Lothrop was thick through the waist, Carl had observed, with a fine black hair line on her top lip. Anything, anything would serve to think about until he could escape to Kristin. He must get back to her. He could see—that is, if he turned and passed the olives to Mrs Lothrop he could see—the curve of Kristin's shoulder and the long, lean line of her arm. Something important happened to him when he saw her. He wanted to return to her quite unbeautiful face and discover what it was about her that he liked. He wanted to arrange to have her sit for him. He wouldn't leave tomorrow after all. Damned if he would! "Oh, yes, Mrs Lothrop, thank you so much, I believe I will." He held out his glass automatically. He'd get her onto canvas first. "The cocktail party was an excellent institution. Yes, Mrs Lothrop, a splendid party. Oh, I'm quite certain people are enjoying themselves—take you and me, for example." He passed her the olives, again, unimpressed by her

125

consumption capacity, seeing only Kristin as he turned with the dish. A fellow-guest joined them. Carl saw his opportunity and escaped. Kristin was still there. He had seen to that.

"Hello," she had said as he came up to her. God, this queer child—but—she's not child nor yet woman, he realized next minute.

"I s'pose I should think of something chatty to make you at ease. I never can." She smiled, unembarrassed, friendly. She had a pale wedge-shaped face, too pale, wide clear green eyes and a small tight mouth which suggested extreme concentration. It was an ugly mouth. Her hair fell solid to her shoulders, fair, uncurled, shiny as the coat of a horse. He took her all in and afterwards cursed his observant artist's eye. Not for him, the excruciating joy of lying awake wondering about the colour of her eyes, the shape of her mouth, or the look of her hands. For him instead, the detailed, photographic image that most men in love desire but cannot recall. Jove, he would do a fine painting of her, a sort of modern Mona Lisa.

"Carl." He came back to the present. She was saying his name, not calling him. Her voice was empty of inflection as if she was merely seeing how she liked the sound of his name on her lips.

"Yes, Kristin?"

She held up her hands. "Carl, do you like my finger nails?"

He paused. "Yes, dear, they are lovely," he said, and waited for the satisfaction to mount to the surface of her eyes. The smile nipped the corners of her mouth tighter, but her eyes didn't change. They were pebbles which had seen neither water nor sunlight.

A low white mist covered the lake so that Carl, looking down from his bedroom window felt he might be looking up into the sky. It was early yet and perhaps the sun would burn through by mid-day. If the mist was as bad on the road as it was on

126

the lake he'd have to allow a good hour for the drive to the station. And he hated driving blind. It made him panicky and God knew he was panicky enough as it was. No one but a panicky man would have scnt a wire to Dick two days ago. He had tried to appear casual, yet feared in so seeming that Dick might consider the invitation unimportant and refuse. Carl had waited, coiled like a powerful spring, for the answering wire, and then it had come. "Delighted meet me noon train." There was nothing facetious, sniggering, suggestive. Just a simple acceptance. How he hated the supposedly humorous digs at marital relationships!

Carl took off his pyjamas and wondered to himself what, just what, he would do with Dick when he came. Until now his coming had been enough. But at this moment, as he walked naked into the bathroom and turned on the tap, he realized that even Dick might make a burlesque of a tragedy. Perhaps he should have barred any intrusion into this very personal sorrow. Perhaps he should have wired to the Fenders instead of Dick. Perhaps . . . perhaps . . .

Carl flung the bath mat on the floor as though he had a long-standing hatred for it. God! God! God! He felt about fifteen years old; unable either to control himself or see any clear path away from what tormented him. Living with Kristin was worse than the agony of a love spurned. Living away from her would mean the partial surrender of the all-important undivided mind. Apart from her he could never again know the complete absorption that so far had been vitally necessary to him. His path lay in either of two directions, both of which were cul-de-sacs. He recognized this to be the end of his love; but what was more important still—for no woman could ever possess him entirely—was that it might possibly be the end of his work. In her withdrawal from him she had taken more of him than she could have in completing and renewing the love he offered her.

With superb contempt for what might be self-dramatization

Carl continued to think, warily, as he washed himself. And the conflict of a superficial defence with a very real and deep pain made the intensity of his hidden struggle greater.

Should he prepare Dick on the drive back from the station for what was to come? Should he say, "Kristin and I are at odds," easily and wait for Dick's reaction? Or should he take him back as if all was normal, delightful and let him find out for himself?

I must not jump so far ahead, Carl thought drying himself with exaggerated care. The thing to do is be but one jump ahead, that is all. I must dwell in the minute to come and the minute that is simultaneously and completely—stretch out the area of my "now" to include one small portion of what would normally be my future. Thus and thus only can I avoid confusion. Stepping meticulously into the footprints of this plan Carl covered the morning. He dressed, breakfasted alone. Kristin was not yet up. He sprayed the charcoal sketch of his new painting—a pattern of intertwined bodies. When one finger of a friend is laid upon your flesh, he thought, then is responsibility manifold. He felt within him that the picture would remain unfinished. But at this moment his "now" had already extended to giving it its initial wash of ochre paint and so he prepared his colour and rag and turpentine. He knew that in some way he had stolen a march on time; that somehow, in the trivial things at least, he was preparing his own fate. And the upper layer of his mind smiled, though the lower layers writhed in mortification. In this self-imposed detachment he could find a momentary peace from the large worry that possessed him. It was as if he were two separate entities, working toward a common end, each with individual unconcern for the other.

The mist lay heavy on the lake. The trees and hills were veiled in nun's veiling when he walked down the gravel walk to the garage. The gravel had colour today—the stones proclaimed themselves personally; the lack of a brighter contrast brought them out in their inescapable pastel display. The red roof of the garage shone through the mist—a glowing patch.

The drive to the station took even longer than he had expected. Opaque rolls of mist swirled out at him on the road, slowing him down to walking speed, stopping him at times. The train was in when he arrived and he was thankful. Waiting on the edge of the track was unendurable. Dick, subdued in the respectable burberry, stood under the shelter of the station-house roof. As Carl saw him he forgot everything but a joy in the familiar outline.

"Heigho!" he called.

"A fine friend, a fine friend, I must say," said Dick. "Drag a fellow all the way down to this god-forsaken corner of nowhere and then leave him standing on the platform holding the bag. Please pardon pun," he added, partly from habit, mostly because Carl seemed to be smiling with his flesh only.

Dick was good, Carl considered. Punster or no he was a clean solid kernel. There was a sharp pleasure in merely contemplating the brilliance of his dark eyes and the contrasting stringently fair hair. Carl, long-faced, sallow, of El Greco proportions, felt a dull dog beside Dick.

"How was the trip?" asked Carl.

"Oh—as usual. How are you Carl, happy?"

Now, thought Carl, now is your moment. Here is the opening. "Yes," he said. "Why?"

"I just wondered." Carl's answer was too evasive. "You—look like hell."

"Right," said Carl, forgetting to keep the "now" extended beyond itself. "Something is wrong. Something has happened to Kristin."

Dick, watching Carl's face as he spoke, noticing the hard line of the tense jaw said, "And I had hoped to have a nice restful week-end. Well, well!"

Thank you, Dick, thought Carl. Thank you for keeping this conversation level. Thank you for staying in the realm of simple things.

And Dick thought, what has happened? There is something here more dreadful than I know. Carl never speaks quietly like this. Something has hit him below the belt and left him winded. He has broken his own pattern. Dick lit his pipe and gazed out at the the white cocoon of a world he was driving through and then launched into talk of the city: of this play, that concert, this book and the ever impudent Tony and his gatherings. He had not seen Carl for weeks. He wanted to talk to him in the old way, effortlessly. He wanted to hear of Carl's work and, too, talk of his own.

The house peered out at them suddenly. The mist had lifted a little. The mallards could be seen clearly now, floating on a lactescent lake; the blue curve of the row-boat was a flute note of sound in the misty silence.

"I've not been here for a year or more," Dick said. "It's good to be back."

Carl turned impulsively. "Whenever I'm not here you can use Birchlands, you know. I'd love you to . . ."

"Thanks," said Dick hastily. Carl seemed to have forgotten Kristin.

"I mean it," he went on, picking up Dick's suitcase. "It's a crime to leave it empty. This place needs living in. It's seen little of life except its own wild life of ceaselessly growing things."

Inside, Birchlands had a smell peculiarly its own, dependent not upon the meal in process of preparation or the soap or perfume currently popular by its owners. It smelled of old pine panelling and an open wood fire.

Dick hesitated in the doorway. From now on he must be prepared to face it; from now on he must be ready to help Carl, help Kristin, whom he'd never met; help them both, if necessary.

Carl opened the door. The old smell was there, at the far end the fire blazed in the large stone fireplace. It was just dark enough for the flames to dance in the copper and pewter of attending plates and kettles.

130

"Hello, Kristin," said Carl. A child with a strange dead face looked up from an armchair. "This is Dick, Kristin, whom I've told you about."

God, thought Dick, he's uncanny. He frightens me more than she does. He's too calm. Something will happen. It can't last.

"Dick, my wife."

"How do you do?" said Dick. I must try to be casual, pretend this atmosphere is one of normality. Not for one moment must I betray the cold fear that prickles in my jaws. "Carl, your taste is flawless and, Kristin, I commend you on your choice of a husband. Take it from me, an old friend, he's not as bad as he looks." Damn, thought Dick, there is something here which stilts me, makes me talk like a book. This is awful. This child is terrible.

A long silence drew the room about them, caught the three of them together and held them, so. Dick clenched his hands in his pockets and knew the weight of Kristin heavy on his heart. He could not speak. And then Carl, easily, spoke again and the weight lifted little by little and Dick's hands unclenched.

"We've just time for a swim before lunch. The water's cold but——"

"Invigorating?" suggested Dick and Carl laughed. "Will you join us too?" Dick asked, turning to Kristin. She didn't even raise her eyes.

"Come on," said Carl. "Kristin won't go unless she's thrown in—will you, darling?" He didn't wait for an answer, Dick noticed, but started up the stairs with the bags, saying as he went, "I'm going to keep you busy, Dick. I want to make a path in the upper woods. How are you with a hatchet?"

"Second only to Washington."

"Right, I'll make you prove it." He was gone. Dick lit a cigarette as he undressed and felt happiness evaporate. He must wait, he knew, until Carl volunteered further mention of Kristin. As he went downstairs and passed her chair on the way to the lake she sat as motionless and unaware as though he had passed in spirit form. And he shuddered and suddenly felt too cold to swim.

Carl was already in the water. A voice from the mist hailed him when he came up from his dive and he struck out in the direction of it, glad of the clean sweep of water on his body, finding in it a momentary escape.

"Race you," said Carl as Dick drew near.

Figures in a mist, figures in a mist, swimming freely but blindly they know not where. Two bodies elongated in water, moving and splashing and the splashing sounding like a watermill—loud and endless.

Dick, for those moments, was conscious of a strangeness but not a fear. It was not until, dressed and tingling, with moisture still clinging to his hair that he knew again the drag of Kristin.

"Scotch and soda?" asked Carl. And Dick accepted eagerly, hoping stimulation would shut Kristin from him and smudge the wedge he seemed to see in Carl's eyes. As they drank, as they smoked beside the fire, Kristin sat still, a shadow between them. By silent, mutual consent she was excluded from the conversation as are the deaf.

"Done any painting?" Dick asked.

"Yes," said Carl. "Not much though. And it's pretty bad—unrelated to the moment, in a way. It seems remote, as if I were painting in a dream. It's," he laughed, "a product of the imagination."

No remark was pointed with sufficient excitement to carry interest; banter fell short of its mark, bringing only pale smiles to their lips, or worse still, hearty laughter that crumbled as it came.

Plates and knives and forks looked out of place swimming in the polished lake of table. Nothing bore the conviction of reality except Kristin, now set in the pattern of eating. She sat at the head of the table, filling the place bodily, gracelessly.

132

Occasionally Dick's eyes met Carl's and immediately he flipped a remark to him—his contribution to the rapidly sinking fund of happiness.

The sun burned through during lunch and when they had coffee on the veranda it had turned into a hot Indian summer day. Carl drummed his fingers on the window-ledge. "We'll start that path," he said. "See, Dick, across the lake, that silver birch by the water?" Dick scanned the shore for the landmark. "That is where we go into the woods." Carl put down his coffee and looked at his watch. "In ten minutes time," he said. "All right? You'll need your oldest clothes." The path is his connecting link with reality, thought Dick, anxious already to be off, to escape from Kristin who had said no word to him since he had arrived two hours ago and too, no word to Carl.

The sun was on their backs as they rowed across the lake and in their eyes was the figure of Kristin at the window; she was not looking at them, or if she were her interest was elsewhere, for a smile and a wave brought no answer from her motionless body. Dick watched her figure grow smaller and smaller until it had dwindled to a small dot in the distance. The fear within him lessened and when grounding the row-boat they turned their backs on the house, Dick felt the weight of her spirit had lifted.

"Here," said Carl, slashing at young willows, "is the beginning of the path. This is the birch you saw from the house." He paused, leaning on his axe handle and looked about him. "One day I mean to clear all the underbrush from these woods so that the trunks of the trees retreat like shadows of themselves."

"And call it Birchlands Park and you'll retire from the world of art and live the life of a country squire."

"Come on!" said Carl, feeling the axe blade with his thumb.

It was easy to begin; easy, easy to throw oneself into this rhythmic movement for a short time. They worked hard, hauling moss-covered logs, lopping mercilessly at branches; working with a strenuous determination which, in Carl, seemed to increase as the work grew heavier and hotter.

"Call a halt, call a halt," cried Dick at last, Carl showed no sign of letting up. "I come from the city and work at a desk all day—remember?"

"Right," said Carl, pushing the dark hair from his eyes with the flat of his palm and sitting where he stood. Dick leaned against a tree and patted the moss before lighting a cigarette.

"God," he said, with the first puff, "that's the way to smoke—occasionally. This might be a Pall Mall—first time in years a smoke has tasted like anything but straw." He tossed his packet to Carl, watched him light up. And then suddenly Carl said, looking over Dick's head and hardly moving his lips, "She's—strange, isn't she? Like a ghost. She moves like the old and her eyes are dead."

It has come, thought Dick, this moment I've awaited and dreaded. This moment when nothing I say will be right. "Yes, Carl, she's strange."

"She was exquisite once. If you could have known her then. Young and so very different."

Shadows were beginning to fall. It grew cold. Dick put his coat on and cupped his cigarette in his hands as though the small glow might warm the chill which engulfed him. And as Carl spoke to him, explaining the old Kristin, the young Kristin, Dick knew no word that could bridge the gap pity had cut between them. To say the child was mad was to hit out in the dark and strike the defenceless. There was no real indication of madness; it was more a magnified withdrawal of spirit. But Carl wanted help, advice, not vague theorizing and Dick knew that he was no use. The only thing he knew with any degree of certainty was that Carl's restraint was unhealthy; there would come a time when it snapped. And he hated Kristin with a fierce hatred for so destroying the very fibre of her husband; he hated this thin slip of a girl with her long legs and her long hands who was wreaking destruction silently and insidiously in the strong male mind of Carl.

Carl pulled on his sweater. "We had better get back," he said. As they walked down the newly made path Carl smiled. "There's a deep satisfaction in manual labour—deeper than the average man admits—after a certain point a peace is reached. And besides, this path is good." Dick gripped his shoulder with a blistered hand. It was an awkward self-conscious gesture but at that moment there was nothing else he could say or do.

The sunset burned in the lake as they returned and the face they waited to see at the window was lost in the reflected glory of the burnished glass.

As Carl said good-bye to Dick he felt he was turning his back on the positive side of his nature and he despised the creature that was left, yet knew no escape from it. Normally he would have gone to his picture; but now he was conscious of no desire to paint, only a desire to want to paint and even that was submerged in the thought of Kristin, Kristin, Kristin. Day and night; inside and out; eating and sleeping—Kristin. The cold finger of ice that burned as it touched and was forever touching everything, everything. Deliberately he sought her out. Perhaps this time . . .?

She was, as usual, on the veranda. Now he could no longer see her objectively; when he looked he seemed to be seeing only a part of himself. Yet propinquity with her started up a rhythm in his mind, stress the casual, stress the casual. And so he talked of the trivial when he longed to get to grips with the issue.

"It is too nice to be in," he said. "Change your shoes and walk with me in the woods."

Kristin leaned back in her chair. "Will you?" he asked.

"N-no," she answered. "I'm tired."

"But darling, you've hardly done anything for days."

"The storm last night tired me. I couldn't sleep. Storms are tiring things."

"Well then, come and I'll take you in a canoe. You needn't move once you get in."

"I'd sooner stay here," she answered.

Carl reached for a cigarette. There was one thing he must know. He must ask. He lit his cigarette and waited until the flame of the match burned down to his fingers before he spoke. "Kristin, are you happy?" From under his lids he watched her face and for one moment he saw it register something close to pleasure. Her voice was live when she answered, "Yes, yes. I'm so near to the trees."

"Then you like it here?"

"Yes."

Carl flicked the match from him. He could have jumped up and kissed her. But he would wait until he had gone further . . . wait until he was sure.

"Kristin, I've wondered—you're not sorry to have married me?" She was far off again, the contact had gone. "Kristin!"

"What?"

"You're not sorry you married me?"

"No."

There again indifference. The wall of his hope was broken by the shadow of her "No". "Then you don't dislike me, Kristin? I was so afraid, so worried." Steady, steady, cautioned his mind. But she was not listening. Already she was gone, escaped.

"Kristin, you must answer me—does it annoy you to have me near?" He waited, fearful, ready for the "No" to fall like a hammer stroke on the air; the "No" that meant nothing at all.

"No." said Kristin.

Carl braced himself. Deliberately he was exposing himself for her to mutilate, but he couldn't stop. "Kristin, Kristin, say you love me a little."

She looked up, puzzled. "Love you?"

136

"Yes, Kristin. Do you love me?"

The puzzled look increased, then as if everything was solved it went again. "I don't understand," she said.

"Great God, Kristin, you must understand. What did you marry me for, what are we doing together at all if you refuse to understand the meaning of love?" He wanted to shake her and shake her—this phlegmatic, disinterested woman. "You told me you loved me, you told me you loved me," he said, clinging hopefully to her words. "Kristin, look at me, answer me."

She shook her head. "I don't know what you mean." Then her face brightened. "Carl, I'm hungry."

Carl swung from his chair. This was too much. No one should be allowed to hurt another to this extent. He would leave, run away somewhere and hide in a crowd. She didn't want him, she didn't even need him. "If she had died," he said aloud, "if she had died I could have found solace; for this wound there is no comfort."

He threw clothes into a bag, blindly, desperately. Downstairs in the studio the new painting stared up from its canvas. When one finger of a friend is laid upon your flesh—no painting should remain and tell the world that his knowledge enclosed this truth. No trace should show. No trace.

With painstaking care he cut the canvas to ribbons with his palette knife, turned and left. He had said good-bye to Birchlands and to Kristin. He would never come back. Never.

The sun and a small wind broke the surface of the lake to glinting sword blades. On the far side, where the trees marched, unchecked, right down to the water's edge, there the lake was a shifting pattern of scarlet, vermilion and burnt orange.

THE NEIGHBOUR

There was silence at the kitchen table except for the noise of eating when the bare leg came through the ceiling. Jeddy was stirring his tea loudly when it came down directly over the centre of the table, so covered with drops of water that it hung like a chandelier. A few splinters and drops fell onto the table cloth and one or two dripped on the sliced tomatoes.

Mr Colley looked up from his hamburg steak, his long nose casting a wedge of shadow on his face as he tilted his head; the light caught his glasses giving the illusion of a face without eyes. "Merrit!" he said and beat his two fists on the table so the plates jumped. "What's he think, eh?" The leg waved about in the air, throwing water spots on the wall paper.

"Leave off of soiling our walls, leave off." Mrs Colley stood up and struck out at the foot with her fork. Her dress was short at the back. When she moved she showed her legs splaying out above the knees and extending into long purplish-blue bloomers. She struck at the bare wet foot and the leg lashed about like a snake.

"Jesus!" said Jeddy, watching the performance. He sat taut with pleasure. "Hit him, Ma," he said. His black hair was cut like a skull cap. He looked like a sadistic dwarf monk.

"Merrit, you leave us be," said Mr Colley furiously. "Always poking in our business. Leave us be," he yelled to the leg, and the leg, as if in obedience, slowly shortened, went up through the ceiling and the water came down all over the table. It came like a great column, melting at its base and spreading out on the floor.

"First the walls and now the tea," said Mrs Colley pulling at the table and upsetting the pitcher of milk; pushing a rag into her husband's hands, jerkily sloshing the wet mop over the worn linoleum.

"What's he think, eh?" said Mr Colley on his knees and Merrit's voice came thick and adenoidish from the hole in the ceiling, "Helpb muh, helpb. I'm in a jeezly bog." You could see his face now when you looked up—the black holes of the nose and the lips hanging like dark fungus.

Mona shivered when she heard his voice and touched the frizzled ends of her hair with chipped scarlet finger nails. The thick wet rubber of his lips, the hands like bread poultices that waited in the hallway for her, waited under the well of the stairs in the darkness and caught her when she came in. She hated it and him, but she always stayed. And now she had seen his bare leg hanging in the light. Something heavy settled in her.

Jeddy ran for her tartan umbrella, climbed on a chair, and, distorted with pleasure, poked at Merrit's face with its point. A low wheezing moan drained out of the mouth like a shaft of dust.

"Leave off of that," Mr Colley pulled at Jeddy's sleeve. Jeddy doubled as if kicked in the stomach, his face stretched with laughter, his feet hitting the floor like pistons. "Jesus, Jesus!" His laughter was high as a tin whistle in the room.

Mr Colley stood directly under the hole, hands on his hips and looked up. "What d'ya think ya doin', eh? Ya nosey bastard. Always comin' where ya ain't deesirable."

"I was ony havin' a bath—jes' takin' a bath," said Merrit. "Helpb muh, helpb. The tub flowed over and the floor's a Jeezly bog. The whole ceiling'll fall, like enough," he added ominously.

Mr and Mrs Colley both looked at the ceiling and then at the room, realizing together what it meant. Mrs Colley started pulling the furniture through the doorway. Mr Colley took command. "Spread the weight out even, like you was on ice," he called up. "Then ease yourself gradual out into the hall."

Mrs Colley stopped tugging at the table. "He don't spread

139

even," she snapped. "All of his weight's in his stomach." And then she began tugging again. Mona shut her eyes and shook her head back and forth quickly. She felt sick.

"Yah! Yah! Ya can't scare me no more now," Jeddy screamed suddenly. "Ya can't scear me no more. Ya big sissy. If ya chase me agin I won't be sceared." He grew large in the room as he spoke, like a pouter pigeon.

"I never did scare you none, Jeddy," Merrit's voice wheedled. "You jes' come up here, Jeddy, 'n helpb pull me outa this here jeezly bog, eh Jeddy?"

"I'll jeezly bog you," said Jeddy hysterically and flung his body viciously about the room till he was dizzy. "I'll Jeezly bog you, ya bastard."

The table was out in the hallway now and the chairs. Mrs Colley was looking at the stove. She layed her hands on it as if for the last time. "That Merrit," she said, but softly. "That Merrit."

"Now work yourself over easy," Mr Colley was saying. Groans, bangs and bumps sounded from above. "He's goin'," said Mr Colley. "He's outa sight." A few last drops of water fell. "Now Mona you get and stuff that hole up with newspaper while your Ma brings the table back."

"I'm goin' out," said Mona, her back turned.

"Oh, no, you ain't." Mr Colley grabbed her shoulder. "What d'ya think y'are, eh? Goin' out! You're goin' ta stay right here and do as I say."

Mona lurched herself free. "I'm goin' out, I tell ya. I'm goin' out."

"You mind what yer Dad tells yer." Mrs Colley was bringing the table back again. "D'ya think it's safe now?" She looked at the stove.

Mr Colley thrust his face up close to Mona's and spoke through still lips. "You're goin' to stay right here and finish yer tea, see? That's what you're goin' ta do." He pushed her onto a chair and she sat with a bump, opened her mouth wide and began to cry.

"Leave me be, leave me be. Ya never let me do anything. I'm goin' out, see. I'm goin' out." But she made no movement, sat quite still in the chair, not even lifting her hands to cover her face.

"Yah! cry-baby, cry-baby." Jeddy was alive again, dancing up and down before his sister. "Cry-baby. Ya can't see your sweetheart. I seen ya in the hallway. I seen ya."

Mr Colley was on a chair stuffing newspaper into the hole in the ceiling. He got down from the chair, found a pencil and paper and licking the lead began to write slowly. "Listen to this," he said, reading. "Listen to this: Mind your own business from now on, see? When we want to see ya, we'll invite ya down special. Signed, William Colley." He laughed so he had to loosen his belt and then climbed on the chair, pulled out the newspaper, stuck the note through and filled the hole again.

Jeddy was sitting at the wrecked table, hunched over his plate, shovelling the cold wet hamburger into his mouth.

"That'll fix Merrit," said Mr Colley settling at his place. That'll fix him." He picked up his fork and wiped it on his sleeve.

"Times like this I miss a phone somethin' awful," Mrs Colley said. "Would I ever like to ring up that Merrit and tell him what I think for spoiling our good tea." Her face was drawn with the pleasure denied her. She took the plate of sliced tomatoes and rinsed them under the tap. "I guess I don't feel much like eatin' now," she said. "That Merrit's leg kinda turned my stomach." She sat down from habit and watched her husband and son.

There was silence again at the kitchen table, except for the noise of eating, Merrit lumbering overhead and Mona's chattering sobs.

141

THE GREEN BIRD

I cannot escape the fascination of doors, the weight of unknown people who drive me into myself and pin me with their personalities. Nor can I resist the desire to be led through shutters and impaled on strange living-room chairs.

Therefore when Ernest stood very squarely on his feet and said: "I'm going to call on Mrs Rowan today and I hope you will come," I said "Yes." The desire to be trapped by old Mrs Rowan was stronger than any other feeling. Her door was particularly attractive—set solid and dark in her solid, dark house. I had passed by often and seen no sign of life there—no hand at a window, no small movement of the handle of the door.

We rang the bell. A man-servant, smiling, white-coated, drew us in, took our coats, showed us into the living-room.

"So it is this," I said to Ernest.

"Beg your pardon?" He crossed his knees carefully, jerked back his neck with the abstracted manner of the public speaker being introduced, leaned his young black head on Mrs Rowan's air.

"It is this," I said. "No ash trays," I said.

"But I don't smoke," said Ernest.

Mrs Rowan came then. There were dark bands holding a child's face on to a forgotten body. She sat as though she were our guest and we had embarrassed her.

Ernest handled the conversation with an Oriental formality aided by daguerreotype gestures. Mrs Rowan responded to him—a child under grey hair, above the large, loose, shambling torso. She talked of candy and birthday cake. She said she didn't like radios.

I said "Music," and looked about startled as if someone else had said it, suddenly imagining the horror of music sounding in this motionless house.

She said, "But you do miss hearing famous speakers. I once heard Hitler when I was in a taxi." She said, "We will only sit here a little longer and then we will go upstairs, I have an invalid up there who likes to pour tea."

I felt the sick-room atmosphere in my lungs and my longing to escape was a strong hand pushing me towards it. I imagined the whole upstairs white and dim, with disease crowding out the light.

Mrs Rowan said, "We will go now," and we rose, unable to protest had we wished, and followed her up the carpeted stairs and into a front room where a tea-table was set up. There was a large figure in a chair.

"Miss Price, the invalid," Mrs Rowan said, "insists on pouring the tea. She likes it. It gives her pleasure." The figure in the chair moved only her eyes, staring first at Ernest and then at me. Her face was lifeless as a plate. Mrs Rowan continued to talk about her. "She's been with me a long time," she said. "Poor dear." And then, "It's quite all right. Her nurse is right next door.' She introduced us. Miss Price sucked in the corners of her mouth and inclined her head slightly with each introduction. The white-coated, grinning man-servant brought in the tea.

"You can pour it now," said Mrs Rowan, and Miss Price began, slowly, faultlessly, with the corners of her mouth sucked in and her eyes dark and long as seeds. She paid no attention to what we said about sugar and cream. She finished and folded her arms, watched us without expression.

Mrs Rowan passed the cakestand. "You eat these first," she said, pointing to the sandwiches; "These second," pointing to some cookies; "and this last," indicating fruit cake. My cup rattled a little.

I pretended to drink my tea, but felt a nausea—the cup seemed dirty. Ernest leaned back in his chair, said, "Delicious tea.'' Miss Price sat with her arms folded; there was no indication of life except in the glimmer of her seed eyes.

"Dear," said Mrs Rowan suddenly but without concern, "you haven't poured yourself a cup."

Miss Price sucked in her mouth, looked down into her lap; her face was hurt.

"No," I said. "You must have a cup too." I laughed by mistake.

Miss Price looked up at me, flicked her eyes at mine with a quick glance of conspiracy and laughed too, in complete silence. Mrs Rowan passed her a cup and she poured her own tea solemnly and folded her arms again.

"Before you go," Mrs Rowan said, "I'd like to give you a book—one of mine. Which one would you like?"

"Why," I said, looking at the cakestand which had never been passed again and stood with all the food untouched but for the two sandwiches Ernest and I had taken, "Why—". I wondered what I could say. I had no idea she wrote. "Why," I said again and desperately, "I should like most the one you like most."

Miss Price flicked her eyes at me again and her body heaved with dreadful silent laughter.

"I like them all," Mrs Rowan said. "There are some that are written about things that happened in 300 B.C. and some written about things that happened three minutes ago. I'll get them," she said, and went.

Ernest was carefully balancing his saucer on his knee, sitting very straight. There was no sound in the entire house.

"I hope you are feeling better, Miss Price," Ernest said.

I saw the immense silent body heave again, this time with sobs. Dreadful silent sobs. And then it spoke for the first time. "They cut off both my legs three years ago. I'm nothing but a stump." And the sobbing grew deeper, longer.

I looked at Ernest. I heard my own voice saying, 'Such a

lovely place to live, this—so central. You can see everything from this room. It looks right out on the street. You can see everything.''

Miss Price was still now, her face expressionless, as if it had happened years before. 'Yes,'' she said.

"The parades," I said.

"Yes, the parades. My nephew's in the war.''

"I'm sorry," Ernest said.

"He was wounded at Ypres. My sister heard last week.'' Her arms were folded. Her cup of tea was untouched before her, the cream in a thick scum on the surface.

"Now, here," Mrs. Rowan came in, her arms full of books—like a child behind the weight of flesh—covetous of the books—of the form of the books, spreading them about her, never once opening their covers. "Which one would you like?'' she asked.

"This," I said. "The colour of its cover will go with my room.''

"What a pretty thought," Mrs Rowan said, and for some reason my eyes were drawn to Miss Price, knowing they would find her heaving with that silent laughter that turned her eyes to seeds.

"We must go," said Ernest suddenly. He put down his cup and stood up. I tucked the book under my arm and crossed to Miss Price. "Good-bye," I said, and shook hands. Her seed eyes seemed underneath the earth. She held on to my hand, I felt as if I was held down in soil. Ernest said, "Good-bye, Miss Price," and held out his hand, but hers still clutched mine. She beckoned to Mrs Rowan and whispered, "The birds. I want to give her a bird," and then to me, "I want to give you a bird.''

Mrs Rowan walked into the next room and returned with a paper bag. Miss Price released my hand and dug down into the bag with shelving fingers. "No, not these," she said angrily.

"These are green."

"They're the only ones," Mrs Rowan said. "The others have all gone."

"I don't like them," said Miss Price, holding one out on a beaded cord. It was stuffed green serge, dotted with red bead work, and two red cherries hung from its mouth. "It's paddy green," she said disgustedly, and sucked in the corners of her mouth.

"Never mind," I said. "It's lovely, and paddy green goes with my name. I'm Patricia, you see, and they sometimes call me Paddy." I stood back in astonishment at my own sentences, and Miss Price gave an enormous shrug, which, for the moment, until she released it, made her fill the room. And then, "God!" she said, "what a name!" The scorn in her voice shrivelled us. When I looked back at her as I left she had fallen into her silent, shapeless laughter.

Mrs Rowan showed us downstairs and called the man-servant to see us out. She stood like a child at the foot of the stairs and waved to us every few minutes as the grinning white-coated houseman helped us into our coats.

"You must come again and let Miss Price pour tea for you. It gives her such pleasure."

Outside, on the step, I began to laugh. I had been impaled and had escaped. My laughter went on and on. It was loud, the people in the street stared at me.

Ernest looked at me with disapproval. "What do you find so funny?" he asked.

What? What indeed? There was nothing funny at all. Nothing anywhere. But I poked about for an answer.

"Why, this," I said, holding the bird by its beaded cord. "This, of course."

He looked at it a long time. "Yes," he said, seriously. "Yes, I suppose it is quaint," and he smiled.

It was as though a pearl was smiling.

146

THE WOMAN

In the small villages in the darkness all the square, flat-fronted hotels were shut. Inquiries brought forth the reply that they closed on Sundays. And the traveller? Doomed to a chromium-fitted night in a city; doomed to enter lonely into lobbies where charwomen with mops and brushes worked among palms and ashtrays filled with sand.

No. John renounced the idea with a thrust of his hands on the wheel. No. Already his left arm ached from use and the hand began to float in its own quite isolated climate. At a garage, large, lighted as a night club, he drew up. The young Frenchman he questioned about rooms ran oil-covered fingers through his hair, leaving a dark mark like a brand upon his forehead. He could phone and ask, he said. As the young man phoned John gazed at the main street. Low hanging lights gathered it in patches to form and shape, released it again to darkness and the feeling of leaves. As far as he could see, the garage alone was bright. There was no challenge here. He must stay.

The Frenchman's voice sounded suddenly loud and reassuring. "Non, non. Il est très gentil. Très gentil."

John realized the man was speaking of him. To someone he had never met he presented a menace. He, John, in his airforce blazer and grey slacks with his damaged arm and bright pink hand.

The Frenchman returned, grinning, nodding, went with him to the car and pointed his finger into the darkness. A great relief enfolded John. He need go no further. He could sleep. He could lie down near trees. He knew at once that he was very tired. And already he saw the room—the country room of his child-

147

hood. Bare boards, wash-basin and pitcher. Slop pail. A window close to the trees.

The woman who opened the door to him stood no higher than the crest on his pocket—dress colourless from many washings, hair colourless from neglect. They stood facing each other in the doorway and he was more at ease than she. She was still afraid.

She stepped back though to let him enter, talked quickly then while she handed him the book and waited for him to sign. He glanced at the names and dates above and saw that he would be alone in the small hotel. He signed his name as she talked, taking his time.

"Before the war, all the time we were busy. Many, many people stayed here all the time. But the business has gone off and now, tonight..."

He barely heard her. And he made no answer. She spoke to release her nervousness. There was no need for him to speak.

She ran up the stairs ahead of him, stopped, beckoning him up. "The room is not ready but—one minute, one minute only." She grabbed his bag with violence as if she wrested a weapon from his hand and ran on again, leading him through a dimly lighted upper hallway with bamboo chairs.

The little room was not as he had seen it but it did look out onto trees—dark masses of leaves and the sound of wind. He stood in the room as she made up the bed, her ridiculously short arms smoothing and stretching, her short legs carrying her quickly from one side to the other.

She ran ahead of him to the bathroom, showing him the way. There she scrubbed and flicked a spotlessly clean basin. He put out his good hand to stop her and she drew away as if burned. So she was still frightened. Very frightened. But would discussing it help her? Were he to way, "I won't hurt you," would it help? He thought not. But he must give her some reassurance. Outside he said, "Good-night, Madam—you have taken very good care of me. I am grateful."

Now he sat on the edge of his bed and found it hard. He took off his shoes without bending down, shoving them off with his toes, gazing about him as he did do. The room was very small: a bureau, a wicker table, a bed. That was all. And down the hall from him, probably locked in her room, was his landlady. Why had she taken him in? Why had she not said she was full up? A store adjoined the hotel downstairs and presumably she had existed on it during the war years. Why then, tonight, was it necessary for her to make two dollars? A dozen reasons revolved in his head, followed immediately by one he felt was correct: she needed the experience of change. He remembered the sentence attributed to him as a child, "I'd sooner be frightened to death than bored to death." There were periods in one's life when that was true enough and others—like parts of the war for instance—when the idea of boredom seemed as sweet as a meadow.

He had wiggled his socks off with his toes by now—a trick he'd got into while convalescing. "Don't favour your arm," they had said to him. "You must learn not to favour it." But that was exactly what he did do. The word had horrified him at first, but he had grown to understand it, grown to know its correctness. Despite all their admonitions, he would "favour" it for many years. He removed his blazer and shirt and examined the arm minutely. Not a pretty sight. Quite horrible still, in fact—but—he "favoured" it. He laughed aloud as he stood and stepped out of his trousers.

Then he thought about the woman again and it even crossed his mind that if his guess were true, perhaps he owed it to her to give her a fright. Not a serious one, of course, but something she could talk about afterwards, something which would, for a time, raise her stock among the villagers. It was a pleasant kind of fantasy to indulge in but sleep was gradually overtaking him. The wind in the leaves was a soporific. He switched out the light by the door. The room shrank suddenly with darkness and he walked in a straight jacket to the bed and lay down.

149

It was good to be lying there, away from the city. He wondered if the woman was asleep. And he slept.

Throughout the night he kept hurting his arm. Pinned between his body and the hard mattress, it would ache and throb and lurch him awake. He imagined himself in the hospital again and listened for the noises of the ward. then slowly the realization of where he was returned to him. Not in a hospital; not in a city. A small place where there were fewer people to stare. And he would sleep again and awaken hurt, reassure himself, hear the movement of leaves and, once, the sound of feet running on earth—a sound that formed a pattern behind his eyes. But later, towards morning, he walked in a meadow and out through a gate and met himself walking in and the old panic gripped him and he greeted himself with so loud a scream that even when it had wakened him it had not quite completed its length and he heard it still—terrible, like a beast in pain.

And then, very wonderfully, came an answering scream: high, shrill, female. As if he had called to a mate and she had replied with immediate urgency. The sound reached him and fulfilled him and he fell asleep then as easily and completely as if he had had a woman.

Not until the sun burst full upon his face did he waken. And he wakened full of the woman, wanting to see her. For now the idea of her answering scream seemed fantastic to him. If he could see her at once, without delay, he would know.

There were no sounds in the hotel as he dressed. The corridor had a sleeping look—forgotten, abandoned. The bamboo chairs cluttered the upstairs hall. Downstairs the room was bare, shabby and empty. No sign of the woman.

He re-climbed the stairs again in search of her and the half-dozen doors stared mutely in his face. He began knocking on each in turn and as he returned from their silence she emerged from the first he had tried—her face still blurred with sleep, her hands grown woolly overnight fumbling, fumbling with the fastening at her neck.

150

He knew nothing from her face and he couldn't ask the question. He said, instead, "I would like to pay for my room." And as he extracted the money from his wallet her expression altered. He felt her small eyes hook and sharpen on his "favoured" hand.

THE LORD'S PLAN

Seumas carried his suitcase in his right hand. It was heavy and his feet were hot—swelling, bulging against the bumpy uppers of his shoes. His toes felt puffy and webbed.

The sun was in mid heaven exactly. It shone on the top of his hat. The dent in his green fedora caught all the sun, held it in a pool. Seumas gave a dusty grin thinking of his suitcase, thinking of the Word of God—the Words of God—packed tightly layer upon layer.

His new sales psychology had worked.

The Lord had given him a plan to sell His Word. Only yesterday, while Seumas was lying in a haystack, airing his feet, the Lord had explained His Plan. He had heard the Lord say: "Seumas, Lamb of the Lord, in order to sell my word you must have a plan." Seumas had jolted forward in the hay. He had tried to convince himself that there was nothing strange in being spoken to by the Lord. But it *had* been strange, none the less.

Seumas had parked his gum behind his ear and stubbed his cigarette and put the butt in his breast pocket—the least he could do for the Lord. And then the Lord had boomed. His Voice had sounded like thunder and Seumas had looked up to the sky and found it blue and clear. The Lord had boomed, "Psychology." Seumas had nodded. It didn't do to let the Lord know he was an ignorant man. Seumas smiled and repeated the word "psychology". It rattled round in his head for a few minutes afterwards. But the Lord had been kind. He had explained the word, just as any Christian gentleman would do, pretending that Seumas knew it all the while.

And—but of course it would, as it was the Lord's Plan—it worked. At the very first house he had come to it had worked.

152

He had stopped at the door of a farmhouse and knocked. A woman opened it. She was pale and immense as though she were made of bread dough, Seumas thought, and had been rising before the kitchen range for years—rising and swelling. Seumas looked at her arms hanging from her sleeveless dress. She had said, "What would you want?" And he had almost forgotten to answer her, almost forgotten the Lord's Plan, because after her arms he had seen her stomach and then he had had to remind himself that he was on the Lord's business. By that time she had noticed his bag and she had said, "Salesman?" How her eyes had folded under the fat lids—how the brown slits that showed through had looked like molasses in the sun; and how close Seumas had come to walking away, then and there, quickly.

But he remembered the Lord's Plan.

He put down his bag and said, "I'm tired, I've walked a long way. Could I—" and he smiled, "come in and rest a minute?"

The buik in the doorway had moved. Seumas stepped inside the large kitchen and sat down. He put his suitcase on the kitchen table. She looked at it once or twice. He pretended it wasn't there. He passed the time of day with her as she beat cookie batter. He watched the flesh of her arms flowing free from the bone, flapping, flapping, flapping; and then her stomach, like a large jelly, wobbling, shivering, under the flowered dress. When she moved one part of her, all moved.

He said, "Could I fetch a cup of water from the well? There is dust in my mouth." She lowered the dipper into a water bucket and handed it to him, dripping. He could see the drops of water on the dipper's lip sparkling. It was all part of the Lord's Plan. He drank. He hung the dipper on the nail again. He thought of that himself. It was as the Lord would have done. He went back to his seat. She kept turning to look at his suitcase. And then he said, "D'you mind if I smoke?" She shook her head. He waited a minute until her flesh had quietened. That one shake

153

had started her arms, her belly, her buttocks . . . He stopped in horror at the words in his mind and he opened his suitcase for his makings. For now, now, did the psychology really begin. As he lifted the lid he saw the booklets piled neatly—booklets of the Lord. But he pretended he didn't notice them and he took out his tobacco and rolled a cigarette. She came over to the suitcase, chose a spoon from a drawer in the table and looked at the booklets in the bag. She returned to the batter, dipped it out into little hummocks on a pan. But in a minute she came back. She put out a finger like a large pale sausage with a little bit of gristle shining at the end of it. She touched one of the booklets and left a smudge of cookie dough on it. "Books," she said.

He feigned unconcern. "Yes, books." He waited, examining the end of his cigarette.

She turned the pages. "Words, words," she said.

"Yes, God's."

"Oh, God's?"

"Yes." He blew smoke out through his nose. "Take a look," he said.

It had all been so easy. But then it had been the Lord's Plan. She bought.

He finished his cigarette fastened his suitcase and walked to the door, but on the way—ah, if only the Lord had helped him there!—as he passed her, his hand shot out and fell on her buttocks, hard enough to start her flesh jiggling again. And he had laughed. She picked up the spoon and brought it down on his head. It had hurt. She used words too—words he wanted to forget, being on the Lord's Business. He had decided she was a very common woman.

He laughed now when he thought of it, even though the sun was hot and the lump on his head ached where his hat pressed on it. If he'd done that to a pretty girl she'd have liked it; and anyway that was *his* psychology—make up to the ladies. True, the Lord hadn't suggested it, but it had always worked before, so he might as well keep on. And too, the next house he had come to after that, hadn't it worked? It sure had. But it was a girl there, young and pretty. Her eyes had flashed when he had chucked her under the chin and she'd tossed her head and said, "You're some smart, you are." Some smart! He'd say he was. Seumas O'Reilly, never seen Ireland, Salesman in the Lord's Business. Some smart! And she was some smart too—some pretty. he thought of her as he walked. He forgot his feet.

At the end of the blueberry plains there was a store. Gasoline pumps outside and signs on the store. He thought of the Lord's Plan. He thought of the sun in a pool in the dent of his hat. He walked into the store. It was dark and he couldn't see much at first. A girl's voice inquired, "Selling?"

"Nothing that'd interest you," he said. He ordered a bottle of Lime Rickey and it walked across the counter to him. Imagine that! He was going to say something to the girl about it but she interrupted him.

"How d'you know?" she asked.

He laid his suitcase beside him and tapped it saying, "Because it's not candy or cosmetics or silk stockings"—but not before he'd noticed the girl. Not too bad, but drab he figured. His plan and the Lord's together ought to make this sale a cinch. He drank up the Lime Rickey and ordered another bottle. Boy, how those bottles could walk!

"How's business?" he asked.

"Not bad," she answered. "How's yours?"

"Good," he said. "Better and better. See a pretty face and business is swell." He watched her as he said it. She smirked and poked a pound of bacon on the counter. And he forgot the Lord's Plan. She walked round beside him. He put his arm round her waist and squeezed her. She pulled away a little.

"Fresh eh?"

He laughed.

"What you sellin?"

He saw her eye his suitcase. "Wouldn't you like to know!"

"Come on, give!"

"Maybe I don't sell. Maybe I'm a college guy hitch hikin' to college."

"Maybe I'm a pair of chickens!"

"Maybe you are." He squeezed her again. She wriggled and looked down. Stuck out her tongue a little. It was pink like a kitten's.

"What's your name?"

"Mabel. What's yours?"

"Seumas."

"Gee! what a handle."

It was the way she said 'handle' that did it. The way her mouth opened and her lips curled. It wasn't his fault. He kissed her. She was like barbed wire in his arms then. The way she pulled away, bristling, spiked with anger. She hauled back her hand and slapped his face. Women! He loved them. He caught her hand, kissed the palm of it, laughing. She walked away. But her hand . . . he still held it. Saints alive! it had come off. She looked black. She stumped away into the darkness, her arm hanging, handless.

He looked at the hand. The skin was rough, red a little, and the nails were like small pearl buttons sewn on the fingers. He was alone in the store with the hand; the hand wearing a gold ring with 'M' on it. He slipped the ring off; he no right to that; it was hers.

And then he remembered the Lord's Plan. And he knew. The Lord was reminding him to use His Psychology. This was the Lord's Way—miracles.

He opened his suitcase and saw the Lord's Word. He took out a booklet and laid it on the counter, with the ring on top of it. He thought of that himself. It was as the Lord would have done. And he packed the hand in the suitcase. That would remind him of the Lord's Plan, remind him to keep about the Lord's Business. The Lord was looking after His Own. Seumas understood.

156

He snapped the fasteners on his bag and put on his hat and walked out into the sunshine. He gave a happy grin thinking of his suitcase—thinking of the World of God—the Words of God—packed tightly layer on layer; thinking of the hand, God's Miracle, God's Reminder.

He pushed his hat back so it didn't press on the bump on his head. He took an old stub from his breast pocket and lit up. Gee! He gave a long whistle of pleasure. Seumas O'Reilly, never seen Ireland, Salesman in the Lord's Business, some smart.

He'd say!

MIRACLES

That evening after supper while Madame rocked on the gallery in the slowly settling darkness Annette took us to see her friends. Lights blazed in the windows as we walked with dust muffled steps along the village street and the air was flooded with green as though chlorophyll lit the evening.

Small groups of youths walked by, serious and stolid as moose in their pin striped suits. "Salud", "Bon soir",—the greetings rang out as they passed. Annette was proud in her acknowledgements, walking with a strange stiff legged self-consciousness. Watching them I was amazed that there were no girls with them—no girls with their heavily powdered faces, extraordinary amateur curls and the stifling smell of cheap perfume.

"They have no girls?" I asked.

Annette was quick to assure me they had.

"But on an evening like this?"

"They are on their way to call," Annette said.

"But they don't go out together?"

Annette swung horrified eyes to God at the suggestion. The curé did not allow it. The curé knew what was right for them and what was wrong. The curé knew everything and looked after them. The curé said it was wicked.

Luke walked, his hands in his pockets, his head back, saying nothing. At first I dragged him in to the conversation but when Annette began to talk of the curé I forgot. Besides, I needed all my energy to keep up with her, to follow the acrobatics of her speech.

"He is a very great and good man," said Annette and her words sounded staccato on the long quiet street. "He performs miracles.'' The speed and extravagance of Annette's language made me feel that I was in some way inside a catherine wheel.

Her face grew long and full of wonder as she recounted her miracle. "Until I was twenty-one," she said, "I was not like other girls. I had not been unwell and I was very weak. Mamma was worried about me. All my sisters were strong, they were getting married, but I was not and each month we waited and I was not unwell. Mamma got the horse and cart from the Paget's and we drove to the town. It was a long way. And it is very expensive to see the doctor. Mamma had the money in her hand and I was afraid when we arrived. It was hot and my head was full and I was ashamed. We waited for him to come and then we told him. He took the money Mamma had in her hand and gave me some medicine and we drove back home again. All that way, all that money, all that way home again. I took the medicine he gave and waited. Each month I waited. Each morning I went to early Mass and prayed but nothing happened. And all the time I got sicker and sicker. Mamma went to the curé then and he came. He said he would perform a miracle. He got a big glass and a bottle of porter and he poured the porter into the glass. Then he added two teaspoons of mustard and he stirred and stirred until it was froth-ing. He handed me the glass. "Drink it down while it is still frothing," he said. But I couldn't. I shook my head. I could not drink that drink. "Drink it down while it is frothing and you will be cured within five minutes." I saw the big glass. Mamma was crying. "Drink it down," said Mamma and she held her head in her hands and rocked from side to side. "Drink it down, Annette." Then I didn't care any more. I took the big glass and I thought of the face of the Virgin Mary and I made the sign of the Cross and prayed inside me and I drank it down. It was bad, that drink. It tasted bad. I wanted to be sick to my stomach.'' Annette paused and gave a great sigh as if she had lived the whole experience over again.

"And it worked?" I asked.

159

The story finished Annette nodded her head sagely, smugly. "Ah, yes. It was a miracle. A miracle in the name of God."

"And you've been alright ever since?" The tale shocked me. In my own head I saw a blackrobed curé—Mamma, great fat Mamma, shaking her head and crying and Annette drinking down a devil's brew with its smoking sulphur coloured fumes that changed her from a child into a woman in five minutes. "Ever since you have been alright?"

"Ah, but yes, it was a miracle."

Had the curé performed other miracles? I wanted to know. What else had he done?

Annette pursed her lips and shrugged. "Ah, yes."

"Tell me," I said. but we had already arrived at the Simone's. Another time she would tell me. Now her mind was on her friends. They were especially beautiful, Annette informed us, for they were blonde. And that was rare. They were the only people in the village who were blonde.

On the gallery sat Mme Simone, frail as a Marie Laurencin painting, her high cheek bones dotted with excited crimson, her hair permanented like the fizz on ginger beer. She rocked more slowly as she greeted Annette and was introduced, insisted that we all sit down, brought forward chairs, smiled nervously and moved her white hands across her apron. Noiselessly, as wherever we went, the children collected—stood in silence, pale, alarmingly pale; each with the dot of tubercular rouge on their cheek bones, their uncurled hair smooth on their heads as butter, their legs and arms motionless.

The ground sloped up from the house beside us—grass and apple trees with yellow apples luminous in the leaves, lying in the grass pale as the children's hair—and everything tinged with the green light, washed in it.

While Mme Simone and Annette gossiped I felt bathed in the blond and green incandescence of this family and its garden, and was fascinated and appalled by the still life of the children, the shyness that held them fixed and their flax blue eyes that

160

looked as shallow and delicate as petals.

"André has bought a truck," Annette said and her pride sat upon her fat and sleek as mercury, before it broke and scattered in excited description. "It is big," she said, her arms enclosing it. "The whole village could ride in it, it is so big. And it is red."

"Agathe told me," said Mme Simone. Her eyelids lifted to hoods and she pursed her mouth to judgment. "He gets a truck instead of a wife," she said. "It is not good."

"It makes a beautiful noise," said Annette, like a child. She turned to us. "It makes a better noise than your car."

"Where is it?" I asked. "Why haven't we seen it?"

"André has gone to the city already."

Madame nodded sagely. "Soon André will live in the city," she announced.

Luke knocked the ashes from his pipe, blew through it a couple of times and put it in his pocket.

The greenness grew deeper as we talked—came up and swamped us until it seemed as if we were under the sea. Mme Simone became nervous, rocked rapidly and suddenly her harsh voice commanded the children: "Get apples for the English." But the children hardly moved. A slight tremor of increased shyness rippled them and froze them. Raising her voice to an alarming volume the mother repeated her command and they scuttled then, uncannily green, into the deep grass, picking the globes of fruit from the ground, reaching to the lower branches of the trees, moving with their eyes still on Luke and myself; shy, offering their harvest with white-green fingers, smiles making masks of their small faces.

I held out my hand to receive the clusters of fruit with the leaves attached.

"They are flower apples," the mother said, and Annette nibbling, explained that they didn't last, but faded like flowers in a few days.

The giant illuminated cross on the hillside sharpened and

brightened as the darkness fell. Proudly they nodded at it, Annette and Mme Simone, drew down the corners of their mouths, told how it burned day and night, day and night and how it was their cross, how each family paid for a light and that light never went out.

In Annette's charge we left when she gave the sign. The green light was deeper now, the children behind their mother seemed no longer strange, but terrible—tiny and fair and lifeless while Madame rocked unceasingly back and forth in her chair, and beside them, on the hillside, the vegetation crept in closer and closer like a wave.

Leaving, our apples still in our hands Annette said, "Eat them. They are good." But I shook my head, feeling the perfectly formed and infected fruit against my palms—pale apple-green and deadly.

"Are they not beautiful, the Simones?" Annette was anxious to know. "Are they not the most beautiful people you have seen here?"

"But surely," I said, sick with alarm, "Surely they are ill. Consumptive?"

"Ah yes," said Annette in easy agreement but bored.

"But Annette it is a dangerous disease. It is catching. It will spread."

"No!" Annette's voice was incredulous. "You joke," she said and laughed.

I felt desperate. I wanted to convince Annette. "In the city," I said, "Those people would go away for treatment. Doesn't the doctor see them, Annette?"

Annette was not interested. "It is nothing," she said. "The Bouchards have it and the Pagets and the..." she listed the family names. "It is nothing. The curé goes and he prays. Sometimes it gets bad and someone dies. Often that happens."

I wanted to cry out at Annette's stupidity. I grabbed Luke's arm. "Say something to her," I said. "Tell her, Luke."

"It is a dangerous illness," Luke said. And the subject was

finished. But something violent and terrible was happening inside me. An anger I had not known before, a fury at the ignorance and pitifulness of people. I had hoped for some affirmation of a similar feeling in Luke. But his voice had been factual and indifferent. I let go his arm quickly, and when he felt for my hand in the darkness and tried to hold it I pulled away, even knowing that he too, needed affirming at that moment.

We stumbled a little in the darkness on the dusty road. A smell of salt blew up from the river and the houses were quiet as though deserted. It was as if all the inhabitants were dead—and the faces of the Simone children arranged themselves before my eyes, lying like wax and butter in a row of green wood coffins.

The curé goes and he prays. The curé is a great and good man. The curé performs miracles. But there are no miracles in the consumptive houses, I thought. No miracles there and I was bitter with Annette for her dreadful acceptance of death. Bitter with Annette and furious with Luke.

AS ONE REMEMBERS A DREAM

It was years since Sadie had put the question directly to her mother. But as if it were yesterday she remembered waking that Saturday morning, stringing the words together into a sentence and carrying them around with her all day. Remembered following her mother from room to room as she dusted and cleaned, waiting, hoping for the moment to come when it would be easy.

"Run outside and play, Sade," her mother had said more than once. "Go along now, there's a love."

And outside it was beautiful. She had *wanted* to go out. Had wanted to push a hole right through the wall and break free from the house, her mother, her whole life. But the chain of words had held her on a long tether, wandering from room to room, silent. Then having left it to the last possible moment when she could safely be alone with her mother, when, at any minute, she might hear her father's footsteps on the porch, she had walked into the kitchen and the great urgency of the question was like a wound.

Her mother was peeling potatoes at the sink and the late afternoon sun shone in the window and made the knife blade glint and reflect in a dancing pattern on the wall. Sadie had crept into the room like a culprit and stood, unspeaking.

"What are you doing, Sade?" Her mother spoke without turning and Sadie had felt embarrassed, guilty almost, as if she were about to ask where babies came from or . . .

"Have you lost your tongue, child?"

She must ask it now. If she waited another minute it would be too late.

"Mum!" The whole kitchen revolved, making her dizzy.

164

"What's the matter with my foot, Mum? My foot, Mum. What's the matter with it? Mum? Mum!"

It wasn't as she had planned to say it. The words had tumbled out, making a great racket in the unsteady room and then leaving it silent except for the little plop as peeled potatoes were dropped in the pot of water. Her mother's hands had continued moving as she said, "Now don't you mind about that, Sade. Light the gas for me, there's a good girl, or tea won't be ready for your Dad."

"But I'm old enough to know. I want to know. It's not fair." Her voice had wailed on the last word and her mother had popped the last potato in the pot, run her hands down her apron with a small exhalation of accomplishment and said, "There's nothing the matter that the boot won't fix, my beauty."

That was years ago. And it was today. Both. She had outgrown three pairs of boots since then and was well into her fourth—black, hideously corrective things that laced half way up her calf.

Time before the boots was non-existant. she couldn't force her memory back at all, except, of course, for that one thing, isolated, different in quality from anything else that had ever happened, and that she remembered occasionally as one remembers a dream. It was a detailed, untouchable thing, floating, forming, fading—crystallizing as sharply and vividly as cut glass —and as suddenly disappearing before it finished—disappearing easily and finally as clouds fade in a blue sky. When it came, it came from nowhere and always, no matter how hard she tried to hold on, it left again, incomplete. The important thing about it was that then—or there—there were no boots. Then or there she had left a pair of sandals under a green tree in order to follow Justy. The grass had pricked the soles of her feet and Justy had yelled impatiently, "Come onnn!" Boots had no place in that picture. If only she could turn around where she stood and retrace her own steps to the original pair—to the moment before them, rather—she felt she could cancel them out. They wouldn't be true. Or if she could force someone to mention her foot—by some violence on her part—a further mutilation of it perhaps—then, the mere objective acknowledgment would settle the thing finally, one way or the other.

She wore the boots over navy blue socks, the high kind that come up to the knee and fold over showing a design. Her mother bought them for her, all the same, ribbed and dark with a lot of grey dots for a pattern. At sixteen she hated them more than the boots. At sixteen all the kids at school were wearing silk stockings. She had glanced at her legs beneath the desk—calves the color of ink—and with her history book propped up in front of her and gazing steadily at the Fathers of Confederation, she had rolled the socks down as one would over ski boots. She knew her legs would be a sickly white but she didn't care. And if her mother said anything she had prepared her answer. But her mother said nothing at all.

Sometimes she tried to catch her mother off guard, mentioned cases of polio and watched her mother's face as she spoke; told stories she had heard at school of monsters being born because their mothers had been frightened or fallen or suffered from shock. She learned to say these things casually, as if it were weather she spoke of, all the time gazing with apparently in-different eyes, waiting for the start, the blush, the nervous betray-ing movement. But her mother replied, ''Poor little mites,'' or, ''Sade, where in the world do you hear such stories? Upon my word, I've never heard of such things in my life.'' And then the memory would return, or the dream, of her own legs running, grass green and soft beneath a tree where apples large and red as balloons hung in clusters or dropped with a thud into their hands, and how the sky became, that day, not a fixed thing, miles away, but something close and blue, almost within reach. And how she had left her sandals under the tree, eager to catch up with Justy.

But now she was folding towels in a laundry, working for

166

a living. Grown up. Now she would tolerate the socks no longer. Now with her own money she could buy stockings, silk ones like the other girls wore. And now people were nothing but legs and feet. The street cars and street were full of them, all shapes and colors and sizes. In her mind she chose the stockings she would have—beautiful, filmy, honey-colored—scorning legs less perfectly clad. She was critical, pitying, amused by turns at the wrinkles, the runs, the textures and tones of the stockings that passed. She cut stocking ads from magazines and stuck them in her mirror, half believing that if she looked at them long enough, often enough, a miracle might happen. And she treated her socks with a certain deference now that she was going to discard them. Folded them carefully at night as if to make up for the day when she would ruthlessly ignore them.

The day she received her first pay envelope she went straight for the stockings after work. People crowded the counter, pushed in ahead of her, were irritable, casual, bored. She leaned on the counter dreaming, growing up. The amputated legs of a dummy waved above her head. She viewed them as a connoisseur; they were neither grotesque nor humorous.

The sales girl's voice sounded brusquely beside her: "Yes? Yes?"

She smiled. Her excitement lay upon her like oil on water. "Some silk stockings, please."

"We have no silk. Haven't had since the war started."

For a moment she was bewildered. Then the salesgirl pushed a box across the counter saying nothing, arranging her curls instead, unrolling them and twisting them up again over her fingers and pushing them into place like so many small sausages in a double row. She looked from the salesgirl to the stockings, slipped a pair from the box. They were copper colored and shiny. They wouldn't do at all.

"You've nothing else?"

The salesgirl shook a disinterested head.

"But the color . . . "

167

"That's the popular shade right now. Take them to the light."

She limped off with them in her hands, feeling their slippery texture. By the street door they looked a little better but they still weren't right. Not what she wanted.

Back at the counter she asked, "How much?"

"A dollar twenty-five."

It was a lot of money. She hesitated. The salesgirl was brushing off her dress, licking her fingers and rubbing.

"Will you be getting others? Others—different?"

"We may. You never know. This may be the last shipment for weeks."

If she waited she might never get a pair. If . . . "Alright," she said and counted the money carefully.

There was no chance to try them on before tea. No chance at all, in fact, until she was going to bed. But a wonderful thing had happened after she bought them: the simple fact of ownership transformed them, made them perfect. All evening she had thought of them in a new way. *My* stockings, she had thought. Mine. The pronoun changed them into the stockings she had imagined.

In her room she waited until she heard her mother's bed springs creak before she took them from the paper bag. Dad was still up but he never barged in, anyway. She laid them over the back of the wooden chair. They hung down silken, flat, while she undressed. She unlaced the hideous boots with her fingers trembling, pulled off the horrible socks and flung them in a corner and then, with the clumsy, unsure reverence of the novice, slipped the long, weightless stockings onto her legs. She lay back on her bed and held her good leg up, gripping the top of the stocking to keep it taut, seeing a future of slim, silk, adult legs. She thought of her mother in the next room, a familiar stranger, her thin body stretched out on her half of the double bed, her rectangular flat hand laid across her eyes. The years of her mother's secrecy and silence had built towards

168

this time when understanding was atrophied, when nothing could be shared. Her mother would ignore the stockings too, Sadie had no doubt. And she felt suddenly bitter imagining them ignored, realizing how not only her failures but her victories would go unacknowledged; how forever and ever her mother would make the land dead level by the simple act of not seeing, pretending not to see, saying nothing.

Quietly Sadie took the mirror from the wall and propped it against her dresser, walked away from it, towards it, turned it on its side for a broader reflection as she walked past it. Next she tried on her boots, laced them carefully, rubbed them up a bit with a piece of Kleenex and walked towards the mirror again. They were solid and ugly as iron. Hideous and heavy over the stockings as they had never been over the socks. They were so hideous that she couldn't look at them. She turned her back in quick revulsion, held her hand across her eyes in a gesture identical with her mother's. In a sudden violent need for action she reached for the scissors and cut the laces all the way down, tore the boots from her feet and threw them across the room, the noise of misery sounding so loudly in her ears that she didn't hear the two thumps they made as they fell. Exhausted, she slumped on the bed. The breath in her lungs was an amorphous solid, hard, difficult to move.

Nothing was said about the laces next morning, not even when Sadie said, "I cut them. Cut them."

Busy buttering toast her mother replied: "You'll find another pair in the left hand drawer of my sewing cabinet. Go and get them like a good girl."

Obediently she had gone for the laces, stooped and threaded their licorice lengths into the boots. In and out through the holes, criss-crossing and tightening, ascending higher and higher up her legs and her fingers moved with them as if climbing laboriously to the tops of two black and sinister ladders. It was then that her mind took a large leap, the extent of which astonished her. It was audacious beyond words, yet so simple, natural.

Once having made it she wondered only that it had not occurred to her before.

She would buy shoes. Other people bought them. Wonderful, high-heeled shoes without toes. Shoes with bows, perhaps, or platform soles. She saw the thousands of towels she would have to fold before it was possible. Great mounds and mountains of towels and the movements her arms would make folding them. But she saw it all speeded up, so that the towels flew about in the air like a snow storm and the days shrank to half their length as she worked with the vision of the shoes before her.

There was another thing too that occupied her mind at this time. It was the dream. Always before the dream had been something of her own, private and personal but now, thinking about it, really thinking about it, not just letting it flow past her, Justy established himself as part owner. He was a real person with a name. Justy Williams. A dream figure no longer. If she could just find Justy Williams, find him and talk to him. Yet he had existed only once so far as she knew; once long ago beneath a tree, eating apples when the sky came low down just over the trees, curving blue. So low you could almost touch it.

"Has anyone ever touched the sky?" she asked.

Justy was scornful. "No one couldn't ever touch *the sky*."

"I bet they could too." And staring at it, it went all funny. It came down low and then it went up high again. She held up her arm as she said, "With a ladder I bet I could. I bet I could get a whole handful on a ladder."

"Oh, maybe with a ladder," Justy had allowed.

The spire rose up then, right into the sky. She could see where it touched. She sat up, pointing. "If I was up there I could touch it."

Justy looked. His eyes grew big. "Geee! I bet I could touch the sky if I was up there," he said as if it was his idea. "Come on."

They ran over to the church. A tree growing beside it spread

170

one branch close to the roof. Justy threw his apple core at the wall of the church, hitched his pants up firmly and began to climb. She watched him clamber up the trunk, go out on his stomach along the branch and swing onto the roof.

"S'easy. Come on."

She couldn't get a start on the trunk with her shoes. They were slippery so she took them off and put them in the grass under the tree. The rough bark tickled the soles of her feet as she climbed. When she tried to wriggle along the branch as Justy had, her dress caught, so she stopped and tucked it into her pants. She had swung herself onto the roof beside him saying, "Gee, that was easy." Looking down the world had flowered green all around her for miles and miles. It must have been then that she had decided God couldn't see so much after all. It had never struck her before how she had come to that conclusion. But it must have been then, on the church roof. From so high up He couldn't see anything at all but trees and houses and maybe processions.

The more she thought about the dream the more it changed. It was undreamlike now. Her background, her past, something solid and real which grew into her present, linked up with it and made it what it was.

That night at tea she put a straight question to her parents: "Where's Justy Williams now?"

She wondered if she detected a slight stiffening in her father. She had tried to watch them both at the same time. Her father's eyes had certainly turned to her mother's but he might well have been appealing to his wife to jog his memory, as he invariably did.

"Justy Williams?" her mother murmured questioningly. "Justy Williams? I don't know any Justy Williams."

"The kid I used to play with when I was little." Sadie was merciless. "The kid who climbed onto the church roof with me. We had a fight up there because we both wanted to be

God and two people couldn't be God. So we fought about it."
She laughed. It had suddenly become funny. And her mother
laughed too.

"You must have dreamed it all, Sade. I don't know what
you're talking about."

Her father was interested. "Who won the fight?" he asked.

"Oh, Justy, I guess. I said there could be two Gods, there
could even be three—God the Father, God the Son and God
the Holy Ghost. So we stopped fighting for awhile to think it
over and then Justy said, 'Well *you* can't be God the Father
or God the Son because you're a girl. You'll have to be God
the Holy Ghost.' I had to give in to that, so I guess he won.
Then he started yelling, 'I'm God the Father. I'm God the Son.'
And I kept yelling, 'I'm God the Holy Ghost.' "

Her father leaned back in his chair and laughed so that his
stomach shook. "That's rare," he said. "God the Son," he
spluttered. "God the Holy Ghost!" He put his hands over his
face and heaved. "Ho, ho, ho," he laughed. "That's rare alright!" And then he pulled his face together and only smiled
and his eyes darted about a bit, not knowing where to settle.
But the wild humor of it struck him again and his body began
to jiggle and rock and the laughter poured out of him as if it
had been pent up too long.

Sadie didn't think it so funny now. He had sucked the humor
out of it with all that laughter. She looked at her mother who
was shaking her head quietly, patiently.

"What a man your father is for a joke," she said. "He'd
even laugh at the Lord God Himself. Here," she reached out
and plucked her husband's sleeve. "Leave off," she said.

"What I want to know," said Sadie relentless, "where's
Justy Williams now?"

Her parents eyes met again.

"I never heard tell of that name before," said her father.
He fidgeted a moment with his spoon. Then, "God the Son!"

172

he spluttered and was off again, laughter owning him, distorting him. And the subject was lost again.

Sadie realized that the route to Justy was blocked, cemented up. Her entire past lay beyond her parents, but through them there was no road. Or even, conceivably, and far worse, a series of blind roads. Their strategy was so subtle and their signposts so numerous that at any moment she could be misled without suspecting it. She could no longer trust them at all. Neither their evasions nor their clues. Her immediate reaction was to leave the maze they had built around her. Walk out.But a maze is not a thing you can leave at once. And she was tied by her foot. It had replaced the umbilical cord. If she could only alter the foot, alter the boots . . . It would be months before she could save enough money for shoes but once she had it she *would* walk out, out and away to that memory of freedom, that recollection or fantasy—she couldn't be sure which—that stopped so abruptly on the church roof. Vivid to that point and then blank.

When finally she did have the money for the shoes she couldn't bring herself to buy them. The importance of the purchase was so tremendous that she put it off. It was the giant step from lame dependence into the world she had dreamed of, a world she already knew by its flavor through and through. The fact that she now had the money seemed to place the shoes further out of reach than when they were urgent, vital and impossible. The very fact that there was nothing to stop her was the very fact that stopped her. She waited, lost, seeking some sign, some indication that the correct moment had come, until passing a shop one day she walked in as naturally as if she had been buying shoes all her life.

Once inside she felt split—child and grown-up simultaneously. The memory of Justy which accompanied her reduced her to the size she had been on the day when they had made their way across the roof to the spire. At its base there was a ledge which she could just reach with her fingers if she jumped. It was firm beneath her grip but she couldn't pull herself up. "Push me!" she called to Justy.

The sales clerk came forward. He was young with pimples and as he bent down to unlace her boots he seemed familiar to her, reminding her of someone. She must be imagining, but he reminded her of Justy.

"I want some shoes," she said and saw herself dangling.

"Any particular style?"

Justy's hands shoved from beneath. It was funny how it all seemed to be happening together—climbing the steeple and buying the shoes. It was mixed, like a dream again.

Above the ledge the base sloped and above the sloping part the slender little spire rose high into the sky. She crawled gingerly up the incline, balancing carefully. Justy—the clerk, she meant—was measuring her feet on a kind of ruler. He made a wry face and she heard Justy's voice yell, "Watch out!" as she climbed higher and higher and grabbed the spire. The clerk went into the back of the store and while she waited she saw herself clearly wrapping her legs as far round the spire as they'd go and starting to shinny up it. It was hard work and the sun beat down on her head like a hammer.

The clerk emerged again from the back of the store. He grinned like Justy and held a pair of spectators on the palm of one hand. She felt a great surge of excitement rise in her and almost choke her. She held out her hands for them and as she did so, realized that she was well above the level of the base. If she let go with one hand and reached up she could touch the sky easily. Carefully, shifting her weight, she tightened the pressure of her right arm, preparatory to releasing the left.

The clerk said, "Shall we try them on?" With the help of a shoe-horn he slipped one onto the good foot. It was perfect.

The sky was right there, she knew. She held her free hand above her head, calling, "Justy! Look! I'm touching it. I'm touching the sky." She could tell by the feel. It was soft, swirling, blue.

The clerk slipped the toe of the shoe onto the bad foot and tried with the shoe horn to force it on. He struggled and she wriggled her foot to help. But as she wriggled she felt herself slipping, losing her grasp on the steeple, and she heard Justy yell and the clerk say, "I'm sorry. I was afraid of that. There won't be no shoes that will fit. You see . . . "

She nodded. There was nothing she could say. But she had time as she fell to watch him as he laced up her boots and tied the bows with a final quick jerk. "I'm sorry," he said again. "I'm very sorry."

All emptiness embraced her. "Thank you Justy," she said, and she felt the swirling blue currents of the air as it rushed by.

GEORGE

All of us in the boarding house were pretty much relieved when George came. We had had, earlier, a succession of house boys, each worse than the one before. Then there had been a long period with no-one. So that night at dinner, when Ladlaw drew George out of her hat like a rabbit everybody felt a good deal happier. Already Ladlaw herself was grinning. He had come that morning, she said, and worked hard all day. A few sceptical eyebrows were raised. We had heard her eulogies before. His references were OK, he'd worked at an Army Camp and likely knew what discipline meant, she figured.

Ernie Arnold suggested we place side bets on George. He began drawing columns on the back of his menu.

"I'll bet anyone a bottle of beer that within a week he's raided my cellar," Mr Jackson volunteered. Mr Jackson was the oldest boarder in all senses. He was also the most affluent.

"There's nobody fool enough to take that," said Mr Cooms. "You've only got to win to lose."

Miss Kirtle was smiling and nodding and looking bright and hovering on the brink of speech.

"Come," said Mr Jackson chidingly. "Miss Kirtle will take me up, won't you, Miss Kirtle?"

She crumbled her roll between her fingers, torn between being a good sport and involving herself in betting.

Ernie was very busy. I leaned over to watch him. Down the left hand edge of the paper he had written our names. He was chuckling to himself. Across the top were various headings: Just Plain Lazy; Kleptomaniac; Dipsomaniac; Religious Maniac; How Long He'll Stay.

"Now, look," he said. "Opposite your own name you put

a tick in the columns you think apply, filling in the final column with the number of days you think he'll stay. Then everyone puts a dollar in the kitty.''

"And if everyone ticks the same column?'' I said.

"Now, wait. I've got this all figured out. Leave it to Ernie. If everyone ticks the same column, then everyone get some of their money back—the amount depending on how many ticks they have that are false and how close they come to guessing the number of days he stays.''

"It all sounds pretty complicated to me,'' I said, "but if you want to figure it out, that's your business.'' He was not listening to me by this time but had taken my menu and was busy at work again.

"Ernie's working out a fancy kind of sweepstake,'' I said, and I explained.

"What happens to the money if George is a complete success?''

Ernie looked up from his writing. "I've got it all figured,'' he said. "If George turns out to be a paragon, we give the money to him.''

'Oh!'' said Miss Kirtle, disappointed.

"This is one hell of a sweepstake,'' said Mr Cooms.

"You don't have to play, you know,'' said Ernie. "Only those as wishes. You'll come in?'' he said to me.

"Sure.''

"And you Miss Ladlaw?''

"What I want to know,' she said, "is why you had to write all over my menus?''

"Emergency,'' said Ernie. But Miss Ladlaw was in a good mood that night.

"There's just one thing,'' I said. "No one must encourage George to develop the characteristics they've ticked. For instance, if you bet he's a kleptomaniac, you mustn't tempt him. It looks to me as if we might make him what we want him to be and be in a couple of dollars and out a house-boy.''

"That," said Ernie, "is in the rules." And he read.

'What I'm curious about," Mr Jackson interrupted, "is who holds the money meanwhile? Being the oldest and most respectable among you I think I should."

"I've thought of all that too," said Ernie. "The money and the betting chart are to be placed in a sealed envelope and put in the cash box. But here, I'll pass you the rules and the chart and you can read for yourself and place your bets at the same time."

Miss Ladlaw raised a few objections at first and then began to laugh and awkwardly walked out to the cash box in the hall desk and returned with her dollar.

There was a great deal of consultation and chat before the chart was finally filled. Miss Kirtle was worried and anxious and timid but Mr Jackson persuaded her it was all just fun. She told me afterwards she'd ticked religious maniac as it was the only *nice* thing on the list but that she couldn't *think* how long he'd stay. She talked about this for some time afterwards. "My dear, when I came to the column about how long he'd stay, I just couldn't *think*."

Miss Ladlaw ticked every column and gave his duration of service as two weeks, explaining that if she lost a house-boy, she'd at least have some money back. Ernie pointed out that he'd have to have all the faults listed before she'd get much back and she muttered, suddenly lugubrious and grim, that she expected he had and more besides.

All the boarders but Mr Coxton antied up. He said, "No thank you," and went on reading his newspaper. That made seven dollars from the house. Then five of the 'regulars' who came in from nearby rooming-houses asked if they could join in too. They felt they ought to get a different rate as they would have to take our word for George's behaviour, but we talked them out of that and Ernie promised if George got drunk he'd phone them up, no matter what time, so they could come and see for themselves. So, altogether, there was an even twelve dollars in the kitty which was duly sealed in the presence of all and put in the cash box in the desk.

That was a Friday night. I don't think any of us saw George on our way to work in the morning. I didn't, anyway, but a deep snow had fallen overnight and as I opened the front door I saw the steps had been carefully shovelled and brushed. If he was Just Plain Lazy, there was no evidence yet. I felt a bit mean about George as I walked to work. If a whole houseful of persons expect the worst of a guy and almost perversely hope it, what chance has he got? But letting my mind run backwards over his predecessors, I felt perhaps we were justified.

I came home well after the lunch hour that afternoon. There on the step in khaki drill slacks and shirt, wearing a green eye-shade, was, presumably, George. He was polishing the brass on the front door. He was very small, very thin, like a bird and had quick movements. No, not Just Plain Lazy, I judged. Not with that build.

"Hello," I said as I came up to him. "Aren't you cold without a coat?" He jumped at my words. His dark-skinned face twitched, he twisted his mouth from side to side, touched his hand to his eye-shade. "Good-afternoon, Miss," he said and reached out and opened the door for me—oh, so obsequious, so squirming.

So that, I thought, is George, and I couldn't help laughing. As I went upstairs I visualized the twelve dollars being handed over to him.

Rita Ferguson was in her room as I passed. I poked my head in. "Have you seen our monster?" I asked.

She looked up from her nails, holding an emery board at an angle. "Not yet. Have you?"

I nodded.

"What's he like?"

"You wait and see. Heaven knows what we're in for now!"

"Well he can clean, anyway," she said. "The baseboard in my room's been dusted for the first time since I arrived."

179

"How do you know?"

"I tried it with my finger when I came in. I always do."

"And let the dust accumulate?"

"Why not? God knows I pay enough for service."

"Well you've got it now, but don't be surprised if you're visited some dark night." I went on to my room. A few minutes later Rita was leaning against the frame of my door. She was still filing her nails.

"Tell me the truth," she said. "Is he really *that* bad?"

"You wait and see," I said ominously.

"Well I think it's disgraceful there are no keys to our doors. I've always thought it was. I'm going out and get a locksmith and have one made today."

"Don't be too hasty," I said. "wait and see. He may be your type."

"You're not a bit funny," she flared up. "Not a bit," and she left. Rita, I thought, is a good careful girl and her family need never worry about her.

I was out to dinner that night so wasn't there for the grand note-comparing that took place in the dining-room. I was told later that Rita had been very angry with me when she got an accurate description of George and that spirits were considerably lower than they had been the night before and that Miss Kirtle was so distressed about her dollar bet now that she'd seen the man that they had had to give it her back, she'd fretted so. Miss Ladlaw's report was that, so far, he'd worked pretty good, and that was high praise from her.

But I knew none of that until next day and after my second encounter with George. I was wakened on the Sunday morning by a tap on my door and a second later the door was pushed open to disclose George, his white jacket making a light smudge in the dark.

"Oh, good morning George," I said. "Come in," and I stretched for the light switch and smoothed a place on the bed. He stood there, confused, the white jacket almost swamping him, holding the tray as if it was a baby and he so unused to them, too. He was terribly embarrassed, really acutely so. He didn't dare look anywhere but at the tray and he seemed unable to move. At last, with a great effort he walked quickly, jerkily, across the floor, deposited the tray like a robot and fled from the room on rubber soled shoes.

Well, I thought, looking at my watch comfortably, he evidently doesn't have to go to early service. I tried to think of his face and couldn't. It was dark-skinned, thin and twitching but his eye-shade hid the upper half with shadow and it was impossible to guess what it was really like. Impossible to imagine it had ever been seen close up, as a barber might see it or a woman who loved him, but he hasn't got a hangover, I reflected as I began my grapefruit, and he doesn't go to early service. Two very good points.

Talk of George had dwindled considerably by Monday. Everyone chivvied everyone else a little over the sweepstake and it was generally conceded that George would get the eleven dollars and deserve it, too. And as the days wore on and the house remained beautifully warm and the snow was beautifully shovelled and the brass beautifully shined, we all felt a little small for having been so suspicious. At last we didn't feel anything about it any more, but took our comforts for granted and went on as usual, Miss Ferguson, however, had a key made for her door.

It was two weeks to the day since George's arrival when I was sitting in the hall after dinner and listening to Ernie telling me about his plans for skiing that week-end at St Saveur. "I'm going to learn to christie if I rupture myself," he said.

Suddenly there was a mass exodus from the dining-room—all the old girls with the feather hats and pearls and their impeccably tailored husbands who came in frequently from neighbouring apartments. As the same moment the front door opened and there was George, bowing his way through the diners, his left hand lifting his bowler hat to the ladies, his right raised in a

V for Victory salute. A carnation shone from his button-hole, he wore grey gloves and spats.

"A beautiful evening," he said, bowing and smiling. "How nice to see everyone," he said. "But you must excuse me, I can't stay to talk," and he moved on down the hall, while behind him, receiving small encouraging phrases like, "That's right, Tom," came a liveried man carrying a parcel. George stepped aside when he reached the cellar door while Tom opened it for him, then he disappeared from sight with Tom following.

"Well!" said Ernie. "The future is looking up," he said.

Ladlaw came into the hall from the kitchen and we told her about it. Ernie acted it out and was very funny.

"I don't believe it," said Ladlaw. "Why, that guy's too shy to speak."

"Not tonight, he isn't," I replied and at that point Tom emerged from the cellar and marched to the front door.

"Who was that?" asked Ladlaw.

"That," said Ernie, "is George's retainer. The one we told you about. Remember?"

When Ernie told the news to the dining-room Miss Kirtle was pretty upset she'd taken her dollar back and Rita smiled in a mean way and I knew she was thinking about her key.

Nothing more happened that night and next day everything was in order. Ernie said, "He's got a split personality, I guess, and it sure is split. As long as he doesn't get the two halves mixed, we're o'kay." But that night, after dinner, just as everyone was leaving, the same thing happened again. In swept George, complete with carnation and spats, his bowler hat raised as before, bowing and smiling for all the world like royalty condescending to the populace. This time however, he stopped at the desk where Ladlaw was sitting. "Good evening," he said and his patronizing air had reached its peak. But before he could go further Ladlaw spoke up in an ugly voice. "You get down to your room and no more of this."

"Me?" said George, only you couldn't think of him as

George any more. "Me?" and he struck a preposterous attitude of wounded dignity. "How dare you speak to me that way?" And he bent right over the desk and glared into Ladlaw's face very close and menacing.

She put her hand on his shoulder and pushed him, "Now get downstairs," she said. "Pronto!"

"Poor soul," he said suddenly and smiling sweetly. "Poor, poor soul!" and then, "Come, Tom, this way," and he went to the basement door, waited for Tom to open it and disappeared from sight.

By now we were all chattering and excited over the two Georges. Mr Jackson even suggested the sweepstake wasn't fair any more—that we'd placed our bets on the house-boy and it had turned out there were two of them. How was Ernie going to figure it out now? But Ernie, presumably, was figuring out christies at St Saveur.

"Nobody's going to win that money, anyway," said Mr Cooms. "George doesn't suffer from any of the complaints we ticked, he has a whole new set of his own." Miss Kirtle smiled happily. "It will depend now on who guessed closest how long he'll stay."

"Oh, dear, and I just couldn't *think*," said Miss Kirtle.

"Never mind," said Mr Cooms roughly, "you're not in the running anymore."

I was out again that evening and didn't get back till late. I was tired when I put the key in the door and I noticed by the desk clock it was after twelve-thirty. As I turned to go up the stairs there was Ladlaw sitting on the top step. Her hair was up in curlers and she was in her dressing gown.

"Are you any good with drunks?" she asked.

"Why?"

She pointed downstairs and said, "Listen."

I listened. "I don't hear anything," I said.

"Wait."

The house was completely still. I could hear the clock ticking

on the desk. In the distance a car horn sounded, somebody laughed on the street and then I jumped nearly out of my skin. A
radio had been turned on full blast so it practically shook the
house. I waited for it to be turned down a bit so it would be
easier to speak and I sat down on the step beside Ladlaw. But
it wasn't turned down. Instead, it was followed by an extraordinary banging and bumping.

"What's he doing?"

Ladlaw shook her head wearily. "It's been going on like
this ever since ten-thirty. I can't get him to stop."

"Is there anyone in?"

"Only Miss Kirtle who's scared to death and Miss Ferguson
who's locked the door."

"I'll go down," I said, not wanting to. "I'll see what I
can do."

When I opened the cellar door the noise came at me solid.
You had to fight against it. I couldn't imagine what I'd do once
I got there—why I was going down those stairs. When I got
to the bottom George's door was shut, the banging and bumping
had stopped but the radio hadn't. I knocked. No answer. I knocked again with my signet ring. No answer. "George," I yelled,
"George!" Still no answer, so I opened the door of his room
and looked in.

What I had expected to find, I don't know, but what I did
find surprised me. The radio, at one side of the room was on
full. The rest of the room was in perfect order. In the centre,
under a strong white light was a table with great piles of papers
on it, all neatly stacked, as business-like as the desk of an exe-
cutive. Behind it, in his khaki drill, wearing his eye-shade, sat
George.

"George,' I said and went across the room to him He leapt
to his feet as he saw me, bowed, took my hand, kissed it with
a great resounding smack.

He was drunk as a coot.

I went over and turned down his radio. "I came down to ask you to do me a favor."

He bowed again. "Anything dear," he said.

"Look," I said. "I can't sleep, George. I simply can't sleep with the radio on so loud. Would you turn it down a little?" I still had on my fur coat and my overshoes but he didn't seem to notice.

"At twelve o'clock," he said, suddenly aggressive and ugly. "I will at twelve, not before."

"But it's after twelve now."

For answer he went and hit the face of the alarm clock with the back of his fingers. It said five past ten.

I felt beaten then. "Look, George,' I said. "I want a cup of coffee. How about having one with me if I make it?"

He was domineering, arrogant. "I want my dinner. Get me my dinner."

"But you had your dinner earlier."

"No, I didn't." He shook his fist in my face and I moved closer to the door. "Ladlaw," he said pulling a face, "wouldn't give me any."

"I'll get you some," I said not stopping to argue. "Right now," I said and I was thankful for a reason to leave.

He looked at me very closely and I saw his eyes for the first time and remembered how I had thought about his face before and wondered if anyone had ever seen it close up. They were minute, brown and slightly crossed, which evidently accounted for the eye-shade, and they had an expression in them that scared hell right out of me.

"I'll make you some sandwiches," I said and I went out of the door as fast as I dared and up the stairs with the terrible care of the pursued who doesn't want the pursuer to know he knows.

Ladlaw was waiting for me when I came up. "Well?" she asked.

"He says he's hungry and that he won't turn the radio down before twelve."

"Twelve?" she said.

"Yes. I'm going to get him a meal. It may sober him up."

We went into the kitchen and I picked up a tray in the pantry en route. Ladlaw went into the cold room and said, "There's lamb or chicken."

"Make it chicken," I said.

She came back and plunked the plate on the table, rinsed some lettuce under the tap. I put the water on for coffee and a slight smell of gas escaped.

"I think you've got a gas leak," I said, but what I meant was that I didn't want to go down into the basement again. I leaned my hands on top of the percolator a few minutes, thinking. Then I began cutting sandwiches.

I cut those sandwiches as if I were cutting them for a lover. The bread thin with plenty of butter, the chicken in beautiful white slices spread with mayonnaise and then the curling green lettuce. I set the tray as if my life depended on it and waited for the coffee to perk and hoped it never would.

When it was ready I said, "Coffee?" and Ladlaw nodded. "Well," I announced, sitting on the stool at the kitchen table, "It's all ready," and I put a couple of lumps of sugar in my cup and began stirring.

Ladlaw nodded at the tray. "Aren't you going to take it down?"

"I thought you would."

She shook her head. "No point in me taking it. I only make him mad. You'd better go. You said you would. He'll be expecting you."

"That's just what I'm afraid of," I said.

We sat there a few minutes. The coffee slipped down warm and soothing. "Alright, I'll go," I said at last, "but you've got to come with me. Right behind."

So we set off down the hall, through the cellar door and

down the stairs. We didn't speak. There was nothing to say and we couldn't have heard each other anyway because of the radio. She turned the handle of George's door for me and I pushed in thinking how scared he'd seemed the first Sunday he brought me breakfast and how neatly the tables had been turned.

He was sitting as before, at his table under the white light. He gave me the creeps rather. I wondered what he was doing with all those papers.

"There." I put the tray down on a table near the door. "There's a nice meal for you."

He made a wide gesture of disdain and didn't look at the tray again. As before he leaped to his feet and came forward. He took my hand, kissing it with the inside of his lips. "You're just like my girl friend," he said and his clutch tightened and I saw those dreadful little eyes for the second time.

"Eat your supper, turn down your radio and go to bed." I pulled away from him and he followed me to the door. "Remember about the radio, George—for my sake." I said it sweetly.

He lunged at me, pressed me to him with a dreadful ardor and I saw the hairs growing out of his dark greasy neck. "Goodnight," he said. "My love!"

I started up the stairs quickly to ensure that Ladlaw would be between George and me. At the top I leaned against the wall, shaking and giggling. Ladlaw said, "Keep going," and we went on to the kitchen and sat with our elbows on the kitchen table and finished the coffee.

"It all began the day he got paid," she said. "He was so good up till then. Sometimes I wonder what's the point of keeping on trying."

We got up then. I slipped a knife into my pocket as we went. The hall clock said twenty-five to two as we passed.

When I got to my room I took the knife from my pocket and tried it in my door. It held fast. I felt better then and made

187

a face in Rita's direction. I was fearfully tired. I sat on my
bed in my coat and lit a cigarette and listened. The radio had
been turned down. I undressed and opened the door onto the
balcony and plugged it so it wouldn't bang and fixed the knife
in the other door and fell into bed. Well, one thing, I thought
before I went to sleep—I ticked dipsomaniac!

I don't know how long I slept but when I wakened it was
suddenly. I listened, hearing nothing. As far as I could tell my
door was still shut. Then I knew what had wakened me. I was
hot. I was so hot that the perspiration was rolling down me.
The floor was hot under my feet as I got out of bed. A thaw,
I thought, and imagined how mad Ernie would be. I flung my
balcony door wide and the air came in like cold steel. No sign
of a thaw. I went over to the radiator and the pipes burned
me. Something was mighty queer. I put on my dressing gown
and slippers and opened my door quietly. There was movement
on the landing and whispering. The temperature in the hall was
staggering.

I found Ladlaw and Miss Kirtle talking. Miss Kirtle was
dead white and her eyes were immense with fear. "He's set
fire to the place," she said. "Oh, we'll all be burned to death."
Her lip trembled.

"Go and get dressed," I said, "at once. And get your bags
packed. Go along." She went like a child, whimpering a little.

"What goes on?" I asked Ladlaw.

She gave a twisted, terrible smile. "He's stoking," she said.
"Must have been for hours. He's standing there stark naked
with sweat running down and stoking."

"Have you told him to stop?"

"He doesn't hear," she said. "He doesn't even know I was
down. He's just stoking."

I ran upstairs and knocked on Mr Jackson's door. He didn't
answer. I walked in, turned on his light and went over and shook
him. "Mr Jackson," I called. 'Mr Jackson." He wakened sleep-
ily.

"Get up," I said. "You've got to help us with George."

He got out of bed hanging onto his pyjama pants with one hand and covering his mouth with the other. Teeth, I thought, and I went into the hall and waited. In a minute he came out, tying his dressing gown cord.

"God," he said. "Is it a heat wave?"

"George is stoking. He thinks he's in a ship or something. You must go down."

I went to the cellar door with him for something to do. I waited. I could hear the shovel going and then Mr Jackson's voice. I waited a long time and then Mr Jackson came upstairs. He was biting his lip and his eyes were focussing on something far away. "Screwy," he said, tapping his damp forehead. "He doesn't hear or see. I've locked the coal cellar and taken the key. That's the last pailful he can get."

"Meanwhile we can burst into flames any moment from the feel of things."

"Run off the hot water," he said, "or the boiler may explode. And open the windows. I'll waken Cooms and see if we can drag him away by force. He's too strong for me, I tried. And don't go down," he added. "Understand."

It was the very last thing I'd have been likely to do. George clad was bad enough.

The water spat and choked from the taps. It was rusty and scalding. While I was in the kitchen I threw out the old coffee grounds and put some fresh on to perk. I wondered about Miss Kirtle and thought I'd better go up and see how she was getting on.

She had one bag packed and was standing in the middle of the room, an empty suitcase in front of her and dozens of garments lying about waiting to be pushed in. She looked quite different from the other times I'd seen her. Her hair was all twisted up anyhow and the top of her knitted suit was on back to front.

"Don't worry, Miss Kirtle." I opened her window. "Mr

Jackson's looking after everything. If I were you I'd just lie down." I pulled the blankets up on her bed and shook the pillow. "Everything'll be alright," I said.

The house was pretty full of steam and the heat seemed worse by the time Mr Jackson and Mr Cooms came up again.

"So help me, he was slippery as an eel," said Mr Cooms. "You couldn't get a grip on him."

"We locked him in his room," Mr Jackson added. Then turning to Ladlaw, "You'll have to give him notice the minute he can hear again."

"The guy's crazy," said Mr Cooms.

We were all standing there as the hall clock struck seven. "Breakfast time," Ladlaw said and we marched into the kitchen. Now that we had time to think we found it hot and cold and everything at once. The steam was clinging to us and the heat fearful but near the windows the air rushed in freezing.

Ladlaw began squeezing oranges and was happier busy. Mr Cooms set the kitchen table and Mr Jackson rocked back and forth over the stove. Every now and then he shook his head and said, "God" in a voice full of wonder.

They didn't talk about George much. I think it must have been because he was naked and that made them shy.

"Something's got to be done," I said. "We can't go *on* like this."

Ladlaw pursed her lips and stirred her coffee noisily. Mr Jackson buttered a piece of toast and cut it in strips. He attempted to look pontifical but his short white hair standing on end rather destroyed the effect. "The preliminaries," he said, waving his knife, "need not be discussed. The events leading up to last night are of no importance. They are trivia," he said. I tried to interrupt but he wouldn't let me. "However," and this he emphasized, "when a man reaches the point where he no longer has any judgment—where he stands up mother-naked and stokes like that—where he endangers the lives of others—then it is serious. Very."

"God knows what he's doing *now*," Mr Cooms added.

We all jumped.

"I've given it my considered opinion," said Mr Jackson, "and there seems to me only one thing to do. We must call the police."

"I think you're right, Jackson. I don't know why we didn't think of it before." Mr Cooms jumped up and Mr Jackson followed. "We can't go through another night with him down there."

"I don't think we can," said Ladlaw.

But we did!

The police came alright. They filled the hall with navy blue and questions. One kept hitting his leg with his truncheon. They lounged on chairs and seemed interested in nothing. Mr Jackson told them what they wanted to know. Then they all looked at each other, got up at once, asked the way to the basement and clattered down the stairs. We heard them banging on George's door, talking among themselves. Then they trooped up again, said there was nothing they could do, explained it was impossible to evict, that if he had been making a public nuisance of himself outside they could pick him up—but not inside, in his own room. No, they were sorry. If he went out and we liked to phone them they'd do what they could, provided he was disturbing the peace.

"Meanwhile he can set fire to the house and it's no business of yours."

The one who kept hitting his leg said huffily that they were only doing their duty, that we had no complaint to make now—he was evidently sleeping. And they left.

"Well!" said Ladlaw but I anticipated her tirade. "I don't know about anyone else," I said, "but I'm going back to bed. Waken me if there's a murder—not unless."

When I did waken it was afternoon. The house was quiet and the Sunday feeling unmarred by our activities of the night before. Snow was falling in enormous flakes outside. I remembered I'd left my cigarettes in the kitchen and went down for them.

In the front hall, before the mirror, giving himself a final assessment, was George. He was immaculate. He wore his good overcoat, white silk scarf, bowler hat and an ice-box rose was tucked neatly into his buttonhole.

"Good afternoon," he said with curt condescension, speaking to me through the mirror without turning. And then, "Brush me off," he said and he pointed to a clothes brush on the desk. Amazed at us both I obeyed him. He surveyed the job over his shoulder, put his hand in his pocket, jingled his change, pressed a dime in my hand and left.

I suppose it was the stoking, I thought, as I went up the stairs to Ladlaw's room. I couldn't imagine how anyone as drunk as he'd been could even raise his head at three in the afternoon, let alone be walking briskly about as if he'd gone to bed at ten.

Ladlaw and Mr Jackson were playing Gin Rummy in a kind of tired silence when I went in. "Look," I said, "I thought you'd be interested. I've just had another encounter with George," and I told them about it, throwing the dime on the card table for proof.

"You say he's gone out?" Mr Jackson asked eagerly and he jumped to his feet exclaiming, "We'll get him now. I'll phone the police right away."

"Don't bother," I said. "He's sober as a fish. There's not a policeman in town'd pick him up now."

I left the two of them with their amazement and after that I had nothing more to do with George. I was invited out for the rest of Sunday and I was glad to go.

The house was quiet when I returned and the only thing that was unusual at all was a note in Ladlaw's handwriting pinned to my pillow: "If you hear the doorbell in the night, don't answer it. Mr Jackson and me have locked George out. He only has a key to the back door and we bolted it.'' So, I thought and I went to bed.

I overslept next morning and didn't have any time for talking or breakfast but I noticed the steps were beautifully shovelled and swept, as usual, and wondered who had been the Boy Scout.

At dinner that night the rest of the story broke. Ladlaw was in the kitchen for the first half of the meal and Mr Jackson, Mr Cooms and myself related our portions of yesterday's adventures. There was a good deal of excitement over the betting. Ernie was sore as hell that he'd missed the fun. He smiled, however, when he heard about the drink. "I ticked dipso," he said.

Miss Kirtle was on the verge of speech as she always was, but no-one gave her a chance to say anything. Miss Ferguson who'd slept through the excitement and not ticked Dipsomaniac was busy reading a magazine. The 'regulars' wanted a full report and they got it. Mr Jackson told how he and Miss Ladlaw had locked George out—but he guessed George couldn't have intended coming back anyway as no one heard any doorbells.

"But he *did* come back," said Miss Kirtle nervously. "He came in through his window." Blushing and stammering with all eyes on her Miss Kirtle began her part of the story. "This morning he was back at work as if nothing had happened. It was just as if we'd dreamed it," she said, her eyes round with wonder.

Ernie laughed. 'We can't divide the spoils yet, then,'' he said. "We've got to wait until he's gone. That's in the rules."

Miss Kirtle was trying to speak again but by this time the conversation had been whisked away from her. She plucked my sleeve. "My dear," she said, "I think they'd be interested. He *has* gone."

"Look," I yelled, "if you'd let Miss Kirtle finish." But Ladlaw came in at that point. I suppose, in the whole dining room, nobody really cared about George going but Ladlaw. Some of us would come to care, doubtless, when the house was in shambles again and the water gushed cold out of the taps just when we wanted our baths. But now all that mattered was the story and the sweepstake. Eleven dollars for someone, no one quite knew whom. Mr Jackson swore he'd won and wouldn't listen when anyone doubted him. For myself, I felt it depended largely upon the accuracy of Ernie's fractions.

Ladlaw picked up where Miss Kirtle stopped. "I told him," she said, and her voice was tired and not a bit excited, "that was the last time he got drunk in my house. I was going to give him another chance what with labor so hard to get. But I'd no sooner said the word 'drunk' than he started jumping up and down like a maniac. He ran down the stairs and up again swinging his arms and screaming. He said he wouldn't work in such a house. 'Go then,' I said. And he went." The story ended there. She told it to get it done with. She was tired as a dog, you could see that, and fed up.

"There," said Mr Cooms. "I said seventeen days and seventeen days it is. Friday to Friday—seven days—"

"Eight," said Ernie.

Mr Cooms pursed his lips and figured on the table top with his finger.

'You haven't a chance, anyway," said Ernie. "You ticked Kleptomaniac if I remember rightly and you never bet he'd drink."

"Go and get the chart," I said. "Go on, Ernie. Work it out now. I've got a bill to pay tomorrow and I'd like the money."

Reluctantly he rose from his table, casting a rueful eye at his plate as he did so. He'd almost reached the door when Ladlaw spoke up.

"Hey," she said. "You'd better save your strength. I forgot to tell you. When George went the cash box went too."

THE GLASS BOX

At eight forty-five exactly the phone rang and she caught it after the first ring.

The voice said quietly, "Ricky?"

"Yes."

"Tonight?"

"Yes. Where?"

"There?"

"Okay" She glanced about her as she spoke. "When?"

"Between nine thirty and nine forty-five."

She was silent a moment.

"Isn't that alright? I can't be more definite."

"That's alright." Her left hand clenched in the pocket of her housecoat. "Goodbye."

"Goodbye . . . "

She walked back to her room along the hall, quietly past Billie's door for fear he was in and called her. She thought back over the conversation on the phone, dividing it into two parallel columns in her mind: what had been heard here? what at the other end? A vague fear gathered about her, increased. She had not said enough, not been sufficiently chatty. She shouldn't have dropped her voice or made it so toneless. She shouldn't have been so close to the phone when it rang. As always this worry was like the soft mouth of a fish nuzzling at her physical outline.

There was no time to settle to anything and no inclination to settle. She drew the blind more carefully and tidied the room for the second time, moving on legs that seemed to have ram rods jammed down them, her hands frozen and streaming with perspiration like hands sculptured from ice and now slowly melt-

195

ing. Her face looked too tense in the mirror as she dressed and too white. Staring at herself she felt suddenly that everything she tried to hide was written all over her for everyone to read. But behind this layer of thought lay another—a layer in which her mind was active and accurate: she had better be ready before nine thirty in case he was early, better meet him outside to prevent his ringing the bell.

She slipped a dress off its hanger and pulled it over her head, thrusting her fingers under the weight of hair caught in the neck, tossing it out so that it fell down heavy and thick on her shoulders. The clock said nine o five. She put on her overshoes and threw her fur coat on the bed. If she met anyone on the way out she ought to have some fairly obvious reason for going—something self-evident, like a letter in her hand. Quickly she extracted a bill from the papers on her desk, wrote a cheque to cover it and addressed the envelope. She took a cigarette from the box and lit it, the fat white tube making her lips project. Unmoving, unreal as a store dummy, she drew the smoke deeply into her lungs. There was silence in the boarding house and the room ready.

Just after nine fifteen she let herself out of the front door and paused a minute on the snowy steps. The strong rays of the street lamp lit her too clearly, fell with a flat violence on the white envelope in her hand. She thrust it into her pocket so that no one, seeing her, would presume she was walking towards the pillar box. Coat collar high about her ears, she turned right on the sidewalk, her overshoes making a crisp squeaking noise on the hard-packed snow. When she reached the corner she stopped in the shadow of a tree, pivotting slightly. An oblique glance at Miss Armitage's window showed a line of yellow outlining the blinds. Miss Armitage was in. Better to know for certain than not know. They would have to come in quietly then, trusting they would not be heard, trusting they would meet no one. If they were, if they did, she would have to break into

196

conversation easily and in that case she had better plan now what she would say.

A group of people rounded the far corner coming towards her. She crossed the street casually to avoid them, stood in front of a shop window, examined minutely the crepe paper decorations and the welter of cheap articles for sale. She was directly opposite the boarding house. If Miss Armitage raised her blind she could see her. Casually again, she moved on to a patch of shadow cast by the Masonic Temple, her eyes sweeping the street from left to right. Great mounds of snow glistened softly in the light and faded grey-white, blue-white in the shadows, sprang glistening and white again beneath the further lights and so on, here, there, for miles throughout the city.

Then she saw him. He rounded the corner by the tree, head down against the cold. He was walking briskly, intently, as if hurrying to work. His shoulders jutted black and square against the snow. She crossed the street again, planning the point where they would meet—a point at which Miss Armitage, if she did raise the blind, would be unable to see them. She hurried across the slippery road and climbed over the snow bank and the snow sank deeply over the tops of her overshoes and settled round her ankles. He didn't alter his pace when he saw her and she fell in beside him.

"Hello," he said. The crook of his elbow nudged against her ribs.

"Hello."

They walked together along the sidewalk and up the steps and she turned the key in the lock and they went upstairs. As they reached the landing Miss Armitage called, "Is that you, Mr Hopper?"

Her heart set up a racket as she called back, "No, it's only me."

Miss Armitage said, "Oh, I thought it was Mr Hopper. That girl friend of his has been phoning again."

She led the way along the corridor and he watched her footsteps, treading when she did. He put out a hand and touched
her shoulder and she jumped under the contact and didn't turn.
When he was inside her room and the door closed, she leaned
back against it, trembling. Her head and shoulders and the palms
of her hands were flat against the wood. The soft grey fur of
her coat moved and fluttered gently with her breathing. She felt
like a moth impaled in a collector's show case.

"Cold?" he asked and she shook her head. "Not only cold."

He ran his hands beneath her coat, holding his fingers wide-
spread across her back. He pulled her away from the door, let
his head drop so that his face was hidden between the fur and
her neck. His breath was warm against her cold skin. But above
the slight movements of her body, above the sound of his breath
and hers, his blood and hers, she listened closely, her flesh a
sounding board.

He slid his hands over her shoulders to take off her coat
and she stood there, unassisting and still tense. He walked her
backwards and pushed her onto the bed and bent to undo her
overshoes. When he pulled, her shoes came off too, and she
sat there in her stocking feet with the dark bands around her
ankles where the snow had melted. He ran his fingers up the
silk of her stockings and cupped his palms over her bent knees
and she saw him for the first time and noticed the small lines
about his eyes, dark, as if drawn with a mapping pen. She lifted
her hand to his face and the fingers of it shook and twitched
uncontrollably.

A tableau, the two of them, under the ceiling light, with
the walls closing in upon them like a box and the walls glass.
Difficult to speak now, difficult to laugh or argue or fool as
they once had. Three hours together and they wore the time
like chains. Imprisoned by it the minutes went clanking by. The
world loved lovers only when they didn't love. Kiss on a street-
corner and the police told you to hurry along. Take a hotel room

and the detective asked you for your marriage license. Thou shalt not commit adultery. Fat chance.

Urgently she got up, reached for his coat, bearing the heavy weight of it with him a moment before he released it, holding it briefly alone.

"Darling, I . . . " The silence came down like a gag.

"Go on."

She stood on the chair and put her arms around his neck. "It's just that we never have long enough, do we?"

"Perhaps, one day." He looked uneasily about the room and back to her again, his eyes lighting as if they had found what they sought. He picked her up and carried her to the bed, laid her down gently and she stared up at him. Her face looked pale and stiff and transparent like freshly ironed white organdy.

"Don't look at me like that. Oh, Ricky, it's not my fault."

"I know, darling."

He threw his jacket on the chair and fell on the bed face downward, his mouth seeking hers.

A bell rang and she jumped like a fish and then froze, her hands rigid on his back. She heard the rattle of Miss Armitage's mules going down the stairs, the front door opening. She strained every nerve listening and the silence was hard and solid like concrete in her ears. Then the rattle of the mules again on the stairs and she sat bolt upright and he vaulted clear of the bed. The sound of her heart was so loud it should have blocked out all noise, but she heard clearly the mounting staccato of the mules continuing along the sorridor. As if there was no dimension to time and everything was happening simultaneously, she put on lipstick, combed her hair, noted that he was sitting on the chair, that the coats were, somehow, now on the bed. She felt as if she was taking shorthand at two hundred words a minute and she went down the corridor, walked as far as Miss Benson's door, saying like an automaton, "Anything for me?"

"A wire."

"For *me*?"

Miss Armitage leaned against the wall, clearly intending to stay until the message was read. Ricky's fingers shook as she opened the gummed flap. "Happy birthday darling wonder what you are doing and if you are happy stop have just drunk your health in Johnny Begg love the family." She heard her mother's gently inquisitive affectionate voice behind the words. She laughed at the stupid family joke about Johnny Begg and handed the telegram to Miss Armitage who said, "Many happy returns. You should have told us it was your birthday, we'd have had a cake." Then after a slight pause, "Say, you can't sit there in your room like that. I'll see if I can find a game of bridge."

"No, no, please. I brought back work from the office." She had spoken too quickly. 'It's awfully good of you but I've got to get this work cleared up."

Miss Armitage surveyed her critically, produced a pack of cigarettes from her pocket and said, "You do a lot of work for a young girl. Why don't you get yourself a boy friend like anyone else your age?" She tapped the cigarette on her thumbnail and said, "Match?"

"I'll get one.'

Miss Armitage followed her. She tried to will Miss Armitage to stop. "My room's in an awful mess. Really awful. I'd much sooner you didn't see it. You'd give me my marching orders if you did. And rooms are so hard to get these days." She bantered, giggled, wondering how she would finally stop her if Miss Armitage insisted upon coming in.

Miraculously the telephone rang. The sharp peal of its bell released the balloons of her lungs.

"This place!" Miss Armitage wailed and clattered away.

Ricky ran into the bedroom. "You've got to hide," she whispered and as she spoke she was pulling the clothes along in her cupboard to make room, taking his coat and hat and rubbers and stashing them away.

"I won't be long, I swear. But don't move until I say your name."

He obeyed her. She picked up some matches and went along the hall, meeting Miss Armitage just as she turned the corner.

"For Mr Hopper again. That girl sure is after him."

"Your match." Ricky was afraid of a long detailed account of the love lives of the various boarders. Feeling hedged into a small space, attempting to appear unhurried, she dreaded every minute the appearance of someone else in the hall; someone else to delay her. Her hand shook again as she held the match and the flame seemed to bounce and jerk about. She wondered why Miss Armitage said nothing.

Miss Armitage took a deep drag of the smoke and held the cigarette loosely in the flabby corner of her mouth. "If I was your mother," Miss Armitage began, took out the cigarette and removed a piece of tobacco from her lip, "I'd see to it you led a different life," Miss Armitage said. Miss Armitage's bulk blocked all exits. Enclosed by Miss Armitage, Ricky was trapped. She wondered what Miss Armitage meant, what Miss Armitage knew. She fought for words to release her, forced them through the tightness of her throat and heard herself saying jokingly, conversationally, "But you aren't, are you?" The exits opened again. Miss Armitage was standing in the hall, quite normally life size—a rather tired landlady smoking a cigarette. Ricky patted her arm warmly and smiled. "I'd better return to my unhealthy pursuits. Goodnight."

She walked easily to the corridor in the way she had taught herself but once round the corner her body began twitching and her head jerking strangely on her neck. She tensed her muscles to control it and said, "Stop it, you fool!" consciously once, only to find herself repeating, "You fool, you fool," over and over again, unable to stop. She tried to make herself think what to do next but the words of the telegram raced through her head. Hope you are happy. Happy! Silly conventional, unreal language. She was suddenly furious with her family.

She opened her bedroom door and stood still a minute before calling him. He emerged looking slightly absurd, his hair disordered and hanging over his forehead in curly bangs. He was clowning a bit about the stiffness of his knees. His laughter made fury snap in her and her face contorted with tears. She turned her back on him and walked away. Sobs started from an unbelievable depth, broke and left her with a rarified sensation in the top of her head as if oxygen was being released beneath her skull.

He went up behind her, wrapped his arms round her, rocked her gently from side to side, held his head close to hers saying, "Darling, darling, what is it?"

The fury abated a little. A kind of tolerant contempt replaced it. "You don't know?" Her voice was chipped. He didn't answer. "Alright, I'll tell you. I just can't take it any longer, that's all. Nothing more complicated than that. For months and months I've done nothing that's spontaneous. Every move mapped out; everyone a spy or a potential spy. Oh Christ! can't you see? Every doorbell, every telephone, every voice in the hall." She covered her face with her hands, shuddering. "Oh, take me out of here," she said and she brushed past him, pulled a blanket from the bed, began tugging at her overshoes.

"She can't find you here or know that you've been—that anyone's been. Can't you see that?" She tied her laces in garbled sorts of knots. "We've got to take a risk—go down the back stairs and through the kitchen. If the maids are still there or if . . . No, you'll have to go that way. If Armitage hears anything she'll be out like a shot. I'll have to go the front way and cover the noise you make." She was getting into her coat with fierce jerking movements and he stood looking at her in amazement. She was trying to think what reason she could give if she were confronted. Lies, lies, she thought. It'll be unnatural to be honest again. She was impatient as he kicked his feet into his rubbers.

"You take this," she thrust the blanket at him, "and this," she fumbled in a drawer for a flashlight. "The lights go on at the foot of the stairs." She glanced quickly along the passage and then pushed him through the door. "Be quick unless you hear my voice. If you do, stay in the back hall until I've stopped talking."

Overshoes muffling her footsteps she started out again. Thrusting her hands in her pockets she came across the bill she had taken with her before. She wondered if the maids had gone, if he was okay in the kitchen. She was furious and humiliated by the deceits and camouflages which had accompanied their relationship from the beginning.

Miss Armitage did not appear. Her bedroom door, opening onto the well of the stairs, was so strategically placed that bad luck alone prevented her from seeing all exits and entrances.

Ricky went down the stairs leaning her weight on the bannister so that the floor boards wouldn't creak. Black silence filled the place.

He was not there when she reached the main floor and, instinctively, habitually, she went to the sitting room window and searched the still, snowy street. Re-entering the hall she saw him. Together, as ghosts might fall into step, they walked to the door. Unspeaking, they moved without conscious awareness of each other as two bird dogs behave identically and independently when concerned with the same bird. The door's closing joined them again and for a split second they looked into each other's eyes and smiled. The fierceness of the cold sprang at them, stinging. Opening their mouths to speak it filled their throats. She noticed his nervous glance about as they walked; the crunch of their heels, sounding like breaking glass, startlingly loud; and his face, white, as if a handkerchief had been tied across it, below the shadow cast by his hat.

Rounding the corner she saw with relief that the frost had made the windows of his car opaque. Even the cold was easier to fight than the long light summer evenings with the glass of the windows clear. The car doors banged, once, twice, against the city.

"My darling." He leaned across to her, knocking the gear shift out of the way with his elbow as he did so. "My very own dear."

But the sense of security vanished again as he kissed her. Perhaps the car had been there too long and someone had seen it. Any one of a dozen people might have recognized it and wondered why it was there. She felt the nervousness growing in him as it did in herself. Pitiful security—frost on panes of glass. He pulled away from her then and started the engine, thawed out the front panel so he could see. "We'd better move on, just to be on the safe side." He engaged the engine and they pulled out into the street, the chains on the wheels rattling a little and clanking.